THE WOLF TRAP

A Wolf Regnum Novel

M. Angel

To John
thank you for coming T?
the festival

Copyright © 2023 M. ANGEL

This book is a work of fiction. Names, characters, places, and incidents either are the product of the author's imagination or are used fictitiously, and any resemblance to actual persons, living or dead, business establishments, events, or locales is entirely coincidental.

No part of this publication may be reproduced, stored in or introduced into a retrieval system, or transmitted, in any form, or by any means (electronic, mechanical, photocopying, recording, or otherwise), without the prior written permission from the author.

There are too many people to thank, too many individuals who helped me gather the courage to write, the strength to keep going and the passion to want to do it again. That being the case I cannot possibly thank them all here. However, I do hope that this novel is but the first of many, thereby giving me the opportunity to acknowledge all those who have brought me to this page.

For now, I will thank the three most directly involved with this work. My amazing daughter Alexis, who lent her artistic eye and skills in the development of the support endeavors necessary for this project. My dear sister Gabriela, my editor, my conscience and the one who kept me honest in my characterizations. Lastly, my loving partner, wife and inspiration Theresa, whose patience, tenacity, love and encouragement were instrumental in bringing this work out into the light...

The moonlight if we are being specific.

CHAPTER 1

Why do they call it "Murphy's Law"? What if I wanted to be mad at the Johnsons or the Smiths? What if I wanted to be angry with the Francos, or the Molinas for having just had my ass kicked? What if I wanted to blame the Carmichaels or the Patels for my running late? I mean it wasn't just losing a fight that had me cranky. It was because I smelled like mud and blood and, was about to walk into a place I hated and feared.

As I stepped out of the car, the humidity fell on me like a wet blanket. Richmond in August was like walking through a sprinkler wearing a parka. Even at two fifteen in the morning the temperatures were still hanging out at a chilly eighty degrees some nights. Being from the balmy hills of upstate New York, I particularly enjoy the feeling of sweat running down my back and into my crack. Just one more thing to add to the mental list of reasons why I hated this place.

I stood next to the car trying to get myself together, hoping that I had done enough, praying that I had served enough to get me out of the insane world I had fallen into. I clung to the idea that I could work my way out, even if in some ways, it was a thing of my own making. Knowing that there was only one way to find out, I took a deep breath and started toward the gate.

There was really nothing about the place that stood out. The postage-stamp of a lawn sat nicely in front of the brick two story row house that looked like every other house. The dull brown paint covering the time-worn brick blended in nicely with just about everything around it. The neat little panes of glass which no one would ever look through were ensconced in white window frames that were neither glossy nor dingy. Two brick columns stood like six-foot sentinels on either side of the wrought iron gate which served as the only access point though the five-foot wall that bordered the entire property. There was a little black metal box mounted on the column to my right, about the size of an average hand. It sat about waist high and contained a microphone sensitive enough to pick up dirty thoughts let alone anything spoken out loud. Below the microphone was a golf-ball-sized speaker under which sat a sort of half bowl of clear plastic.

I approached the thing, leaned over and spit into the bowl. I was rewarded with a sharp click from the speaker and an all-too-familiar voice.

"When will you stop doing that?" The voice from the speaker was rich, a bit deeper than mine with the slightest hint of an accent I couldn't quite place.

"When you stop checking my genetic ID at

the door. Especially considering that you can see me right there," I said tapping on the small camera bolted to the column just above the box. Most everyone else was content to drop a strand of hair or some other bit of themselves that would satisfy the elaborate DNA security scan. I found it more satisfying to provide a sample that would have to be cleaned up by some minion before dawn. Probably not the best "how do you do" considering the conversation I was hoping to have, but sometimes I just can't help myself.

A buzz followed by a click came from the gate and it sprung slightly inward. The plain looking walk took me to a plain looking door that popped open with another buzz-click as I climbed the five steps leading up to it. Soft light spilled out onto the landing which would have, in other circumstances, been welcoming but in this case felt as cold as the man I was about to see.

Closing the door behind me I smelled it immediately; a mixture of smells really, but faint as they were, the underlying scent hit me like a hammer. I exhaled through my nose forcefully to clear the stench. My rational mind knew it wouldn't work but I did it anyway. It was like smelling old, wet clothes left balled up in a corner for a few days combined with what can best be described as the opposite of fresh cut grass and lastly, blood.

A wall sconce on my right held two candles that shed dim light down a narrow hallway. At the end of the hall, and from a wide doorway on the left came more candlelight letting me know where I was to be received. I slowly took the three short steps to the threshold and lingered there, wishing I were somewhere else. Finally, I took in a lungful of air and stepped into the room.

Standing at the opposite end of the room, in front of one of the many bookshelves that lined the walls of the large room, was the man whose voice I had heard through the speaker. Dressed in dark gray slacks and a white dress shirt, he kept his back to me as he ran a long, graceful finger over the spines of the many leather-bound tomes, all of which were probably older than me.

"I apologize for any discomfort, Wolfgang," he said as he pulled one of the books from its place.

"I've asked you not to call me that."

"It is your name, is it not? I would have thought, given your penchant for sarcasm, that you would appreciate the irony."

He was still facing the bookshelves as he began flipping through the book's pages, so all I could see was his black shoulder length hair and the outline of his graceful, almost feminine jawline. I did catch the slight tilt of his head though, which, along with the tone of his voice, let me know that he was enjoying himself. "Wolfgang Aldous Regnum. Your mother's doing, if memory serves."

I never cared for my first name. For that matter, I did not care for my middle one either. So, I had taken to introducing myself as Ray, a kind of shortened version of my last name. It never lasted though, because as soon as anyone got wind of my real name, they would just start calling me Wolf.

"Your are late," he said turning from the shelves and making his way to a high-backed leather chair in the center of the room. while still managing to not bother looking at me.

"I had a flat tire."

"Is that how the blood ended up on your shirt?"

Like a lemming following the herd over the cliff, I immediately looked down at my shirt and saw nothing. Then I followed my nose and there it was, blood on the outside of my collar. It lingered in my nostrils since leaving the parking lot, but I hadn't bothered to track it down. In my defense, I had other things on my mind at the time; like not turning into an uncontrollable killing machine.

"It was a rough neighborhood," I said finally. It had been well over a year now and it was obvious that he still enjoyed keeping me off balance. "I do appreciate the candles though," I said, making my way to the chair opposite his. "They do help a little."

I stopped just in front of the chair and watched as his hazel brown eyes slowly met mine. I made sure to look right at him as I sat down without asking. It annoyed him and I knew it, but I felt the need to establish some measure of control. Speaker Man just smiled, looked down at the book he had selected and flipped casually through some more of the pages.

"I brought you the reports from Simon's---"

"Set them on the table next to you," he said with a wave of his hand. I did as he asked. "Is there some other reason why you are still here Wolfga... well is there?"

"There was a journal," I said. "I was able to get it out of the house before anyone else noticed it was even there."

"I suspected as much or you may have been on time," he said without interest. Then his eyes brightened, flicking up to meet mine. "Have you read it?"

"I flipped through it to make sure there wasn't anything in it I needed to know but---"

"I wonder," he said by way of interruption, his eyes narrowing. "Did you feel any sort of kinship with Simon's creation?"

"I'm not sure I know what you mean," I said evenly. This was not what I was here to talk about, and the exchange was getting away from me.

"Well, you were both recently..." he paused as if searching for the word, "inducted into our little world and I thought that perhaps..."

"He was given a choice."

"Ah, yes," he said, tilting his head back slightly. "Still, I would think his plight might have been analogous to yours in some way."

"I really didn't know the guy, so I didn't really feel anything," I said, still struggling to find some way back to what I wanted to talk about.

"I see," he said, looking away. He almost looked sad, and I started to think I might have a shot.

"Now that Simon's... creation has been dealt with I was hoping that I could transfer a bit closer to..."

Speaker Man's face grew dark and he began to speak as though to himself. "Simon was good for us. He was old and he was wise. It is a pity that he had to die trying to rid the world of his mistake. But it is the risk we take when we choose to make another. We take great pains to choose wisely in the hope that our creation will make the world around them better." He let the lids of his eyes fall slowly, closing them gently. Then his eyes snapped open, meeting mine with an intensity that made me shrink back into my seat "It is sad that greater care is not taken by your kind when selecting those who will be changed!" His voice boomed in the large library.

"I was not selected, I survived," I said, recovering. His accusations deepening my own self-loathing.

"With your kind there is just naked lust matched only by your savagery and blatant disregard for—"

"I was not chosen!" I yelled, interrupting him before he could insult me further, my words trailing off into a low involuntary growl. Without knowing I had done so I found myself sitting bolt upright in the chair as if preparing to launch myself across the room.

"Of course not," he said, his voice soft and even once again. He smiled as he spoke, having proven his point. "And as such, you have no loyalties to any breed, nor any love lost." He stood up slowly, making no threatening movements. It wasn't out of fear though, I was pretty sure I would have smelled it on him if it was. It was more like he was trying to avoid staining his carpet with my guts. "That is why you were asked to join us, to watch over the rest of our brothers and sisters. To help police them, if you will pardon the pun," he said, moving casually back to the bookshelves and placing the book back in its designated location. "To clean up the inevitable messes that turn up every so often."

"I wasn't exactly asked."

"Encouraged then, if you prefer," he said, turning to face me.

"Well, since there are no other active...you know, supernatural cases in our area—"

"Really? Tell me again how you ended up with blood on your shirt," he said with a knowing look.

"I was wondering if now might be a good time to transfer me a bit closer..." I hesitated not wanting to repeat myself. "Some place where I might be of more use to—"

"You will be transferred when I am done with you!" The echoes of his booming voice faded into silence before he continued in a softer, more sinister voice. "And, until then you will watch for us. You will watch them, and I will watch you."

With that, my hopes were dashed by my boss... My boss the Vampire. It sounded like a bad musical.

CHAPTER 2

The fresh air outside the Speaker Man's cozy little love nest was a welcome relief. My clothes reeked of the place, and I suddenly felt the urge to roll around in the dirt for a while.

My phone chirped and, after digging around in my jacket pocket, I pulled it out and saw the half-dozen or so missed calls. I could guess what he was trying to tell me.

"You ok man?" He answered his phone so quickly he must have been holding it in his hand.

"Why didn't you tell me who it was, Jo?", I asked, my voice sounding strange to my own ears, tired and beaten.

"I didn't know, man, I swear. One of our Custards called it in as a car in the parking lot. He described it, but I didn't make the connection until you were already out there!"

"How many Aston Martins are rolling around Richmond fucking Virginia Jo?"

"He described it man," he said, loud enough for me to realize I had been screaming into the phone. "How many Custards you know can tell an Aston Martin from a Ford Pinto?"

Custard was his nickname for anyone who was serving time as one of our eyes and ears in the world of Gremlins, Vampires and Werewolves. It was short for Custodiatis - some Latin word that I had no idea what is translated to in bad english. Any of the aforementioned creepies who bent or broke the rules were punished; those that committed relatively minor infractions usually ended up serving time as our little spies.

"Whatever man," I said, not feeling very forgiving even if there was a logical explanation.

"So...did you get him?"

"What do you think?" I asked, getting loud again as I got more irritated. "You don't get Markku!"

"I just meant---"

"Meant what? It's not like I can make him do anything even if I did manage to..." I stammered as I spoke, the memory of the confrontation infuriating me. "And as for stopping him? No... Hell no! He kicked my ass all over the parking lot. Is that what you meant?"

"Look, we're not getting anywhere," he said. "I assume you're all right since you're just as much of an asshole as usual." He took an audible breath before continuing in a slightly calmer voice. "Everything taken care of?"

"There was a body, so I called in the I.D. guys as well as disposal."

"He killed someone?"

"Doesn't he always?" I was getting irritated again so, I took a deep breath of my own before going on. "She was hanging halfway out of his Aston Martin, Jo." The image of the poor girl spilling out of Markku's car filled my head: the vacant eyes, the blood streaming down the side of her face, the vicious gash on her neck where her carotid used to be. "Now that I think of it, I suppose we'll have to clean his damn car too."

"That part is already taken care of," he said, sounding graver than he had before.

"How?"

"You're still on a kind of ... probation. Everything you request or get sent out on has to go through me."

He was right. I had almost forgotten that I was not a full-fledged member of the spooky club. I wasn't sure if there was a secret handshake or some mantra I still had to learn, but the bottom line was I still had a handler; that was where Jo came in.

"Ok, then why were you surprised about the dead girl?"

"Because, smart ass, these clean up disposal types are just that and nothing more. They don't give detailed reports or anything. When you call these guys, they come out and make an entire incident disappear. It's their job and when they are done that is exactly what they call and say 'Done', that's it."

"Well then, sounds like you people have got this stuff down to a science." I could not quite put my finger on why, but I was still angry. "And what about the Custa...I mean... whoever called you about the car, do I need to track him down? You know... to be sure no one else saw anything."

"It has been handled, kid."

"But what about---"

"There's nothing more you can do for her, Wolf."

His words rattled around in my head like razors. I was powerless and I couldn't shake the feeling that I failed the girl I left hanging out of an abandoned sports car in an empty parking lot.

"Wolf?"

"Yeah," I said. The sound of my name bringing me back to the present.

"I know it hurts man, but there was nothing more you could have done."

"Alright. Listen Jo, I'll talk to you later, okay?"

"Yeah sure."

Joaquin Ramirez, Jo to his not-so-close friends, had nailed it. It was like he could read my mind even after I had pissed him off to no end by being ... well, by being me. Almost two years of working with him and I still had no idea how to stay on his good side. My rational brain told me that yelling was probably not the best way, but I rarely listened to that side when I got angry... or anytime really. I shoved the phone back into my pocket and tried to clear my head, but I couldn't quite get there; instead, I stood there reliving the whole thing, wishing I was back in upstate New York.

Ramirez had called me just as I was getting ready to head home. One of our freak power brethren was doing something he shouldn't and our Cust… God I hated that term, one of our spies had called him. There was no way he was going to get there in time, so he tapped me. As soon as I pulled into the abandoned parking lot, I knew I had a problem. When all was said and done, I was left looking down at the lifeless body of what was once a beautiful woman after getting my ass handed to me by the guy who had done it.

It would have been nice to be able to say that she looked graceful, a perfect image of peace. It would have been nice to be able to say she was draped across the front seat of the car in some elegant way, beautiful even in death. But this world is not nice. Nice does not leave a young woman spilling out of the front seat of a car. Nice was not a corpse with her skirt hiked up around her waist, legs splayed wide open, one over the back of the seat and one hanging off the front. Nice was not a blank stare from eyes that will never see anything again, a face without emotion as if drugged, her blouse open to the waist exposing blood covered breasts. Two years ago, I was naive enough to think that this world was at least sometimes nice. That was before I learned that monsters were real; it was also before I was turned into one of them.

A light rain started to fall, making me acknowledge that I really was in a world of crap, and that I couldn't just stand there. Ramirez was right though; there was nothing more I could do for the girl. The car had been towed and would be cleaned.

The I.D. guys would figure out who the girl was and come up with a story consistent with her history and the wounds on her body. Whoever called in the sighting would start asking around to see if anyone saw anything that might raise questions. So I took a breath and headed to my car.

Arriving at the driver's side door, I stopped to take a last look up and down the street. I had no idea why I felt the need to, but I did. Maybe I had seen too many movies, or maybe I was just paranoid. I didn't even know what I was looking for, but now that the dramatic pause on a barren street was checked off my list, I eased myself into the car. The Dodge Charger's engine roared to life, and I was reminded of how much I loved this car, pity it wasn't mine.

It was coming up on two in the morning and the last callers were starting to hit the streets. My little pitstop as arranged by Jo as well as my little chat with Speaker Man had worn me out and I was not in the mood to take things slow. I shifted into drive, hit a switch on the dash and accelerated. The blue lights began flashing;consequently, anyone in the area doing what they shouldn't be would think twice. I wasn't interested in drunk drivers or petty crooks tonight, but I had to admit that sometimes it was convenient being a cop.

CHAPTER 3

The rhythmic clicking of the ceiling fan's chain against the light globe was not enough to lull me to sleep. My mind was going back and forth between Speaker Man's denial of my request to get the hell out of Richmond and the utter ass whooping Markku had given me to begin my evening of pleasures. The funny thing about getting your ass kicked is that you can't help but go over it again and again, trying to figure out how you might have won. You analyze everything, every step, every swing, every miss and when that doesn't work you go back a little more and see if you could have avoided the fight altogether. Even after all of that, I still couldn't come up with anything I could have changed. It all happened as though there was no other way it could have gone down.

Laying in my bed I went over every detail in my mind, but the question I kept coming back to was why had he let me live. Thanks to his father, Markku could act with impunity taking out anyone who interrupted his feeding, even a newly minted detective in the Richmond Police Department. Markku was untouchable. It didn't even matter that

I was also working for the Speaker Man. In fact, that particular relationship is why I was placed in the Police Department in the first place, watching the other freaks and beasties of this world. So, why was I still breathing? Then I remembered what he said to me.

"You are not afraid of me." It was a statement, albeit one of surprise. *"You might actually be a useful little dog,"* he said as he pressed my face against the driver's side fender of the Aston Martin, my right arm twisted painfully in a hammer lock behind my back. *"There is something happening Detective, something that has not happened for quite some time. Pay close attention to what you see and hear over the next few days. You have a long day ahead of you Detective, so I suggest you get some rest."* He released me and I crumbled to the asphalt landing so close to the blonde prostitute's throat that I could see the puncture wounds still oozing blood. *"And go kill something, would you please. You look terrible."*

I kicked off the sheets and got out of bed. My thinking was that if I was going to have a case of insomnia I may as well try and figure out what I was dealing with. I headed out of the bedroom and into the kitchen. The kitchen table doubled as my home office so I flipped open my laptop, punched the name Van den Broek into the search engine and waited. The Wi-fi was crap in my apartment but eventually the name Hadrian Van den Broek, President and CEO of Caesar Holdings, Incorporated popped up on the screen... Markku's father. If there was anything happening in the city, he would know about it.

A long list of articles about the highly respected businessman and real estate mogul -all of them resoundingly positive- filled the screen and ranged from acts of altruism to an uncanny ability to come out on top of whatever venture, deal or merger his company was involved in. If the Speaker Man was a sort of seriously anemic Yoda for our side, Hadrian was the Emperor for theirs.

Screen after screen scrolled by and still no luck. The more I clicked the more frustrated I became until I finally came to an article mentioning Markku, Hadrian's one and only son. Apparently, he was more of a black sheep than a spoiled rich kid. The article detailed some kind of rift between father and son that manifested into memorable moments ranging from embarrassing footage on webcams and photos in the trash tabloids you saw in the check-out line at grocery stores, to outright statements against his father's deals and incitement of protests.

The alarm clock blared in my room, and I almost jumped out of my chair. Evidently, time really does fly when you are having fun. The welcome sound of steam puffing and liquid gold dripping into the carafe of the coffee maker had me almost convinced that it was going to be an alright day when my phone started buzzing and beeping. I snatched up the phone to look at the name on the screen; all my ringtones were the same because I had never figured out how to change them. Hell, I could barely figure out how to turn the thing on.

Once I saw who it was, I had to fight the urge to throw the thing across the room. The little angel on my right was a bit louder than the other guy this time and I hit the green talk button.

"What could possibly be worth calling me at this hour when I will be at my desk in forty-five minutes?"

"Good, you were going to work." Ramirez's voice was even, but there was an edge of tension in it. "After getting thrown around a bit I wanted to be sure you weren't calling out sick or something." He was neither sympathetic, empathetic, or any other kind of -thetic I could think of.

"I kind of earned a day don't you think?" I asked.

"Skip roll call and come down to the Sheraton Hotel and Conference Center."

"How am I supposed to explain that to---"

"I'll square it with your Lieutenant. Don't worry about that." There was a cacophony of voices in the background as he spoke. "We have a mess down here and we need some damage control." He hung up before I could ask for any more details.

"Damage control" meant that someone from our side of the reality tracks, the creepier side as I liked to call it, had screwed the pooch. It would be our job to make sense of it while keeping the normal people in the dark so to speak, or at least most of them. Then we had to find whoever was responsible and dole out some otherworldly justice.

"Justice", I thought to myself, unless your name was Markku Van den Broek.

CHAPTER 4

The scene was the typical kind of crazy one would expect to find around a dead body, and it didn't help that the hotel was enormous. It took me almost five minutes to make my way through the gaggle of reporters. It then took me at least another two to find a uniformed cop who could give me directions to where I might find Detective Joaquin 'Jo' Ramirez.

The large conference room had been set up with about twenty round tables that sat about ten people each, but, no one was sitting. Photographs were being taken of everything from the body itself to the contents of a mop bucket that was found near it. People were milling about in all directions, and every single one of them was working extremely hard to justify their own existence.

I found Ramirez directing traffic around the body. He had his work cut out for him since the body had been found in what looked like a broom closet. He had about five people talking to him at once, so it took him a while to notice me standing just outside the fray. I heard him bark out something like, "just get it done to some poor kid in uniform before he headed over to me.

"Jo! What do you got me doing here?" I asked once we were out of earshot.

"You're the new kid on the block, Wolf."

"I know so teach me something. Let me watch and learn, man," I said, trying to sound sincere and not like someone who simply hated the job. "And stop calling me Wolf."

"I need you to take the lead on this one, kid. I have been instructed to have you—"

"And how is that a good idea, Jo? I don't know what I am supposed to do here!"

"It's been requested by..." he looked around before continuing, "by you know damn well who!"

"Requested?" Now I was getting concerned. "What exactly was requested, Jo?"

"Look, like it or not, you're the lead on this one, so take your thumb out of your ass and get to work," he said, turning away from me.

"Wait a second," I said loudly, placing a hand on his arm but not grabbing it. "Lead on what? I don't even know what this is."

"Damn it kid!" He faced me, then checked to make sure no one could hear. "Listen up. I count two bodies so far that I have to explain because they look like they've been drained of every bodily fluid possible to the point where they look like week-old raisins. The only bright spot is that they are in separate parts of the hotel so I should be able to keep anyone from connecting the two. Hell, I may even be able to keep them from being called murders for a while."

"Are they murders?" I asked and regretted it immediately.

"Why in the fuck would we have been called in if they just tripped down the damn stairs?" He looked at me hard. "One was found in a suite on the sixth floor, and the other was in that maintenance closet you saw." Ramirez scanned the room to make sure we still weren't being heard. "What I need you to handle is the kid that survived. He was here attending some kind of sales conference motivational crap when some woman came out of the closet where we found contestant number one, walked up to our boy over there," he pointed to the other side of the room, "and wigged out on him. Now, I don't have time to babysit so get on it."

Ramirez stormed off toward a group of people gathered by the front desk while I stood there wondering what I was supposed to do next. All I knew was that someone had been attacked and survived, and that shortly thereafter the body in the closet had been discovered. I looked back at Ramirez and could see that he was addressing some reporters near the dead body in the closet.

"The three incidents are being investigated independently until we can make concrete connections," he said to the group.

Turning my attention to the guy that survived, it was pretty obvious he was in shock. He wasn't really focusing on anything. I started making my way over to him slowly, keeping my eyes on him as I got closer. He was still looking around like a lost kid in a mall. I caught his scent, and I was surprised at what my nose was telling me; he wasn't scared. I was still getting used to interpreting the different smells humans had for different moods but this one was kind of confusing. It didn't make much sense but if I had to guess, I would say this guy was feeling pretty good.

"Sir?"

"Yes." The guy looked up at me and started to stand. I eased him back down with a hand on his shoulder then offered him my hand in a very clumsy introduction.

"My name is Detective Regnum. I understand you may have gotten a good look at our suspect."

"Suspect?"

"The woman you were talking to just before the screaming started."

"Oh…Oh yeah." The guy started smiling like a five-year-old after you ask him who his girlfriend is.

"Could you describe her to me please? It would help a good deal." I was slowing down my speech so that the space cadet could understand me.

"Sure, sure, she was beautiful…She…" He cocked his head slightly looking confused.

"Sir?"

"Yes."

"What did she look like?" I asked, starting to lose what little patience I kept in reserve for morons.

"She had brown eyes." He was smiling again, and I was getting really frustrated.

"Thank you for that. Now what else can you tell me?"

"I don't know."

"You said she was beautiful. Do you remember that?"

"Yes," he said, still grinning.

"Then could you tell me what was so beautiful about her?"

"Her eyes," he said, grinning even bigger now.

"Her brown eyes?" I said making no effort to hide my sarcasm.

"Yeah!" He said, as if he was talking to someone who finally understood what he meant. "But they weren't just brown, man, I mean they were... brown like...I mean really brown almost like..."

"Aw jeez will someone get this guy an artist and a drug test," I said out loud to the room, interrupting the space cadet. "Maybe she wears an eye patch or something that could narrow down the search for his 'brown eyed girl'." Markku was right; it was going to be a long day.

CHAPTER 5

It was well past three o'clock in the afternoon before I made it back to the precinct. Most everyone was out in the field, so Major Crimes was not as crowded. As I got closer to my desk, I could see Ramirez going through the photos of the bodies from the hotel. I passed row after row of empty desks before grabbing the chair next to him. That's when Ramirez almost flew out of his chair squealing like a five-year-old at a clown convention.

"Damn it man! What are you trying to do to me?" He yelled trying to regain his composure.

"What's your problem?"

"It was like you came out of nowhere. You don't catch on real quick, do you? Jesus!" He slumped back onto the desk holding on to his chest where I imagine he thought his heart was. He was a little north of the mark.

"Catch on to what?" I asked, losing my patience.

"You move quieter than everybody else now, Wolf," he said, sitting up and looking intently at me. "You have to make an effort to be noisy. You can't go walking around like a predator all the time or someone who knows something is going to figure it out, and I hope I don't have to tell you that most humans don't like us very much." This last part he said while looking over his shoulder as if someone might be listening. "Jesus! They need to set up some kind of monster school for guys like you." He was right of course, about the monster school, but I simply wasn't in the mood to hear it.

"Did the car get taken care of this morning?"

"The Aston Martin? Sure. The guys in clean up weren't too happy. Getting blood and that smell out of carpets and leather ain't easy."

"They've seen it before," I said, not caring about the woes of some idiot cleaning cars for murderers.

"I was going over the damage to the prunes we found back at the hotel, and it does narrow things down a bit." Ramirez was flipping through notes as he spoke. "There are very few of us out there that can do this kind of thing, but whoever it was would have to be real motivated, if you follow me."

"No, I don't follow," I said, letting my weight fall into my chair hoping to make enough noise. Ramirez didn't take the bait but closed his notebook and looked down at me.

"Let's just say that the kind of time it would take to do this to a man would mean some serious hatred, or anger, or whatever."

"Whatever?" I said, honestly perplexed.

"You ever heard of a Succubus?"

"A what?" I said sitting up straight.

"A Succubus. Didn't you watch any horror movies growing up?"

"Nah, kung fu theater and Bruce Lee movies."

"Look, Succubi are some of the oldest supernatural things on earth. They're supposedly a type of demon that prey on men, sucking out their life force and leaving them looking like a ten-year-old corpse."

"Demon?" I couldn't keep the sarcasm out of my voice. "You mean like a minion of the Devil?"

"I'm just telling you what the damage was most likely caused by. You got a problem with classification, semantics, or maybe you are just some kind of monster bigot, I don't give a shit but whatever did this did it fast and did it well."

"I'm still lost, Jo."

"Christ you've got a lot to learn," he said, standing up and taking a few paces away from my desk. Joaquin Ramirez was about my height at five foot eleven with walnut skin and hard, dark brown eyes that were surrounded with crow's feet from scowling all the time. He wore his hair like he was a Marine and usually barked out orders like one as well. He was wiry and quick in the nervous twitch kind of way and even though I carried more weight on my frame, all things being equal and no super freak powers, I would not want to tangle with him. "Look here," he said, laying out the photos of the three bodies on my desk. "These two, broom-closet boy and the knucklehead survivor you spoke to, they were there for this sales motivational thing, right?"

he said, turning back to look at me again.

"Yeah." I was nodding my head trying to get him to cut to the chase.

"Well, they were both seen through the first half of the meeting. These things are designed like shows or cheap books. When the preliminaries are over, they make the second half shorter to give the illusion of the entire presentation picking up steam or excitement." I was staring at him, still not getting what he was shoveling. "The rest of the meeting was only about forty-five minutes. That is some fast juicing!" Now I was finally catching on. "And it happened in the janitor's closet with people walking by the whole time, so it had to have been done real quiet like."

"And all that tells you that this was done by some demon?"

"It tells me that whatever it is, you don't want to piss it off."

"Fine, so what about the guy you found in the hotel suite?" I asked, taking a closer look at all three photos.

"Here is where it gets tricky," he said, taking a deep breath.

I felt my empty stomach roll. "What do you mean tricky?"

"You wanted to know what made me think this was a demon, right?"

"Yeah, so?"

"There was no record of anyone checking into that room. And yet..."

The sing-song tone of his "and yet" was a little dramatic for my taste, but when he pulled out a disc and dropped it into the DVD player of my computer, I figured he had something real.

He stared at me for a second before I thought to tap on my keyboard and log in so we could watch the playback. "This," he continued, "is the security footage for the lobby of the hotel from midnight to seven this morning." The screen brightened and a four-panel display filled the screen showing different lines of sight into the lobby. "Move forward to 4:42 AM."

I did as he said then watched as the footage rolled. The lobby was deserted except for the desk clerk typing away at his computer. Then the revolving door started to move, and in she came. Long and lithe, graceful, and so full of power; she moved like a whisper, as though not one muscle exerted any effort save what was absolutely necessary. A man walked beside her, but he was almost invisible; there was no mistaking that she was the predator, and he was her prey.

"Now," Ramirez's voice snapped me back to the here and now, "watch what happens when she gets to the desk clerk."

The kid behind the desk was still clicking away at his computer when she stepped to the counter. It was about another three seconds when he looked up casually as if it were a bother to do it, then froze. From the camera angle behind the kid, I could see the woman speaking, but it was too far away to make out what she was saying. It could not have been more than a sentence or two, but the kid looked down, picked up a check-in sheet, removed the key card from it, and handed it to the woman.

"See that?" I jumped when he spoke this time and looked over at Ramirez to see if he had noticed. "Lots of these hotels and resorts will fill out check-in sheets and program key cards over the night shift for the incoming check-ins that are coming in the next day."

"So, the kid gave her one of those rooms," I said. "And since the key was already programmed, he didn't have to check her in or take any information if he didn't want to, but why would he do that?"

"Didn't you see him?" Ramirez sounded almost shocked. "The kid went all slack jawed when he laid eyes on her. Oh, and I almost forgot." He leaned over and took hold of the mouse. "Take a look at the guy with her." He rolled the footage back to when they approached the counter. "Look at his face. See anything familiar?"

I looked closely at the man struggling against the urge to look at her and only her. "It's kind of far away but I don't think I've ever seen the guy."

"No, not the face so much as his expression."

I looked again and a flicker of recognition came to me. "You're right." I was still grasping for what my brain was trying to put together. "It's right there but I'm not picking it up."

"He's got the same look on his face as the

bonehead survivor you had to interview."

I looked at Jo then back to the screen and there it was, as obvious as if it were stamped across his forehead. "What the hell?" The realization overwhelmed my ability to connect the rest of the dots. "So what does that mean?"

"I don't know, kid, but I think we need to take your boy to see someone."

"My what to see who?" I asked.

"Your witness," he said, staring at me for acknowledgement. "The chowderhead?" Ramirez raised both eyebrows and let his mouth go slack, mocking me.

"The kid from the hotel?"

"Finally!" he said. "Maybe we need to send you to regular school before we start worrying about monster school."

"Nice of you to look out for my best interest," I said. "And who are we taking him to, the department psych?"

"What is in your head, kid? If we take him to a shrink and they somehow get to and believe anything about a supernatural being, we are screwed!"

"Ok, then who?"

"Look, there's somebody I know that might be able to help us out." He looked away slightly as he spoke, which made me nervous. "She's human but... well let's just say she plays on our side of the tracks."

"What does that even mean?"

He looked around again before speaking.

"She's kind of a medium."

"What, like tarot card and crystal ball stuff?"

"Just trust me, will you?"

Shaking my head, it didn't seem like I had much choice. "Alright, and how do we do that? I mean, I assume this person is not connected with the police, so how do we justify to the witness us taking him there?" I asked.

"We kidnap him."

"What?"

"We kidnap him." He suggested it as if it were stopping by a convenience store on the way home.

"Why do we have to kidnap him?" I was losing my patience again.

"Not really kidnap, we just have to take him somewhere and convince him that it is official police business."

"Damn it! Look, this thing didn't even happen in my precinct," I said, running both hands through my ragged hair. "What the hell do they have me working this for?"

"Regnum!" The obnoxiously loud voice came from the end of the aisle behind us, and I recognized it immediately. Ramirez and I both turned, dreading what was to come.

"Hey Lieutenant. What's up?"

"There is a homicide I need you on." Lieutenant Gregory Bowman, an impressive man standing around six foot three with the build of a hockey player, was looking at me and holding a file. There wasn't a hint of anything but business in his expression, which surprised me.

"Sir," I said, searching for the right words. "You know why Jo and I are here...I mean the real reason." I knew we were alone, and I still felt compelled to look around. "We kind of have something going on right now."

"The hotel thing?" he asked, still with little to no expression.

"Yes sir."

"That's Ramirez's case."

"I know but it's one of the special---"

"Regnum," he said, interrupting me. "I know exactly what you are and what you mean." Now his expression did change and where I thought I might see fear, I saw anger. "I am one of the few people who have to bear the burden of knowing that things like you exist. But let me clue you in on something. I will be professional. I will not discriminate against ... whatever the hell you are. But I will also not discriminate against every other cop in this place just because you have some extracurricular things going on. They have their cases, and you have yours." He began to turn and in fine Columbo form, turned to face us again.

"And one more thing, just because I know something does not mean I am obligated to like it. In fact, to be completely honest, I don't like it at all. There are plenty of cops that deserve that desk a hell of a lot more than you do, kid. So shut up and work the damn case!"

CHAPTER 6

Ramirez and I agreed on a time to meet up later so we could take the chowderhead to his séance then went our separate ways. My way just happened to be to a new murder scene. I had been assigned to crime scenes before but never as the lead detective, and for that matter, never as any kind of detective. Up until now my investigative skill set had consisted of knocking on doors asking if anyone saw anything; not much to go on when you find yourself in charge.

I started looking at the faded numbers on the front of the houses as soon as I turned onto Q Street. I had not been in the area long enough to know the city, and I was too nervous to remember to punch the address into my GPS. The row houses went on and on, each one looking as ragged and unkempt as the one before it, paint peeling off the eaves in huge patches that would eventually fall to the ground like toxic maple leaves and front steps that looked like they were put together with driftwood by a circus monkey. Various pieces of stained and dry-rotting furniture lined the curbs; some even still had their owners sitting in them, drinking out of bottles wrapped in brown paper bags. I almost felt rescued when I saw the flashing lights of the crime scene a few blocks ahead of me.

By the time I arrived on the scene, there were two units parked out front and the forensics team had already begun their preparations to go in. The only thing that seemed to be missing was me and I had no idea what I was supposed to do.

I got out of my car, slamming the door as if I were annoyed at the inconvenience and walked purposefully to the front door. The news crews were still setting up, so by the time they noticed me I was thankfully already through the front door.

The wind had picked up outside, slamming the door closed behind me with more force than I intended. The noise made everyone in the room stop what they were doing and look straight at me. Recognizing who I was, I saw just about every eye in the house glaze over with the same look that every fifteen-year-old gets when a substitute teacher walks into their history class. "Here comes the putz," is what their expressions said to me, "the guy that doesn't know palm from pussy," and this time they were right.

I mean, everyone thinks that when the guy in charge shows up after the grunts have already been working for hours. I know, I have been that grunt. And normally, the grunt pays his dues before becoming the insufferable prick that walks in the front door criticizing how everything was done and demanding to see who turned his crime scene into Grand Central, but not this time. This time, the guy walking through the front door has no clue what to do next. This time, the guy walking through the front door has not paid his dues, has not seen all there was to see, and has no idea how to run an investigation.

"Sorry about the mess, Detective."

"What?"

"I said sorry about the mess. I don't know how anyone could live like this."

I turned to my left to find the strong, young face of Officer Shepherd. He was a patrolman I had run into a couple of times since being assigned to the 1st Precinct, and it seemed he was the first on the scene.

"What's the story?" I asked, trying to sound like I had already figured out what he was about to tell me.

"Not a whole lot to start with, sir." He paused as if he were wondering whether or not to continue speaking.

"Then let's start with what you have so far," I said, trying to sound gruff and unimpressed. I motioned for him to lead me to whatever it was I was supposed to be looking at, and he started meandering through the filth.

"Ok, first thing is that she was bludgeoned to death, but that's not the problem," he said, stopping just inside the doorway of the kitchen and gesturing toward a white sheet covering what had to be a body.

"So, what is the problem?" I asked, ramping up my feigned frustration.

"Well sir, it seems that the weapon used was her own cooking pan."

"So... the murder wasn't premeditated?"

"There's still not enough to be conclusive but... I don't think so."

"Anything else?" I asked.

There's one more thing you might find interesting."

"Show me," I said.

He nodded, turned, and walked with a purpose given to one who sensed the opportunity to prove himself, leading me through the filth that someone had called home and forged ahead.

Stepping out of what I had to guess was the living room, we passed through the kitchen. Except for a lone frying pan, one plate, a knife and a fork sitting neatly in a dish drainer, the entire room was a disgusting five by eight foot collection of dirty dishes and laundry piled so high that it was impossible to tell soiled from clean. From there we stepped into a room where it was obvious from the feces all over the floor that a dog was kept. The smell was enough to make me cover my nose and mouth, stifling the urge to vomit. Turning left, I found myself in a laundry room with Officer Shepherd looking at me as if I could answer whatever question was written all over his confused face.

"Well?" I asked, trying to discern what it was I was supposed to be noticing.

His eyes shifted a bit, and I saw his confidence waiver as he spoke. "I just thought it was odd...Wait, let me show you the rest." He darted off back to the main part of the house and took a right down the hall that led from the giant ashtray of a living room where I had walked in initially. "You see?" he asked, standing in the left side doorway at the end of the hall.

I was looking into what had to be a child's bedroom. I felt an odd sensation in the back of my mind, a thought that had not formed but was there nonetheless.

"These two rooms are the only ones in this whole house that are clean."

CHAPTER 7

It had been the most obvious thing in the house, and I had missed it! The whole charade I had been trying to construct while at the crime scene, had fallen apart miserably. In that moment, I was nine years old standing in front of a room full of my fellow Sunday School students with my mouth hanging open. The Sunday School teacher had finally come up, after what seemed like hours, and rescued me from my stage fright giving the report that I was supposed to have given.

"We're here," Ramirez said, jarring me back to the present. He didn't take his eyes off the road as he pulled into a parking spot just in front of the chowderhead's apartment building.

I was a bit concerned about how we were going to get the kid to come with us, but it turns out there was no need to be. You would be surprised at how easily people follow you when you are a policeman. Ramirez and I walked right up, knocked on the door, told him we needed to take him to a consultant, and he just got in the car. We stayed in metro Richmond proper, but just barely. The whole city was a confusing intersection of no less than seven different counties with Richmond being sandwiched in between them.

We headed into the Shockoe Bottom neighborhood which sits right along the James River near the southeast corner of the city. As we passed the Edgar Allen Poe Museum along East Main Street, I could not help but think that Mr. Poe had known a little about our world. Maybe that's what made him drink too much and end up in a gutter half crazed and all dead.

We finally arrived in front of an apartment building that could charitably be called livable. The complex was old and smelled of urine. We all got out of the car and headed toward the entrance. Ramirez stopped about halfway to the door and turned. "Now, you're going to have to be patient with this one," he said, speaking to me in a slow and measured pace as if explaining something to a preschooler. "We need her to get into this guy's head, but she may not be too pleased with us visiting her."

"What are you saying? Didn't you call and let her know what was going on?"

"It's not so much me she'll have a problem with," he said, turning and heading toward the entrance.

I had no idea what he was talking about, but I was about to learn real fast. After two flights of stairs, he knocked on a door at the end of a hallway. A woman's voice yelled from behind the door and included a few words in Spanish. She spoke so quickly that I could not understand either language, but I had definitely heard the tone before. I heard the clip clop of heels approaching the door, and a second later it opened to reveal a dark-skinned black-haired woman who did not seem at all happy to see us. She was short but not small, with strong thighs that led up to generous hips that may have looked large on another woman but perfect on her. Her ample breasts completed the voluptuous package and the expression she greeted us with confirmed the attitude and fire of a Puerto Rican. I was no expert on the Latino community, but I had seen plenty like her all over New York. There was no mistaking it.

"¿Mira, que quieres ahora cabron?" She turned away as quickly as she spoke. Her voice was deep and strong, and the words were coming out so rapidly it seemed as if she had spoken just one.

"Un favor negrita." Ramirez spoke slowly enough that I could pick out 'favor' as he followed her in. I realized he had not let her know why we had come.

"Siempre con favores y 'ayudame negrita...'" I was just starting to understand her when her eyes found mine. That is when she froze. "What the fuck?" She almost fell backward screaming out the words. I stopped in my tracks. The bonehead witness ran right into the back of me.

"Niña!" Ramirez called after her as she bolted to a room at the end of the hall and slammed the door.

"What the fuck you bring into my house!"

"Stop fucking cussing at me!" Ramirez was

yelling now too.

"Animal! You bring a killer into my house!" There was a lot of noise from behind the door like she was looking for something. "You, I help, but that thing is a beast! They don't control themselves."

"He's with me. He's okay!"

At that moment the door opened, and a handgun was being leveled at my head. I was moving before her next words escaped her lips.

"I don't give a sh---" The door swung inward opening to my right. I saw it all happen slowly. Her left hand was letting go of the knob and moving up to get a two-handed grip on the revolver that was pointed up and away to get clear of the swinging door. The sweeping motion of her hands as she brought the gun to bear, made her overcompensate. Her initial aim would have placed the shot just past my right shoulder, had I still been there.

I jumped to my left, my legs propelling me just behind Ramirez at an angle so that I landed next to him. My left foot planted where the wall met the floor and my hand against the wall. I made myself small, coiled my body for power and launched forward. I was under the woman's right arm with my right hand around her throat before she could correct aim, the gun still pointing at an empty space where I was a split second before.

"What is your problem, lady?"

Her eyes were wide in surprise, but they darkened so quickly it was almost feral. "Go on you fucking lobo cabron! Tear my throat out!" There was no fear in her and, as I recognized that, I also realized that she knew what I was. "Me cago en tu madre!" She knew what I had become, and she hated me.

CHAPTER 8

Ramirez sat on the edge of the couch next to our walking vegetable and the woman, whose name I learned was Milagro, sat in a threadbare recliner in the corner of the room farthest from me. I was standing at the entrance to the living room still coming down from the rush. She could see it in me. I felt her disgust and I knew that she, of all mortals, knew what I was feeling and knew how close I was to changing.

"We need to know what is in this man's head, cariño." Ramirez said, his calm voice breaking the silence like a bull horn.

"And you want me to get it for you. Look at him!" She waved her arm at our vegetable dismissively. "His mind is almost gone, and if it is not, then there is something else in there and you don't know what it is." She stood up and started pacing back and forth, careful not to get any closer to me as she maneuvered around the room. "Now you want me to go in there and stomp around some man's head without knowing what else is in there?"

"Look chica!" I said, losing my patience. "Speak English for those of us who don't know the hocus pocus lingo, okay?"

"I'll use small words, Fido," she said, swinging her head around so that she could spit the words out at me. "And, if you sit and shut the hell up like a good little dog, I'll give you a fucking biscuit." She was seething with as much anger and hate as I had ever witnessed. "If this man's mind has been touched by something …not human, I will see that other mind too."

"That's a good thing, right?" I said without thinking.

"That depends on what the hell messed with his mind now, doesn't it? Some of the things out there feed on minds, and if you try and read them, you wind up hugging yourself in a pretty white jacket singing 'it's a small world after all' with other nut jobs. Entiendes?"

"The only thing I understand is that you are either going to help us, or you're not. Now, I need to figure it out quick, because I have way too much to do with someone running around treating people like human juice boxes to stand here and screw around with you."

She stared at me with a peculiar look on her face. I couldn't tell if she was confused or surprised, but there was something there that wasn't there before. After what seemed an eternity, she stood up and went towards our little chowderhead.

"Mira, Joaquin. Keep Old Yeller off me while I do this. I don't want him to mistake me for a Milk Bone."

"The name's Ray," I said.

"Whatever, Dog Chow!"

She knelt down in front of the man we brought with us and took his face in her hands. The touch seemed so intimate as she moved her face closer and closer to his that I found myself holding my breath. They were so close that it seemed she would kiss him, but her eyes were wide open, as were his. It could not have been more than three seconds when the girl collapsed. It was like her body crumbled, and the only thing that saved her was Ramirez catching her head before it hit the hard floor. He moved with such a casual ease that I could tell he had done this many times before.

"What the hell was that?" I asked.

"That is what we came here to ask her to do."

"To take a nap?!" I could not keep the disdain for this woman out of my tone. She had insulted me, accused me, judged me, and sentenced me without so much as an introduction.

"If she wakes up, we'll have what we need." Ramirez said as he held her head gently in his lap and stroked her forehead.

"If?"

CHAPTER 9

We took the kid back home after we were sure that Milagro was going to be alright. She wasn't able to tell us much, but Ramirez explained to me that sometimes it takes a day or two for her to get her head back on straight. Still, what she did tell us made no sense. Even after I got over the fact that I was trying to track down what might be a demon, it still didn't make any sense. We knew that whatever this thing was had left at least one body, probably two and then let some guy live. We just didn't know why, and I had nothing more than the hazy memory of a guy who was apparently still under some kind of mind-numbing spell.

Ramirez had not said a word since we dropped off the kid and I was too tired to push. It was pretty obvious that he had a lot on his mind, and I was not about to go poking around where I wasn't wanted. If it was important, he was going to tell me, or he wasn't, either way I needed to get home and clear my head.

We pulled up in front of my building and he did not even put the car in park. It was a three-story old Victorian with the top floor being an attic that had been finished to make another apartment. That was where I lived, the top floor; in case I ever wanted to throw myself out the window, though Ramirez assured me it wouldn't do any good.

"Hey Jo, I'm going to cook up something. You want in?"

"Tempting but I'm heading home to look up a few things and check on Milagro on the way," he said.

I could tell he was holding back something, and to be honest, it was a weak attempt on my part to try and make nice. We had both been trying to find some common ground since we were teamed up, and it was not working. I just could not shake the feeling that there was something he didn't like about me. I guess when I thought about it, it made sense. There was a whole lot I didn't like about me either. "Cool," I said, trying to sound casual about it. "I have to get on the frying pan murder the Lieutenant gave me in Chimborazo. The M.E. report should be ready in the morning, so I'll check in with you around lunch."

"Got it," he said and eased away from the curb before giving his car any gas.

After jiggling the key in the lock to make it work, I stepped into my apartment. There wasn't a whole lot to look at, but it was quiet, and it was mine. I flipped on the radio, which was still tuned into the local public radio station, and made my way to the kitchen. A soft piano played beautifully, giving part of my brain something to chew on while the rest tried to figure out what the hell just happened and how could I even believe it, let alone act on it.

I went over to the refrigerator, opened the door and started pulling out vegetables and a container of tomato sauce. Grabbing a small pot from under the sink I filled it with water, salt, and a cap full of olive oil. I could not help thinking of the really happy girl with the smile and her own cooking show saying, "and don't forget the E-V-O-O." I set the pot on the range, put the flame on and went to my cutting board to start chopping up vegetables for the sauce. If there was one positive thing I could say about my situation, it was that even if I hated being a monster, at least I wasn't a vampire. They aren't able to eat anything other than blood. I think I'd lose it if I couldn't cook a thing or two now and again. But I was still a monster.

Reminding myself that thinking like that did not make for a good night, I refocused on what I knew about the case. "The case," I said aloud to no one in particular. "Which one?" Why was I getting my first homicide so soon after stepping into my new role as detective? On top of that, the head creep of our little creature squad made Ramirez give me this demon deal.

"It was in for the kill," I thought to myself. In fact, it was so hungry for this guy, it was apparently about to expose itself to dozens of people just to take this kid after drying up two bodies already. So, what else did I have? According to what little we got from

Milagro, this thing liked variety. Other than that, all I could really work with was a loose timeline and witness statements.

The first victim was taken at about four in the morning; the body was found in one of the suites. When we inquired about who was in the suite, the desk clerk had no record of anyone having checked into it.

The second body, the one in the broom closet was found after the attack on the chowderhead kid. Either this thing ate a lot, or there was something about this guy that made him irresistible. But what? As far as we could tell the guy was a class A moron. Then it hit me. In Milagro's vision, he was having a conversation with it, and something about him was frustrating the creature. Did he know he was being targeted and trying to talk his way out of it?

I had to talk to the headcase again. I decided to give Ramirez a call and set it up, especially since he also might know if this mush mind thing was temporary. If we could get the chowderhead to the voodoo girl with his head on straight, we might get a clearer picture and he might even be able to explain it a bit more.

Then I remembered Milagro's reaction. She was repulsed by me. I remembered her face as she recognized what I was, and she loathed me. There was fear and anger and hatred in her eyes, and she didn't even know me. It was just what I had become, the thing in me, this part of me that I can never get rid of. The part of me that was a monster. In her eyes, it might as well be all of me.

I shook my head, trying to clear the images from my mind, then looked down at the cutting board. I saw blood. Without realizing it, I had sliced open my thumb and was bleeding all over the garlic. I sighed, knowing it didn't matter since it would heal in a few minutes anyway; another part of what Speaker Man called my gift.

"Gift," I thought to myself as my hands started to shake. Grabbing the blood covered board I threw it across the room, peppers, onions and garlic spun in small circles with specks of blood flicking off most of their edges. I watched it fly through the air and immediately knew how idiotic of an act it was, but I felt better having done it. I was never much of a reader, but something I read a while back, maybe when I was in college popped into my head. Hemingway, '*What an animal a man is in a rage.*"

"No shit," I said out loud.

"You smell good."

I spun around lowering my center of gravity preparing to attack or run. Halfway through the move, the sound of the voice struck a chord. Even with my new speed, I knew who it was before my head swung around to lay eyes on him. Sitting in my window, one leg swinging idly, was Markku Van den Broek.

CHAPTER 10

"Your blood, it means you eat well." Markku Van den Broek had somehow climbed up three stories, opened my window, and flopped himself comfortably on my windowsill, all without making a sound. "Now, what you're cooking? That does turn the stomach a bit."

"I went heavy on the garlic," I said, looking at my thumb then back up at Markku. "I seem to have developed a taste for it over the last 24 hours." I turned back to my kitchen counter and reached for the paper towels, then, realizing my bleeding had already stopped, grabbed the wooden spoon instead.

"You know it is just annoying to us."

"Every little bit counts," I said, stirring the pot literally and figuratively.

"Let's go for a walk, Regnum," he said dropping silently into the kitchen from his comfortable perch in the window.

"What for?"

"I want to talk."

"Talk here," I said, plopping myself down on one of the three chairs surrounding my oval kitchen table; the peeling veneer giving off what some would call character, and the rest of us would call cheap. I put my feet on the table and crossed my arms, trying my best to look uninterested.

"Call it neutral territory." He was smiling as he spoke, and I did not know him well enough to know whether I should respond in kind or grab a weapon. "You and I would do well to keep each other informed."

"As far as I can tell, you are keeping me pretty much in the dark."

"All in good time, Regnum." He smiled with just his eyes and the left corner of his mouth.

"I don't have a lot of time, and none of it is good nowadays." I sat up trying to get a little more control of the situation, and considering he had just got the drop on me, it was no easy task. "Why don't you start with whether or not you know anything about this demon thing that left me two pieces of human jerky and one basket case."

"Ah, you mean the succubus."

"Yea, the suck me off, whatever." Bingo! Confirmation! I was getting good at this detective crap. "Where did she come from, and what does she want in my town?"

"Your town?" He stared into my eyes hard, and I felt the power behind those eyes, but I did not look away. "Regnum please, I may not know you, but I know of you." He smiled, regaining his easy composure. "You want to be here no more than pigs want to be chops." His eyes searched mine for a reaction. "Don't defend this town as your own to me.

Save it for your dirt-eating friend Ramirez and the turn-key vampire that pulls your strings."

"Do you know anything about her or not?"

"No... but I will keep a weather eye out, of course."

"No? Then how did you know what kind of demon I was asking about?"

"I keep informed," he said, leaning casually against the wall. "I know the state in which your so-called victims were found, and therefore know how they were killed. Only one creature kills that way and so... Succubus."

At that very moment, and many times after that, I wondered whether he was trying to help me or torment me. "What do you want?" I asked, not knowing what else to do.

"Walk with me." He watched me intently as I sat motionless. "I want to show you something that may interest you."

"Now you know what interests me?"

"I know that you are more than what you seem." Markku leaned forward, demonstrating his sincerity, furrowing his brow as he spoke. "I know that, while you speak like an ignorant slob, your mind works much faster... faster, you hope, than your opponent's does." He turned away from me, looking out the window and speaking as though he were addressing a child. "But remember this, Regnum. Though I may seem young to your eyes, I have walked this earth for more than five hundred years, and I know a worthy adversary when I see one. Do not play the fool with me!" He turned his face to me, our eyes meeting once again. "I haven't the time for it. Now, if you please, walk with me."

"You can wait until I have had my dinner!"

CHAPTER 11

The streets of Richmond seemed almost peaceful. It was an odd feeling to walk a dark street at night without fear, knowing that you were at the top of the food chain so to speak. It also didn't hurt to have a full stomach, not to mention the pleasure of having had Markku sit and wait for me to finish my meal.

"What do you know about my father?"

The question came out of nowhere, and I didn't immediately know how to answer. "Not as much as I'd like."

A sly smile crept across his lips. "That is very slippery of you, Detective." He made a point of looking around before he spoke again. "Most of what you see around you has his hands in it. He has interests in both worlds, and none of it is for anyone but himself."

"So, what's your problem with it? I imagine you're in line for it eventually. Oh, wait," I stopped for effect, placing my hand to my chest in feigned pity and my best falsetto voice. "Are you the tortured son here to save the world? Are Daddy's evil ways too much for you so now your conscience demands that you act?" I leaned in conspiratorially and whispered, "you must be the silver spoon with the heart of gold!"

"Not quite," he said, laughing softly. "But what good is it to be next in line to someone who is virtually immortal."

"You could force the issue," I said in my normal voice, resuming our walk to wherever he was taking me. I was testing the waters and I figured that he knew it, but I had to make a move. I was being led around like a dog on a leash... no pun intended.

"Hmm... Once again, very slippery, but I'm not interested in what he has or does."

"Then what are you interested in? I mean other than slaughtering helpless girls in the back of expensive cars."

"That is exactly what interests me!" He had stopped walking and turned to face me. "There was a time when we feared the human race. There was a time when they could see us and possessed such knowledge as to be our greatest enemy and threat." He turned away, spreading his arms in grand fashion indicating all the world. "Now look at them. Your dirt-eater partner walks among them in full view with horns and the legs of a beast and still no one sees."

"They're little horns and anyone looks good in Dockers."

"What happened to this once worthy adversary? Where is that lethal cunning thing that kept us underground?"

I could see the contempt in his eyes, but there was something else...regret? "Look, if what you're looking for is someone to keep you on your toes that's my job now, and you still have to answer for that girl you---"

"Would you like to see what these mortals have allowed to fester in their very midst?" He interrupted. "Would you like to see acts that make my little snack look like jaywalking?"

I kept silent.

"Oh, come now. If you have not realized that there are degrees of right and wrong, then you will soon enough."

We walked down Leigh Street then took a left. We ended up deep in the places where anyone who was not looking to get buried, stayed far away from. The street sign read 'Q' street. I knew it well since it was the street that ran right behind the station where I worked. I tried not to seem shocked while at the same time paying close attention, just in case Markku showed me something or said something I could use to nail him. We stopped at the corner of 25th and Q, literally a stone's throw away from the precinct headquarters. Markku motioned with his chin to a dilapidated two-story building on the corner diagonally opposite the one on which we stood. The siding was falling off in wide swathes with garbage strewn on the steps, and a foul stench coming from the very stone it was built from.

"That is one of my father's exclusive clubs,"

he said, sliding his hands in his pockets, feigning innocence and looking over at me to gauge my reaction.

"You're shitting me," I said, looking from him to the building then back again. There were no expensive cars parked in front, and the smell of the place was so overpowering that, even at this distance, I couldn't smell anything else. Then it hit me. That was the point.

"You see the vagabond woman heading slowly towards the building?"

"Yeah." What looked like the most run down and disgusting bundle of rags was dragging a squeaky old-fashioned handcart behind her.

"She's 497 years old and a professor of interpretive dance at Virginia Commonwealth University. She is one of his best customers."

"So why does anyone go through it all?"

"It is simply the price of admission. Follow me." He began walking toward the house, toward the doorway Professor Bag Lady had just gone through. It was a small side door with no awning, no porch or stoop and no number.

"Your Dad is not going to be happy with you taking a cop into his, I have to assume, illegal club."

"You have no idea. A...cop, as you call it, would be handled decisively." He smiled at me as he spoke the last word as though it excited him. "But you are more than just a cop, aren't you?"

"Either way, I'm a cop. Whatever group you want to throw me in, it's still my job to stop guys like you from doing bad things."

"What are they called, this group you work for? And I am not referring to Richmond's finest."

I said nothing, and Markku looked at me with genuine surprise. "You work for them, and yet you know nothing about them?"

"We have an… agreement," I said, not wanting to go deeper into what was my debt to the Speaker Man. "All I do is clean up the messes made by you people."

"You people?" Markku abruptly spun round, looking at me with an intensity that almost made me take a step back. "Regnum, you will realize soon enough that you are just as we are. You are a predator, and there is nothing that will change that." His face softened into a knowing smile. "In fact, you may have been one before you were even bitten."

"And what the hell do you mean by that?"

"Do you ever wonder how it is you survived?" His eyes searched mine.

"Survived?"

"Your attack, the one that made you what you are. Do you ever wonder how you were able to fend off a Werewolf with nothing more than a well-placed stick in the eye?"

"You seem to know a lot about me, so why don't you tell me what it is you want with me."

"To make you see the truth," he said and headed for the door.

The first floor of the place looked like your average, run down, very poor house with a little extra filth thrown in. The smell hit you as soon as you stepped in and only got worse as we walked down the hall passing the kitchen on the right. Unwashed dishes were piled in the sink. The garbage had been knocked over, and the flies had taken up permanent residence. As we moved into the living area, the wonders continued with discarded cups and food wrappers of all sorts adding to the charm of the place. A threadbare couch sat in the middle of the room facing an oversized television, the only clean thing in the house.

Markku walked through without looking around, obviously having been here before. He stepped to a door in the right rear corner of the room. The door opened to a basement that smelled a lot better than where I was currently standing, but I could pick up something else, something familiar but I couldn't place it. The scents were all masked by the filth above, and I started to see how effective the filth was at covering up anything that might give the place away.

"Understand Wolfgang, that if you walk down these steps events will be set in motion that cannot be stopped, and you will have to decide where your loyalties lie."

I was getting a little tired of all the mystery nonsense. I had two bodies and nothing to go on but the advice of someone who had kicked the crap out of me this morning and my chowderhead who was still in a trance. So I nodded without really caring whose side I was on and started walking down the steps. Then I felt the pin prick in the back of my neck.

CHAPTER 12

I heard a voice, rhythmic and soothing. It was repeating something over and over. I didn't recognize what was being said at first, but it was there.

"Calm..."

I had not yet opened my eyes, but that feeling of too little blood flow to a limb kept pinned too long was in my head.

"...not here..."

My chin was touching my chest. Willing my head up, it lolled off to the side not answering to the commands my brain sent.

"...hurt you..."

My eyes snapped open, and I lunged at the darkness responding to the words while not yet seeing.

"Calm down Regnum, I have not brought you here to hurt you."

The same voice, rhythmic and patient. There was no threat in it, and yet I found myself immobilized.

I was in a plush chair with what felt like suede leather covering the arm rests and enough cushion on the seat that my bottom felt like it was floating. That floating thing might also have been the drugs. All of the luxurious comfort was fouled only by the fact that I was tied to it.

"Regnum?"

"I hear you!" I said, half snarling the words and jerking at my restraints.

"I say again, no one is going to hurt you, but I need you to pay attention." Markku was standing to my right, leaning against the corner of the room with his arms crossed. He was looking at me with the most sincere expression I had seen from him yet. "I had to restrain you to give you the opportunity to see all that I have to show you. I need your trust for---"

"Tying me up is a great way to build team fucking spirit!" I railed against the ropes that bound me, the fibers tearing at my flesh as I felt my anger growing.

"It is only a precaution. If you feel threatened, you can transform and easily free yourself." He was right; there was no way the ropes that he used could hold the monster in me if I let it out. "The restraints are your price of admission, Regnum. If you want to see what I have to show you, then you must remain calm and watch without interrupting. If you allow your rage to change you, you will remember very little of what I am trying to show you."

I looked into his eyes which belied his easy posture, and I saw belief. He truly believed that what he was doing was right, and he was asking me to listen. "Why the restraints?" I asked. "Why not just tell me or show me, or whatever?"

"You are a police officer; I could not risk you putting duty over prudence." He looked away from me to his right through a blacked-out window that allowed us to see out and none to see in. "I need you to see this, and if you were free, you would be obligated, foolishly so, to try and stop it."

A chill hit me, and I was now looking out the window as well. He was making sure that I would not stop whatever was about to happen. Markku knew that in order to stop anything, I would have to become that which I hate, a beast, and in doing so, I would corrupt my memory of all that happened. I wouldn't be able to trust any of what I would remember. Rage at that level forms the memory of events into what we feel, be it justification or guilt, but they are rarely what really happened. If I wanted a true account, I would have to sit there and watch, no matter what took place. It was brilliant, and I hated him for it. Looking back on it and what he made me witness, I can say that I still have not forgiven him for it.

My temporary prison was about the size of a walk-in closet. The window I was looking out of was eight feet across and three feet high, tilting away from me like the box seats at the New Meadowlands stadium; I had won a seat there from a sports radio station. It was an anteroom looking down into the basement which ran the full length of the house under which it sat.

"My father uses this room, on occasion, to observe the… activities. To be sure his patrons are enjoying the services he provides, so to speak."

"So, you're showing me your father's illegal activities, is that right?"

"Yes." Markku looked back at me and smiled knowingly. "You are very astute."

"Why? And why me?"

"Because very few people even know this place exists and even fewer know of this room. As for why you, be honored. You are the first being outside my family to set foot in this room since it was built, well before you were born."

"I'm thrilled."

Movement below drew my attention. Creatures from the world of which I was now a part of had begun entering the space from four doors that stood at the four corners of the room. Vampires moving slowly and easily as creatures without respect for time do. Werewolves in human form, languid and sensual, feeling the vibrations of the very earth their feet touched, and creatures I had never seen nor smelled before, moving and gesticulating in ways particular to whatever it was they were, filled out the group. It seemed that all the pieces were in place for whatever show was about to begin.

The crowd, now about forty strong, parted to allow a sharply dressed vampire through the center of the rectangular room.

"I must say," Markku said, breaking the

silence. "I do not know how you will react, though I will admit to being extremely interested. That said, I feel compelled to remind you to try to remain calm. I need you to see this." Markku spoke these last words so slowly that I could almost feel the weight of them.

The Dapper Man raised a wireless microphone to his lips and began speaking. It seemed that the blind room I was in was also soundproof. He made large gestures and smiled a lot. Then the crowd parted again. A human woman was brought in by two very large creatures I could not place and was presented to the Dapper Man. With a flourish, the Dapper Man indicated the human woman now standing next to him. My mind started to reel as I imagined the various things that could happen to her in a room full of monsters. She was trembling, but her eyes did not show fear. Was she drugged? She did not seem to know where she was or what was about to happen to her.

More gesturing and the crowd came to life with gestures of their own. Watching alternating hands rising into the air and the gestures by the Dapper Man, I quickly realized that she was being auctioned! The rage began to rise in me, and I fought to maintain my control. I had to remember this night. To do what with it, I had no idea, but I had to remember.

The bidding continued for another few seconds before a man dressed in loose fitting jeans and a T-shirt was named the winner and stepped into the middle of the room. He stood just out of arm's reach of the Dapper Man and the girl. Dapper Man said something into the microphone, raised both hands and was greeted with applause from the audience as he stepped away, still smiling.

Despite all the activity around him, the winner of the auction did not take his eyes off the girl. His chest was heaving now as his breath quickened, and still his eyes did not leave hers. With a quick snatching motion, his shirt was thrown to the floor and his hands were feverishly working his belt. Visibly trembling now, I watched as he struggled with the button and zipper but soon, the jeans dropped to his ankles, revealing his already transforming body. His change seemed driven by rage. Any strong emotion could trigger a change; anger, fear, hate, lust, or pain would result in the same monster. He was a werewolf, and he was angry. Throwing his head back, his mouth worked into a scream of agony as his entire bone structure shifted to accommodate the monster inside of him tearing its way through his body. His rage was seeking release and I could feel the tears welling in my eyes as I felt his pain and anticipated hers.

His right arm, now completely changed, did not wait for the rest of him and lashed out, opening the poor girl's belly. Lovely in life, she could now only look down at herself, the blow so fast as not to inflict immediate pain. Her eyes came up once more to behold the creature now manifesting itself before her, and she realized what was about to happen. Still dazed, she placed her hands over the gaping wound, her face now registering the harsh reality of inevitability. Her mouth opened as if to beg for the very life that was already pouring out from between her fingers. But no one would hear her, because the beast's left hand, now fully formed and jealous of the right, slashed up and across the girl's lovely face. Her eyes, wide and astonished at the pain she could not have imagined in a thousand nightmares now coursing through every nerve of her body, stared at nothing.

Finally, her legs gave way and the beast, now complete in its hideousness, engulfed her with ripping claws and tearing jaws. All that could be seen were sprays of blood and the furious movements of a creature that could only come from the depths of hell. I should know... I was one of them.

CHAPTER 13

I threw myself against the restraints, heaving my weight back and forth trying desperately to break free. "I've seen what you want me to see, now cut me loose," I said, trying to hide the tears of shame now running down my left cheek.

"You need to see a bit more to truly understand what it is that goes on in... what did you call it? Oh yes, *your town*." His words dripped with sarcasm as he stressed the 'your' and I could only sit there, seething, while I waited for whatever it was that he wanted to show me.

The carnage was cleared away with an old fire hose; hunks of flesh and bone slid over the concrete slab and into drainage grates strategically placed throughout the inner circle. The auction continued, but this time it was a man that was brought out. He was strongly built with a dark complexion and brown medium length hair.

"Ah, this should do nicely," Markku said, his posture changing, almost it seemed, in anticipation. The bidding started up again and went on just like before. "She has specific tastes and when she sees something she likes..."

Markku's eyes were tracking someone making their way through the crowd. I tried following his gaze, but there were too many bodies for me to make out the one he was watching. Then a graceful arm went up, and I saw her. Looking back at Markku for confirmation, I then followed his eyes to none other than Professor Bag Lady. Dressed in a form fitting mesh dress that covered only the tiniest of spots across her chest and between her thighs, there was an aura of lust emanating from her. Her hair, hidden from me by rags and a hood outside, was just past her shoulders and a sensual amber red, her eyes green and fierce. Even I couldn't help but be aroused sitting there tied up and still very angry.

The bidding ended and she was named the winner. Not standing on formalities, she slipped out of her black heels and was peeling off what little clothes she wore before taking the first step towards her prize. Dapper Man raised his hands once again and the crowd became even more animated than before. By the time she reached the center of the room her victim's eyes, showing obvious signs of having been drugged, grew wide while a grin played across his face. Her body was even more exquisite naked than in the small scraps that had left very little to the imagination.

Running a gentle hand across his chest she guided him to the ground. He lay before her willingly. Kneeling beside him she caressed him softly, almost lovingly, as his eyes closed, and the grin became a smile that spread broadly across his lips. Hunger burned in her eyes as she smiled back. She leaned forward and licked his chest in long strokes, her tongue flicking across his nipples making him shiver. Slowly she worked her way down, caressing his body with her lips and tongue. Finally reaching her destination, she took him into her mouth and began rolling her head and neck in circular, quick, up and down movements. His eyes rolled back into his head. The crowd roared with arms raised in praise of the raw lust displayed before them.

I could feel my whole body swelling as the change began to take me. Lust was taking me over, and I grit my teeth fighting against it but unable to look away.

"Stay calm, Detective. This emotion ends in blood, and I know you well enough to understand that you do not want blood."

He was right, I had not killed anyone since my first, and that first had cost me more than I could have imagined. The lust subsided enough for me to look back into the pit. The Professor was staring at her prize, smiling. A bit of saliva dripped from her full bottom lip, and she slithered her way up his prone form until her full breasts covered his face, his mouth desperately searching for each nipple and finding one. She eased herself onto him; his body arched, and her mouth opened in ecstasy, exposing the telltale fangs of the vampire.

Back and forth she rocked, her hands on his chest giving her leverage. Her prize swung his head side to side, unable to do anything but enjoy the pleasures of the goddess that was taking him closer and closer to the gates of heaven.

Her pace quickened and the crowd urged her on. Her prize cupped her bottom, clenching his teeth, fighting his release to make the pleasure last just a bit longer. She leaned back, touching her own breasts, pinching herself in the most sensitive spots and increasing her pace. Her prize now wide mouthed, shook uncontrollably releasing all that was in him. Then beauty became pain, lust became horror, and life became death as she lurched forward, her fangs tearing into his throat. His eyes, an instant before having gazed at paradise, now witnessed the hell of all hells, the nightmare of being eaten alive.

CHAPTER 14

Sitting at my kitchen table where the evening's terror had begun, I trembled from the whirlwind of emotions coursing through me, the memory of what I had seen. Markku had kept me there, watching her gyrate on her victim even after tearing out his throat until finally collapsing and being pulled off of the glassy eyed corpse that had been her lover. The look of euphoric ecstasy lingered on her face even as she was carried out of the room, her pale skin covered in crimson streaks and nothing else. Did she look at me as she was carried off?

I forced the memory from my mind as I felt the tightening between my hips, a not-so-unpleasant ache in the lowest part of my torso that made the less evolved parts of my brain crave, made them want. But I could never want like that again, and I knew it.

After cutting me loose, Markku had simply pointed the way up the stairs. When I asked why he had shown me all of it, the question coming from different places in my head, he simply said something about opening my eyes. So, I was left to walk from the Kill Club in a daze and now, staring at my table, I tried desperately to hold on to some semblance of reality. There were monsters in this world, creatures that took pleasure in the pain they inflicted on others. Hunters, predators, beasts that protected themselves were a different story; their actions were dictated by the environment in which they found themselves. No, these beings were sadistic imitations of life that sought out the screams of other things, searched for the horror of existence and paid handsomely for the opportunity to send another to hell… and I was one of them.

Pain, anger, hatred, lust, loathing, hunger, and rage surged through me. She had kept going! She kept on rolling her hips over his, even after he was dead! I could still see her. I slammed my fist hard on the table, and the corner of it snapped off.

Too much life… I could smell it all around me: the old lady across the hall, the slight man two doors down, and the newborn babe next door, all of them just steps away. I could taste the scent of them, the strong, the weak, the young, the old, my mind classifying each in the order of easiest to kill. How long had it been since I had allowed myself to change?

I stood and shook my head, trying to force the visions out. Why did Markku show me that? Why did he make me watch? She was fondling her breast as she rocked back and forth on him, her mouth open to catch the squirts of blood erupting rhythmically from his torn carotid artery.

I heard a muffled pop, like the cracking of knuckles, but coming from inside my chest. Then I felt the spasms. It was happening! There was nothing I could do. I felt it growing in me and I could not stop it, could not stop the wanting of it. It was coming and I needed it to. Knocking over the table I lunged for the front door, nearly tearing the knob from the housing as I ripped it open. That was when the first wave of pain hit me, forcing me to the ground.

She looked at me while she took her prey, she looked at me! Her mouth was open, catching squirts of blood while letting the rest spatter over her neck, her heaving breast and stomach! I had to get out! I had to make it to the woods!

I stumbled out into the hallway; the smells of life were stronger now. The wave of pain intensified as I tripped onto the first-floor landing, the stabbing in my stomach radiating to my shoulders and hips.

On the street, I caught sight of my car and took a step towards it when the next wave of pain sent me to one knee and forced from me what should have been a scream but came out, a primal roar. I ran. The nearest woods were south, and I headed that way on instinct as fast as legs could take me. My speed was inhuman, but I did not care if I was seen. My vision was turning, the pupils allowing in more light Her rocking hips and powerful thighs pushing harder and faster! Peripheral vision was replaced, more and more by hearing and smell; my sight, though narrowed, covered more distance, focused on what there was to kill. Her nipples erect, one covered in blood! My mind was clouding, becoming simple; narrowing to a singular and terrible purpose, to hunt. I struggled to maintain my mental hold and understanding just long enough to get to the woods. I smelled the trees, the thick grass and all of the life within. I was close. Her lips parted, fangs bared and smiling as she threw back her head. My mind slipped away from me, emotion and instinct ruling my every move, pushed me to where I knew there was prey. My very humanity faded from me as I entered the woods. My skull was already changing shape; cracking bone that became a snout and was picking up the scent of prey. I was in the woods, I let go, followed the scent and hoped that whatever it was, it was not human.

CHAPTER 15

The grass beneath me was cold and wet with dew. I shivered but kept my eyes shut, hoping to drift back off to sleep. A voice that I dimly recognized as not a threat, was trying to break through, but I held on to the darkness hoping the voice would go away.

"Wolf!" It was Ramirez, whispering so loudly that I felt my skull vibrate in my head. "C'mon man, get up. We gotta get you out of here."

I was lying on my side when I finally acknowledged his voice. Rolling onto all fours the pain hit me instantly, like tiny bits of glass in every joint, cutting all at once. The echoes of my scream bounced around me from all directions.

"Jesus, man," said Ramirez. "Keep it down."

Once able to breathe again I looked up to see Ramirez looking around nervously. With the agony of my joints subsiding, I eased myself back onto my knees. Something soft fell away from my body, and the full chill of the morning air sent more shivers through me. Looking to the ground I saw the blanket, and remembered that I was stark naked. I slowly picked it up and wrapped it around myself.

"Why does it hurt so bad?" I asked.

"It has something to do with the ligaments in your body having to realign for the change."

"How long have you been here?"

"I was on my way to your place when I saw you run out of your apartment," he said as he crouched down beside me to help with the blanket.

"You've been here all night?"

"Not all night. I waited for you to change back, and then I went to your apartment to get the blanket."

"Thanks, man."

Suddenly my mind whirled in panic. I had changed back! "Oh God, what did I kill!?" It was not controlled! I didn't have time to get out of the city. It could have been anything, or anyone.

"It's okay, man."

"No! I killed something!" I stood searching the ground around me, the pain in my joints forgotten. "If I changed back, it means I killed someone!"

"Hey, hey it's okay, it was—"

"What the hell did I kill, Jo?!"

Ramirez put his hand on my shoulder, calming me. "It's alright. It was a small deer." He was indicating a spot off to my right, and when I looked, I saw the carcass. The wounds on the poor creature brought back faint, clouded visions of what I had done. Like trying to remember a bad dream, I could see flashes of the hunt. I looked at the claw marks on the shoulders and flanks where I had pounced on the creature taking it to the ground, holding it as I sank my teeth into its neck. Then with a quick jerk of my head and jaws, the neck snapped. The other wounds were feeding marks, and as I looked down at myself, I saw that I was covered in blood from my mouth to the middle of my chest.

A twig snapped behind us and I sprang up from the ground, landing on the balls of my feet ready to run or attack.

"Easy, Wolf!" Ramirez quickly stepped in front of me, his hands up. "I'm sorry, but there was no way I could've known you were going to change!"

With great effort, I slowed my breathing and looked over his shoulder. I could see a small hand, the fingers digging into the bark and then slowly a face eased out from behind the tree. Her eyes were wide, and her mouth hung slightly open. The expression of horror on her face made it difficult to recognize her at first, but it was Milagro.

"She was with me last night." Ramirez slowly lowered his hands to hover cautiously over his thighs. "By the time we caught up to you, the change was... you were changing back. I needed her to watch you while I went for the blanket. She wouldn't leave even when I tried to send her back to the car."

Ramirez picked up the blanket and covered my bloody skin again as she stepped out tentatively from behind the tree, keeping her eyes on me and her terrified grip on the tree. She closed her mouth, and I could see her throat working as if she was having difficulty swallowing, but she had regained some of the courage I had seen in her apartment. There was something else in her eyes now, not loathing but something else. It was as if she was in awe.

Ramirez took me back to the apartment, though I don't remember much of the trip. I lay in the back seat of his unmarked police cruiser, moving as little as possible while Milagro sat up front with Ramirez. Dozing in and out I noticed the clothes I had torn off on the way to the woods crumpled up on the floorboard. Ramirez must have grabbed them. After all, it was important to gather up that kind of thing or someone might think there had been a killing or something. I laughed at my little joke, and the tiny connective tissue holding my ribs to my sternum screamed. It was a pain I had never known was possible from a body part I never knew existed. I remember everything after that very clearly. Ligaments, sinews, cartilage, so many things in the human form that we take for granted until they hurt or stop working.

*****

Back at my kitchen table -Ramirez having placed it back in the center of my eat-in kitchen- I held on to the coffee cup in my hands like it was the last thing I owned on earth. The pain in my body was subsiding, but now I could feel the kill. The trembling in my hands was not all from the cold, but from the life that I had taken and the exhilaration of the change.

"Wolf, are you with me?" Ramirez's voice held genuine concern, but I was not in the mood for pity. "Wolf?"

"What?!"

"The kid's gone."

"What kid?"

"The chowderhead from the hotel."

The pieces started to fall into place, and I suddenly realized that things were going south faster than they had already been. "Gone, like left town?" I was struggling to make sense of it. "I mean, where could he have gone?"

"We think he was taken."

"We? Oh, now she's a cop? Why did you bring her here in the first place?" I was angry, I was ashamed, I was exposed, and I felt like a leper.

"Look man, let's keep it together, okay? She came to me last night because she now knows it was a Succubus."

"Yeah? I put that one together already," I said, still embarrassed.

"Anyway, something she saw in her vision didn't make sense."

"What?" I asked, without really wanting an answer.

"She called the kid Adam." He looked at me like what he had just said was supposed to set off some kind of light bulb in my head.

"And?" I said, losing my patience quickly. "In case the blank stare isn't saying it, I have no idea what the hell you're talking about."

"This is a Succubus man; she feeds on men. She shouldn't have let him live, much less talked to him. And she sure as hell wasn't supposed to call him by--."

"What man? Spit it out!"

"His name is Todd. The kid's name is Todd!"

CHAPTER 16

It would have taken more time to figure out what Ramirez was trying to tell me than I cared to invest. My report on the bludgeoning murder should have been on the Lieutenant's desk already, and I had barely started writing it. On top of that, I had no idea what the hell it mattered that our man juicer called the kid Adam. I mean what was the big deal if she called him by another man's name? I am pretty sure that is not the first time that's happened in the world of men and women. What if he just looked like someone else? What if the guy was in some kind of witness protection like in the movies? Ok, maybe that was a stretch. Either way, I had to get to work on my real-world case and leave the fantastical to Ramirez and Milagro for a while.

Pulling into the parking lot, I could see Lieutenant Bowman's car was already in his reserved spot. My report was late, but I had hoped that if I got it done before roll call, I could slide by. Now it seemed as though I was going to catch hell on my very first case. My joints were still burning, my senses were going haywire from hyper-sensitivity, and my mouth tasted like I just finished a turd sandwich, but either way I had to give it a try.

I headed straight for my desk as soon as I saw the coast was clear.

"You know all I need is an excuse to bounce you out of this unit."

I let my head drop forward, chin to chest in resignation, fingers still on the keyboard as soon as I heard the lieutenant's voice.

"And then," he continued, "the people you work for will have to go through a lot of trouble to find someone to replace you."

I could picture him standing behind me, legs slightly more than shoulder width and his hands on his hips. "And from what I hear, when you get fired by those people, you don't really hang around long enough to tell anyone about it." I turned around to take my ass chewing like a man and there he was, hands on his hips.

"Now see, I heard there was a really nice severance package," I said, unable to control my sharp wit when confronted by the Peter Pan pose from hell.

"Oh yeah, well even if you do walk away from it, in your world, you either have power and authority or you've got lots of problems," he said, mercifully dropping the Peter Pan thing and folding his arms across his chest. Problem was, now he looked like the Genie from Aladdin.

"Lieutenant, when I come out of the back door to this building and look down 25th Street, it looks like it is pretty much the same in your world."

"Where's your report, Regnum?" he said loud enough to get the attention of the few early arrivals to the building.

"I'll be adding the final touches after roll call and have it on your desk by lunch, sir."

"Your first case and you are already screwing it up. Get on the stick, Regnum, or I'll cram one up your ass." That last bit he added for the benefit of the other officers and detectives who were now all ears. He knew full well what I was and how he would be better off beating himself with his stick than even flinching in my direction.

"Yes sir. Thank you, Lieutenant."

No matter what, we were technically on the same side, and as for the other law enforcement group I worked for, the relationship with the real cops was important. It allowed us to get ahead of any incidents we didn't want the public to know about. I did wonder who approached whom to propose our little alliance. Did some vampire walk up to the Chief of Police and introduce himself? "Hi there, I really want to snap your neck and turn you into a sippy straw, but I wonder if I could place a couple of freaks on your police force? You know to catch other freaks who... want to snap your neck and turn you into... well you get the idea." I also started to wonder why the Lieutenant kept reminding me of Disney characters. Sleep. I obviously needed some sleep.

Lost in thought, I caught a scent close to me and snapped my head around.

"Holy jeez! You scared the hell out of me."

"I'm getting that a lot lately," I said, relaxing. Officer Shepherd stood about five feet from my desk. At least, that was where he landed after I had apparently freaked him out.

"You're like, really fast. Were you a boxer or something?" he asked, taking a tentative step toward me.

"Uh...yeah," I said thinking it sounded like as good an excuse as any.

"Maybe you could give me some pointers sometime," he said, finally reaching my desk and setting down the two files he carried.

"Old injury keeps me out of the ring, sorry. What are these?" I asked, changing the subject so I would not have to expound on the lie.

"These are the files you asked for yesterday. I had dropped them off in your box before I went out for the rest of my shift. This morning, I came by to make sure you found what you were looking for, and since they were still there, I figured I would deliver them personally."

"Right the files on the woman and..." I was searching and not remembering what the other file was for.

"...And the boyfriend, or at least, that is what we think because of the mail addressed to him and some addressed to the woman. Only the woman is on the lease."

"That's the one. Right?" I opened the file on top with purpose and let my eyes scan the page without really reading anything. Then I spotted, remembered, and registered what I had forgotten. "The child!"

"Uh, yes sir. I dispatched Child Protective Services to the school to pick him up after we finished working the crime scene. Uh, just like you asked," he added quickly. "He was in school when it happened so he couldn't have seen anything, but he might be ready to talk now." His voice trailed off as though he was afraid he had overstepped.

"Let's hope you're right." I heard him let out a sigh of relief. "I'll head over right after roll call. Where is he being kept?"

"The address is on page two of my report, Detective," he said with just a bit more confidence.

"Thanks Officer, and good work."

"Yes, sir," he said as he turned to leave. He seemed so happy, I thought he might salute. Still, he seemed like a good kid, and he was really careful to keep saying that I had asked him to do all those things when he was the one making all the suggestions.

Now I had to go see a scared and orphaned little boy. How was I supposed to talk to a kid whose mother had just been bludgeoned with a frying pan? What was I going to say to him that would make the least bit of difference? How was I supposed to make things right?

CHAPTER 17

The GPS I still used to get around this strange city, called out lefts and rights in its mechanical voice. The kid had been taken to a Social Services facility on Jefferson Avenue, just off of 25th Street. Going down 25th, you get to see a few different sides of Richmond. There are buildings that are literally falling apart next to freshly painted houses with manicured lawns. You can see buildings almost as old as the country itself next to buildings that are less than a year old.

Stopping at a yield sign, I found myself waiting for drivers who had no idea how to navigate a roundabout. After they managed to find the accelerator, I finally entered the circle and got off on Jefferson Avenue. I found the building on my left and had to execute a U-turn to get back to it. It looked like a typical government outreach building with dark brown brick and plenty of glass. It was well lit and with wide walkways leading up to the oversized doors that were meant to look welcoming but were anything but.

After checking in with the front desk, I was directed to one of the dorm rooms they kept for battered women or abused children that by some miracle or other, were able to get away. Social Services was expecting me, so when I walked in there was a modestly-dressed counselor sitting opposite the door watching everything like a hawk. It amazed me how some counselors could be as protective of their charge as a lioness and yet still soothe children with soft voices and kind gestures.

The kid was seated at a desk angled with his back to the door, as well as to the counselor who was now staring critically at me from her chair. He was writing something on loose-leaf paper while consulting what looked like a textbook. Apparently, they were keeping him busy with schoolwork while they tried to figure out what to do with him.

"Hi. I'm Detective Regnum, Richmond Police Department," I said to the middle of the room, not knowing who to speak to first.

"My name is Ms. Evans, and this young man here," she said, indicating the boy, "is Isaac."

Isaac laid his pencil down and looked at me. When I turned to look at him, his expression changed very slightly. He cocked his head to one side and placed his hand back on the desk, almost as if he were steadying himself. Isaac was about nine years old with light brown hair styled in the worst at-home bowl cut I had ever seen. He looked straight at me with deep blue eyes, darker than most, and a mouth that looked like it had not smiled in ages.

"Hello Isaac," I said, moving to his side of the room.

"Hi," he replied.

"I was wondering if we could talk a little bit."

"About what?" he asked, picking up his pencil and resuming his schoolwork, turning his back to me as he did so.

"You know, stuff," I said. I felt him close up, but also sensed fear at the same time. "What are you working on there?"

"Social Studies."

"You like it?" I asked, trying to get him to engage.

"No."

"No?" I asked. "Why not?" He shrugged his shoulders, and I knew I needed to keep pressing. "What is your favorite subject in school?"

"Music."

"Okay, why music?" I asked, hoping that this was my in with the kid.

"Because the other kids are not allowed to tease me in music class."

"What, they're allowed in your other classes?"

"Not really, but..."

"But what?" I was onto something here.

"Most teachers are too busy to notice when the other kids whisper stupid stuff to me during class."

I watched him hang his head slightly as the words left his lips. It was difficult to imagine how teasing affected a kid until you saw him talk about it. "So," I said, trying to bring him back before he shut down, "this music class is pretty cool?"

"Like I said, the kids don't tease me in there."

"Fair enough, kid," I said, dreading the line of questioning I had yet to start. "You know why I'm here?"

"You have to ask me about my mom," he said as his head sank a bit lower, his voice cracking slightly. "Ms. Evans told me you were coming to talk to me."

"That's right, champ." I said without thinking. Isaac looked over his shoulder at me, a quizzical expression on his face. "Do you know if anyone was angry with your mom, or if she had an argument with anyone?"

"No," he said, now doing little more than doodling on the loose-leaf paper he had been working on.

"How about people hanging around the house that you don't recognize?"

"Nope." more doodling.

"What about your mom's boyfriend? Did they have a fight?"

"They never fight. When he comes home, he sleeps most of the time. He works on the fishing boats, so he is gone a lot."

"When was the last time you saw him around?"

"He just left on a trip. He won't be back for another week or two." He turned completely away from me to face the desk and pulled his textbook closer.

"I thought you said you didn't like school," I

said, trying to lighten the mood.

"I never said I didn't like school," he said, clearly getting upset. "I don't like some of the kids, and I don't like talking about my mom right now!" His voice cracked and my heart felt heavy in my chest.

"My mistake, champ, you never said you did not like school. But hey, the kids in the music class have to be okay, right?"

"No, my teacher is the reason I like music class. He makes the other kids stop."

"This teacher sounds pretty cool, and the kids sound like jerks."

"They are," he said, looking back at me with a tear in his eye. "I used to call them monsters, but my mom said that monsters were much worse." His eyes fell to the floor at the mention of his mother. "She was right."

"What do you mean?"

"She was right!" he yelled, his eyes locking on to mine but not in anger. "Monsters are much worse, like the one that killed my mom." He burst out crying.

On instinct I reached out, then hesitated. Looking over at Ms. Evans I did my best to ask permission with just my eyes. She nodded, and I laid my hand gently on Isaac's shoulder trying my best to console him.

"Why did you call me champ?"

"I'm not sure," I said, fighting back my own tears. "I guess because... it's what my dad used to call me."

CHAPTER 18

Walking out the door of the shelter, the ache in my gut was only getting worse. All I had were questions, and the biggest one was "what am I supposed to do next?" What I did know was that this little boy was in more pain than I was, and I didn't think I could handle someone else's pain just yet.

What was the right thing to do? Hell, what was the wrong thing to do? As long as it took the kid's pain away, I really didn't care.

My head was starting to hurt; too many thoughts and too many emotions wrestled for my full attention. Champ... I called the kid champ. I said it without thinking but why? I wanted the kid to feel at ease, but maybe I was the one who needed to be put at ease. My father used to call me champ anytime things didn't go my way or when there was bad news to be delivered. One time I remember we were watching a boxing match with his favorite fighter, Julio Cesar Chavez. He said, "A champion is not someone that never loses but someone who keeps going even when he is losing."

I got to my car and just stood there, holding my keys in my hand. I was struck by the fact that

I had no idea where I was supposed to go. There was no one direction that seemed better than any other. Everything I saw screamed at me that it was only getting worse and I'm in over my head. It seemed that everything was out of balance; the man standing at the corner across the street with his sign scrawled in black marker 'HOMELESS PLEASE HELP', the girl trudging toward me wearing worn out sandals, sagging pajama bottoms that were almost falling off her bony hips, and a paper-thin tank top that would have shown through any bra... had she been wearing one. Everything was tilted.

I almost jumped out of my skin when my cell phone rang. I checked the screen before answering.

"What's up, Jo?" I could hear the noise of the squad room in the background before Ramirez even started speaking.

"What are you doing?" he asked.

"What do you mean?"

"I mean that I haven't heard from you, and we have some serious otherworld baddie juicing dudes like they were squeeze boxes!"

"What are you talking about, man?" I could not help raising my voice in frustration. "You heard the lieutenant; I have to work my case. And to tell you the truth, if I gotta choose between trying to figure out a flesh and blood killer or freak of nature, I feel a hell of a lot more comfortable with a human. I told you I'm not ready for this!"

"Who gives s shit?"

"What?" I was completely taken aback.

"WHO... GIVES... A... SHIT!?" Ramirez let the silence hang for just long enough before continuing. "You show me a time or place where bad things happen and any of us are ready for it, and I'll name you governor of that little fantasy land. That's why they're called bad things and not just inconveniences!"

"Hey," I interrupted, "all I'm saying is that someone else would be better---"

"There is no one else! You think that this thing you got is the only thing going wrong in our great big world?"

"No... I mean---"

"I'm done talking to you until you pull your head out of your ass."

I opened my mouth to continue defending myself when I heard silence on the other end. I looked at my phone as if I could get Ramirez back by sheer force of will.

Then the question popped into my head. Why did I care? What was any of this to me?
When all was said and done, I had a lonely kid whose mother had been murdered for no apparent reason, two bodies that looked as though they had been put through a juicer, and of course the chowderhead who could barely remember his own name.

The mother had been bludgeoned to death with her own cooking pan, and the juicer corpses were so dried up that the medical examiner was having difficulty establishing a time of death since there were barely any bodily fluids to regulate the body temperature. The orphaned kid was no witness at all, the space cadet was about as useful as a guitar with no strings, and Ramirez was still looking into the succubus angle but with no real proof yet.

I had nothing, and what pissed me off was that it seemed other people knew more about what I was working on than I did. Shepherd knew more about procedure and how to go about a homicide investigation. Ramirez knew what to look for when it came to the things that hid under little kid's beds, and Markku knew even more than Ramirez, but he wasn't talking. If I could just talk to him, I could get some nugget of information that might help me figure out what the hell was going on.

Unfortunately, I had no idea where Markku was or how to reach him. But it occurred to me that I did know where there was someone I could talk to. He would, of course, lie just as soon as tell the truth, but I had to say I tried.

CHAPTER 19

Downtown Richmond was cleaner than you might expect. In larger cities, downtown often meant buildings surrounded by run down homes and street people who had no home at all. These buildings were well-maintained and a few of them had some fancy landscaping or sculptures in front of the main doors. This was probably because the business district was just one street over, running along the James River. It was almost inviting with all the "Virginia is for lovers" flags and pretty banners along the main street. Still, this was a business district and the faces of anyone walking by reminded you that this was a place where money was made or lost. And if you looked closely enough you could still find street people huddled in alleyways, waiting for the lunch rush so they could handle their pans. If you wanted to see happy faces with idealistic minds, you had to go a couple of blocks over to West Broad Street, hang a left and visit the university.

I pulled up to one of the more impressive office towers, parked and headed toward the main doors. My thinking was simple; if I couldn't get answers from the son, I would try to get them from the father. Markku had been trying to warn me about something, and if there was anything sinister going on in the city, Hadrian would know about it.

"I'm here to see Mr. Van den Broek," I said, walking confidently up to the reception desk.

"Do you have an appointment?" The woman behind the desk asked the question as automatically as the rest of us breathed. She was attractive and sincere with light brown, almost honey colored hair and she was having none of it. I considered turning it up a notch, but being self-aware enough to know my limits I simply reached into my jacket pocket for my badge.

"My name is Det---"

"That was not the question." The new voice came from my left, and the hair on the back of my neck stood. Her skin was the color of the dark, her eyes mahogany, her hair, shorn close to the scalp, was as black as midnight. Even without the two-inch heels, she was at least as tall as I was. She moved slowly toward me, her full lips parted slightly, revealing perfectly white teeth. She moved like a cat, dressed in billowing blue slacks and a cream-colored button up blouse. The blue jacket she wore was kept open as if she were armed, but catching her scent, I knew immediately that she did not have to be.

She was perfect, she was stunning, and I was almost too lost in her beauty when it occurred to me that she was not just moving slowly... she was stalking me.

"Do you have an appointment?"

My upper lip curled instinctively, but I managed to get myself under control before I let out a full snarl. She was like me. If the situation escalated any further, she would change.

"No, I do not. It's very important that I speak to Mr. Van---"

"Then we cannot help you," she said, now circling slowly to my left, coming between the receptionist and me. "Please accept our apologies." Low, guttural clicking filled the room as she pulled her lips back baring her teeth, warning me.

I was about to make what I am sure would have been a very convincing argument when a voice from the intercom on the receptionist's desk beat me to it.

"Please show Detective Regnum into my office."

The receptionist, who had seemed little more than annoyed as two lycanthropes contemplated the best way to eviscerate one other, led me to a large set of double doors. Opening them she promptly turned and walked back the way we had come.

Hadrian Van den Broek sat behind his massive desk at the far end of his cavernous office. There was no pretense of being busy by shuffling papers or closing files; there was no smoldering cigarette in a crystal ashtray like in the movies. His desk was clear, and he was sitting there staring at me.

"I had an interesting conversation with your

son two nights ago," I said, walking toward a chair conveniently set opposite him.

"I doubt that any conversation with my son could be very interesting Detective Regnum."

"Really," I said as I continued my slow approach. The closer I got to him, about a third of the way now, the more I saw the slight resemblances - and many more differences - between father and son. "As a matter of fact, I found it very interesting. Now, that could have been because a lot of what was said was over a human woman with her throat ripped out."

Hadrian Van den Broek's face revealed nothing, but he leaned forward, stopping me in my tracks. Placing his elbows on the desk and steepling his fingers, he continued staring into me without blinking. I say 'into me' because that is what it felt like, like he was looking deeply into places that I instinctively did not want him to. His eyes widened a bit, and I could feel the deep, hazel brown eyes penetrating my very being. Those eyes reminded me not of Markku, but of the Speaker Man. There was less of the brown in Hadrian's, but there was no mistaking the similarities. Markku's eyes on the other hand, were a hazel as well but with flecks of blue, and his hair was a vibrant blonde whereas Hadrian's was muddier, as if a bad dye job had been performed too many times and was now permanent.

My heart slowed to a mild thump in my chest when Hadrian finally leaned back in his chair, losing none of the elegance he showed as I walked in. He smirked a bit, an expression that took nothing away from his regal bearing.

"Honestly, Detective, we do not make messes of our meals. We leave that to...less evolved creatures."

Even though I did not particularly like what I had been turned into, the barb stung.

"That is really not the point, it---"

"Then what is the point, Detective?" He never moved but his voice deepened, sounding almost like two voices at the same time, one deep and spoken, the other more like a roar. I could not stop my eyes from widening in awe. I got the point.

He had taken the opportunity to remind me of who he was, and I did not have to be told twice. If this guy's son was able to throw me around, Van den Broek senior could fold me up like the morning newspaper and pitch me across the street. Add to that the fact that he was probably equally, if not even more powerful politically. I had to change tactics.

"I apologize for the inconvenience, of course," I said, assuming the submissive role in the exchange, as was my place. We are, after all, animals and I could still accomplish what I had come to do without being the aggressor. "I realize that you are extremely busy, and I thank you for seeing me." I could feel the intensity in the room lessen considerably. I continued cautiously. "Your son spoke of the coming few days and warned me that there was going to be, well he did not use the word trouble, but he said I should be mindful."

I chose my words carefully. It was no secret that there was no love lost between father and son, and if the younger was trying to help me, I didn't want to give too much away. The trick was giving enough to get something in return.

"The young are often given to the dramatic." His body language gave nothing away, but the scent in the room changed.

"I am sorry to have disturbed you, but I have to be thorough." He was deflecting, and I needed to press a little harder, but it was a fine line. "I assume you are aware that yesterday morning, there was a killing that could be nothing other than one of us. So, there is nothing to be concerned with… in… our world?"

"I am not aware of anything that would be of concern to you, Detective."

There it was again, the scent change. That along with his condescension told me more than all his words put together.

CHAPTER 20

I knew going in that there weren't going to be any miraculous revelations after talking to Hadrian, but I did get what I hoped for. I caught a scent, literally and metaphorically. He knew something about what was going on. He may not have been directly involved but he knew who or what was.

Sitting in my car, trying to figure out my next move. I knew that I had to get back to Ramirez and start pushing the investigation in the right direction. I just didn't like the taste of crow, and I was going to have to eat a lot of it if I called him. Still, there was no doubt that I was starting to run short on time; sooner or later, Speaker Man was going to have to be updated, but I figured I at least had until nightfall.

"Have you pulled your head out of your ass already?" Ramirez's charming voice came through loud and clear. "I didn't hear any popping sounds."

"Look Jo, I'm sorry about before, but I need you to meet me so we can talk." All I could hear was the hum of traffic on the other end of the call. "Jo, I think I learned something, and I don't know what to do next." More traffic hum.

"Where are you?"

"Uh…" I was hoping not to get into this particular part of my story just yet. "I'm on Cary Street."

"What part of Cary Street…? Wait a minute! Did you…?" I could swear I heard his jaw tightening over the phone. "Legends."

"What?"

"Legends on East 7th Street. It's on the other side of the Manchester Bridge from where I hope you weren't stupid enough to go." He hung up before I had the chance to say another word. This was not going to be a pleasant conversation. I put the phone in my pocket, started up the Charger, and headed for the bridge.

At first glance, Legend's Brewing Company was a plain square building with its back to the James River. A simple yet inviting deck with metal mesh tables and integral umbrellas ready to be opened to protect the patrons on the hot summer days was attached and available for dining al fresco. It was in an industrial section of Richmond with a great view of the business district across the James. Pulling into the parking area, I caught a glimpse of a set of stairs on the side of the building. The stairs led to a loading dock with large vats where, true to the name, beer was brewed. The loading docks were no doubt built to take deliveries from passing watercraft in days gone by.

As I made my way to the front doors, I looked across the river and spotted the very building where my confrontation with Hadrian had taken place, a sobering reminder that I was not there to enjoy the view.

Stepping inside I began scanning the large room. A dark wood bar, complete with brass rail, sat below an impressive overhang covered with shields and decorative claymore-style swords. Behind the bar, shelves were lined with beer steins, each one bearing the name of what I assumed, had to be regular patrons. I spotted Ramirez toward the back and began making my way through the hustle and bustle of the lunch hour crowd. One of the patrons got up from a table just in front of Ramirez, revealing the foul-mouthed mind reader that had tried to shoot me.

"What, is she attached to your hip or something?" I asked, sitting down and looking right at her.

"Don't be a dick, Wolf. The way you left us alone at your place, I didn't know if you would have any questions for her when you got back."

"I don't," I said, still staring her down.

"Listen," she said, her eyes sad and wide, "I'm sorry about..." She reached across the table to touch my arm, then thought better of it, "...about the way I was before."

I looked away from her but did not stop listening. It was childish, but I was not going to make this easy on her. That didn't mean I didn't want to hear it.

"I saw you cha..." she continued her voice

trembling. My eyes met hers not knowing where she was going, but mindful of all the ears around us. Her eyes got a distant look and she seemed like she was in pain, as though she was remembering something she didn't really want to. "You were fighting with yourself. It was like you wanted to tear yourself apart."

"It hurts more when you fight it."

"Then why do you---"

"I always fight it!" I snapped without thinking, feeling terrible when she shrank away.

"...you fought," she continued softly, "and you ran. You ran like... like you were terrified, but you *raged* at the same time." Her voice cracked. She looked up at me again, her eyes were holding too much water and were threatening to tear. "You didn't want to change, and you... you screamed," she said shivering. "I have never heard a scream like that. You were in agony, and you were begging, not for the pain to stop, but to make it to the woods." Every word she spoke was heavy with terror and pity as the tear finally fell from the corner of her eye and ran down her cheek. I felt her pain as sharply as I remembered my own. I reached out and touched the hand that had stopped only inches from my own. Milagro let go a sob before taking a deep breath and squeezing my hand in hers.

"If you two are done with your greeting card moment, I would really like to ask Romeo here what the hell he was thinking going to see the most powerful being in the city!" Ramirez said. Milagro and I let go of each other's hands.

"I had nothing else to go on!"

"So, let me get this straight. You're told by our boss to find out how a couple of guys got turned into raisins. Then you get assigned a murder investigation, a bludgeoning of the most basic variety, and you think the best thing you can do with your time is to go whine to Markku's daddy about how he kicked your ass in a parking lot?"

"That's not why I went to go see him," I said, feeling more and more like a scolded child than a supernatural being capable of wanton destruction.

"Then please, enlighten me, Wolfgang!" he said, using my first name to get under my skin.

"Look I knew the guy wasn't going to spill his guts or anything, but I did learn something."

"Yeah? And what was that?" Ramirez sat back crossing his arms, as if he were daring me to say something stupid.

"I don't think he is behind any of it, but I can tell you that when I asked him about the killings and about Markku's warning, he lied when he said he didn't know anything."

"Really? And how could you tell that?" Ramirez was not giving an inch. "Did your puppy-sense start tingling or something?"

"Well, now that you mention it... yeah, it sort of did, you arrogant ass!" I said, obviously forgetting to bring my couth filter along. "I caught a scent, and I mean that literally." I watched him uncross his arms before I went on. "He knew something about what was going on. He may not have been directly involved, but he definitely knows something."

"You have my attention, but you still have not said how you know that he lied, so get to the point."

"Look, you know how when humans lie their bodies do things that, for the most part, they can't control? Their heartbeat quickens, the blood vessels dilate, and sometimes even the speech pattern changes. Well, when a vampire lies, I guess their bodies do a couple things as well. You taught me that a vampire's natural defense mechanism is that their skin tightens right?"

"Yeah, so?" he said, raising an eyebrow.

"You said it is almost like armoring the body. Now, since the vampire feeds on blood and since their bodies function generally the same as humans, their bodies smell sort of like blood. You know, as it comes out of their pores and all that." Ramirez's mouth opened slightly, and I was guessing he was picking up what I was putting down. "So, when the skin tightens it would make sense that they would sweat less right?" I didn't wait for an acknowledgement. "To a sensitive nose, it's a tell."

Ramirez leaned back and furrowed his brow, tilting his head to one side as if he was trying to decide whether or not I was full of shit.

"Do you hear what I'm saying, man? Vampires sweat blood, I mean like really sweat blood and when the skin tightens like Hadrian's did when I asked about the next few days and told him what his son had said, there was less blood in the air. I could smell it! He lied!"

Ramirez looked around the room without seeing anything. Apparently, he was not quite sure what to make of what I just told him when his eyes found something that grabbed his attention.

"You have a fan," he said, thrusting his chin in a direction just over my left shoulder. I fought the urge to look around and spoke as evenly as I could.

"Talk to me," I said.

"He's staring right at you, and he doesn't look happy." Ramirez kept his eyes on my so-called fan as he casually raised his glass to his lips but did not drink. "Dark brown hair long, but not yet to his shoulders, black t-shirt, fair-skinned."

"What's going on?" Milagro asked, looking back and forth between Ramirez and me.

I had turned in my seat to face the bar which had a mirror that allowed me to see the rest of the restaurant. Ramirez was right; the guy was staring at the back of my head, and he wasn't blinking. I was having difficulty picking out specific features with just his profile to work with until he turned and looked at the mirror glaring at me with those same unblinking eyes.

"Detective," a familiar voice said from behind me. I whipped my head around and saw something that almost always means a bad day, another werewolf.

CHAPTER 21

Hadrian Van den Broek's security woman... lycanthrope... guard, was standing directly behind and looking down at me. There was no anger in her eyes, so I slowly released the death grip I had on the rocks glass in front of me, along with most of the intent I had to slam it into the side of her head. Her eyes lingered on the glass, then came up to meet mine only after I had let it go.

"He wants to see you," she said.

"I just left him, and he wasn't in a chatting mood when I did." Turning away from her I locked eyes with Ramirez. Once I confirmed that he was watching her, I was able to play it cool, making like I was more interested in my drink than whatever she had to say. If she made a move, I would see it on his face. "If he had anything to say to me, he should have spoken up somewhere in between you trying to throw me out and him threatening me."

There was a palpable silence, followed by the sound of her clearing her throat. I didn't know if she was taken aback or insulted by my disinterest, but her next words got my attention and made me rethink a lot of what I thought I had already put together.

"It is not the father I represent here."

My head snapped round, and after about ten seconds of staring at her I was able to close my mouth and form big boy words. "You're here for Markku?" The words coming out of my mouth did not make any sense, but it was also the only thing that did make sense. "What does he want, and who the hell are you?"

"My name is Inyoni, and as for what he wants…I have been instructed to extend you an invitation to meet with him tonight. Will you come?" Her face held no emotion, and I couldn't get a feel for how much trouble I was about to walk into.

"Do I have a choice?" I asked, both to buy myself some time and to gauge her reaction.

"In this instance, you do." Her face never changed.

"Fine, say when and where and I'll think about it."

She stared at me for a long time before producing a business card out of what seemed like thin air, placing it on the table in front of me then turning to walk away. She strode through the crowd easily; people moved out of her way on instinct, never really looking at her but moving all the same. I waited until she was out of sight before reaching for the card. I was just about to read it when I felt more than saw Ramirez staring at me in disbelief.

"You're not actually going to meet him, are you?"

"Look," I said, slipping the card into my shirt pocket, "I'm pretty sure I'll be alright. I'm gonna see what he wants."

"What makes you think you'll be alright?"

"This guy has had the drop on me twice, and I'm still breathing."

"Third time's a charm mean anything to you?" Ramirez said without smiling and went back to examining the inside of his glass.

My phone chirped letting me know there was a text I probably did not want to read. I hated text messages. Pulling the oversized rectangle out of my pocket, I swiped my finger across the screen and saw that it was from Shepherd. I was right. I really didn't want to read it.

"I gotta go," I said as I stood.

"Yeah, what for?"

"A patrolman I work with needs my help. After my shift, I'm going to stop by and see Speaker Man, and report what I---"

"Who?"

"Speaker Man, you know, our boss?" I said as I turned away.

"You don't like using his name?"

"I don't know his name," I said over my shoulder.

"How could you not know his--"

"I never got around to asking for it."

I got about five paces when I remembered the guy in the black t-shirt. I had meant to casually glance over and get a better look at him but there was nothing casual about this. He was staring right at me, so I took a detour on my way out of the bar.

"Can I help you?" I asked him as I walked straight at him.

"No," he said, holding my stare without blanching.

I looked into those eyes and was immediately struck by an unnerving feeling in the pit of my stomach. "You know that staring is considered rude in most places?" He did not speak. "Why have you been staring at me?"

"Because I choose to."

"You choose to?" I repeated the question not expecting what I had just heard. "What's your name? You know I'm a police officer, right?"

"You may call me Sean, and yes I know exactly what you are." He still hadn't blinked, and I could feel the power in his gaze. At the same time something else hit me. He had no scent.

CHAPTER 22

Traffic was light for once and around fifteen minutes after I left the pub, I was pulling up to my second crime scene in two days. The house was one of those quaint little two-story jobs with a flat roof and a porch that ran the width of the entire house. It seemed well taken care of with decent paint, a shiny mailbox, the whole nine yards. It all would have been kind of inviting had it not been for all the flashing lights and yellow police tape.

"Sorry about the text message." Officer Shepherd, the one who saved my ass on my very first homicide, was walking toward me from the side of the house.

"Don't worry about it," I said looking around at all the commotion typical of an active crime scene. "But I gotta ask, what am I doing here?" I spoke in a low whisper, trying desperately not to seem even more out of place than I already felt.

"It might be better if I showed you," he said as he turned toward the front door.

I followed him through the front door and past a couple of guys wearing standard-issue mesh vests marked 'POLICE' who were too busy dusting for prints to pay much attention to me. Inside, the place looked like a normal, well-kept home. The first room served as a living room and everything was in its place; nothing seemed out of the ordinary. The furniture was not too expensive, but it wasn't the particle board stuff you can buy at the local warehouse stores either.

From the entryway, you could continue down the hall or hang a left into the next room which was obviously the dining room. Every chair was polished, and each napkin was folded in a neat little triangle. I could see that no one ever sat there, except for today. At the end of the hall was the kitchen, and that's where I saw the body. The sheet covered most of it, but from what was still showing, I could tell it was a woman and that she was sprawled out lying on her stomach as if she had been shoved forward and never got up. She had gone down near the back door on the right-hand side of the kitchen. There were a couple of suits standing over her, so Shepherd and I stepped to the left, walking as quietly as we could.

"Here, take a look at this," he said, grabbing the handle of the dishwasher and opening it up.

"Ok, what am I supposed to be looking at?" I asked, staring into the nearly empty machine. "The only thing in here is a..."

"Yeah, just like the dump we were in a couple of days ago!"

"How was the woman killed?" I asked, hoping against hope that there was some way out of this.

"Looks like a blow to the back of the head just li---"

"Just like the lady in the dump..." I finished the sentence for him. My mind started whirling as I looked for anything that might make this not true. "Does she have a kid?" I asked.

"Yup, and about the same age as the kid from the last murder scene," he said, putting his hands on his hips.

"Give me a second," I said, trying to gather my thoughts. I kept staring at the lone frying pan, dish, glass, and single set of flatware sitting in the dish rack of the machine. My mind whirled with possibilities, each one less desirable than the last. "Alright Officer Shepherd..."

"Call me Shep."

"Alright Shep," I said, looking around trying to think on my feet and failing miserably. "I have got to be sure about this before I even think about talking to the lieutenant about this and even if this turns out making some kind of sense, the chances of anybody believing it are slim to none."

"Detective," he said, looking as if he might explode, "let me set both files side by side and find anything that crosses over." His enthusiasm was infectious. "I'll bring you whatever I find, and then you can figure out how to convince the Lieutenant."

"I just don't think..."

"I'll meet you at your desk after roll call tomorrow morning," he said and walked away, not giving me the chance to protest further. I stood there for what felt like hours. I looked around at all the rooms; they were all full of cops, and it felt like they were all staring...at me.

CHAPTER 23

"Succubus?" Speaker Man had seemed mildly annoyed, even bored up until that very moment. But no sooner had the name left my lips did it become obvious; I had his full attention. "Succubus." He said the name again quietly to himself.

"I am sorry to have to wake you up." In truth , I didn't give a damn, "but from what I am told this thing is a pretty big deal."

"My kind does not really sleep," he said dismissively, "it is more of a meditative state." He was sitting in the same armchair he'd been in the last time I had the pleasure of visiting, and he was wearing a robe that looked like it dated back to a time I could only guess at. That being the case, it was still in beautiful condition.

He rubbed his temple with his right hand as his left rested motionless on the arm of the chair, his eyes seemingly far away. "A pretty big deal?" He said more to himself than to me; the expression sounded strange in the European accent that I still hadn't placed. He leaned forward in the chair, studying my face to the point where I began to feel really uncomfortable.

"Look," I said standing up, "I don't understand any of this, so I would really appreciate it if everyone would stop assuming that I have any idea what any of this means!"

He stared at me a moment longer before leaning back in his chair once again, serene and diffident to the point of being annoying. "The word Succubus comes from the Latin tongue, and it literally means to lie beneath." He spoke slowly, gesturing with the hand that had previously been rubbing his temple as if lecturing to a slow pupil. "These creatures rely on their beautiful appearance and the uncontrollable lust of weak men... or those gifted who are also weak," he said, gracing me with a crooked smile. "In the days long past, they were blamed for many things including stealing the seed of chaste men." Noticing the bewildered look on my face, he explained further. "Anytime a monk or priest would have what your modern vernacular calls a wet dream, he would claim that a Succubus attacked him in the night taking his seed."

"And why would they want to do that?" I asked, sitting back down, genuinely curious.

"The stories of the Succubus vary, but one of them is that they take the seed of men in Succubus form and then seduce women in the form of an Incubus, a male version of the same demon, planting their now corrupted seed and bringing a demon spawn into the world."

"And what is the truth?"

"The truth is they are more like vampires

than anything else, but where we live off the blood of living things, the Succubae are able to feed off of a being's lifeforce. When they feed, placing their mouths over the mouths of their victims it appears as if they are taking a deep breath, a breath of life, giving themselves more as they take it from their victim."

It was fantastic, mind blowing, and scary as hell. I sat there with my mouth hanging open, wondering how this story could possibly be true. How could a creature like that still be around? And how the hell was I supposed to put a pair of handcuffs on it?

He stood and walked over to a writing desk. "I will note this as unresolved killings by gifted persons. Allowances can be made for visits from creatures like a Succubus. It will not reflect on you poorly or affect any decisions regarding your performance here."

There was a slight change in his tone. Was he daring me to go after her? "We have some sex pot psycho demon running around turning guys into beef jerky, and you think I'm worried about my numbers?" I said, trying to contain my frustration. "I mean, how many more bodies is she going to drop on us before she decides to move on to the next buffet?"

"Please spare me the ubiquitous 21st century dramatics, Wolfgang," he said, picking up a pen and making some notes in a very large book. "A Succubus is a cyclical being. She arrives in an area to feed. Usually there are two or three victims, then they disappear for decades, sometimes even as long as a century." He paused as though trying to recall something before continuing to write. "You mentioned that you found two bodies so far. Therefore, she may very well have already moved on."

"Not likely. It looks like she may have kidnapped her third."

"Kidnapped?" He stopped writing and looked up at me. "She took someone?"

"It would seem so. She went after some kid after her first two victims; I guess those were the appetizer and main course, but then she left him alive. Apparently, she's ready for dessert now, because the kid's missing."

"That does not make sense." He laid the pen down looking at the book but somehow not seeing the words, his mind working out the inconsistencies.

"Yeah?" I said, standing up and heading for the door. "Well, I haven't run into a whole lot of things that make sense around here so welcome to the club. I'm going to find this kid."

"A Succubus is not something you go looking for ,Wolfgang."

There was that tone again. I stopped and turned to look at him. "I'm not looking for her. I'm looking for the kid." I had already started moving toward the exit but stopped a few paces from the hallway. "How do I stop her?" I asked over my shoulder.

"Stop her?" He laughed. "No Wolfgang, we stay out of her way and clean up the mess."

"Now that makes even less sense," I said, turning to face him again. "You force me into this little creature crew as part of our agreement, shove me into a police department where the lieutenant is just aching to get rid of me, and after all that you don't want me to do my job? You don't want me to stop a monster that is killing humans and breaking what you called 'the first and most important rule'?"

"Detective, there are few beings that have even the slightest chance of surviving a confrontation with her, and you are certainly not one of them."

CHAPTER 24

The annoying voice coming from the GPS feature on my phone was telling me to 'TURN LEFT'. That's when I caught sight of the building. I pulled over and took out the business card Inyoni had given me. The word "Office" was printed just above an address and, sure enough, this was the place. Stepping out of the car, I looked up at the building and couldn't help a little head shake.

"You have got to be kidding," I said aloud to absolutely no one and chalked up what I was looking at as just one more thing in this world I simply didn't understand.

"Wolfgang!" His cheerful voice echoed off of every ornate wall as well as the acoustically perfect ceiling as I walked through the heavy front doors. Man, I really do hate that name.

"A church? Your office is a church?" I asked, still not believing what I was seeing.

"I wanted to give you some time to digest what I showed you last night. Now, I am hoping we can discuss it intelligibly," he said, ignoring my question as though it were too ridiculous to even acknowledge. He was standing with his back to me at the end of the center aisle. Dressed in a gray suit he looked like a Wall Street heavy, preparing to bare his soul after a crooked deal or two. "Why didn't you tell my father about what I did?"

"Excuse me?"

"During your meeting this afternoon," he continued, turning to face me as he did, "why did you not tell him?" Markku was smiling but his eyes were inquisitive.

"Why did you take me there if you thought I would?"

"Call it a calculated risk," he said, tilting his head to one side and narrowing his eyes.

"Then does it matter? I saw what you wanted me to, and I didn't tattle on you to your daddy. What difference does it make?"

"A considerable difference," he said with a sincerity that surprised me. "Intent is everything." He began walking slowly toward me, his hands out to his sides as though professing to an audience. "People stumble around doing the right thing all the time, and some seem to stumble around doing the wrong things as well. I want to be sure of who I am dealing with." He stopped walking while furrowing his brow in a show of deep concern, and I couldn't tell if his expression was genuine or not. "You're not a stumbler, are you, Detective?"

"So, you are saying that it was right to keep your little antics secret?"

"Yes," he said with a monosyllabic laugh. "But did you do it for the right reason?"

I studied him, hoping to get a sense of what he wanted to hear. Problem was, I wasn't getting anything, and the longer I waited the more obvious it would become that I was doing it. "Neither you nor your father is a friend to me. So, if one of you is willing to dish on the other, I will take all the information I can get. If it's worth anything, I use it but only when it's in my best interest."

His face broke into a broad smile and, before I knew what was happening, he let his head fall backward and laughed from deep in his gut. It was a melodic sound that filled the cavernous church. "You see," he said, still laughing as he spoke. "You are exceptionally wiser than you let on, Detective."

"Yeah, I'm finishing up my thesis on bullshit, and you're giving me great material," I said, no longer enjoying the chat. "What do you want?"

"What is the nature of this world, Detective?" The smile on his face remained but with a shine to his eyes that looked like a bag full of crazy, or passion, and I couldn't tell which.

"I'm not here to discuss philosophy with you," I said, turning toward the door to either get out or force him to get to the point.

"Predator and prey."

I stopped walking and half turned, waiting for the rest of what I was sure was going to be worthless information. "And of course, you are the predator."

"Not always," he said, his smile broadening again. "That's the beauty of it."

"Beauty of what?" I said growing irritated.

"Why am I here?"

"Chaos."

"What?"

"Why do we hide ourselves?" He took a step toward me. "Do you even know? You are wise, but you are also young and may be ignorant of what and where we come from."

"Because humans cannot know we exist."

"Why?" Another step closer.

"They would hunt us down."

"Hunt us? Do you hear the words coming out of your mouth?" Another step. "Do you hear how absurd it sounds?"

"But it's true," I said, feeling him closing in but not feeling threatened.

"Precisely!" His hands once again went out to his sides, palms up, waiting for me to come to the conclusion he had carefully led me to. "We hide so that we can grow soft and lazy." He brought his palms together and touched the tips of his fingers to his lips before tilting them forward just enough to allow his words to flow. "We cower so that we can live in luxurious anonymity."

I didn't know where he was going but he had me. I wanted to know what was in his head. "That's how it is. It's been that way for centuries, right?"

He sensed my hesitation, smiled warmly, then took the final step that brought him right beside me. We stood shoulder to shoulder now, facing opposite directions so that each word could now be whispered. Leaning toward me he whispered,

"There was a time, Detective, when we hunted openly and were hunted as well. There was a time when the humans could recognize us on sight; some were so attuned, they could even sense us. Even you, with your virile and healthy appearance, would not have been safe. They would smell you out and fall upon you en masse before you could complete your change, tearing you apart."

"What's your point?" I said, getting my bearings back and remembering the slaughtered girl I found him hovering over not two nights ago. "You just talked yourself in a big circle. That is exactly why we hide."

"Wrong!" he said, turning on his heel and stepping back toward the pulpit, his arms raised high as though preaching to the world. "That is why we can no longer hide."

I had to consciously close my mouth, but I couldn't hide the confusion on the rest of my face.

Turning to face me again, the echoes of his grand proclamation fading away, he leaned casually against the nearest pew to my left crossing his arms and legs. "I could walk down any street in this city with blood dribbling off my chin, and no one would give me a second look. With films, books, romantic notions and clever marketing, our natural appearance, once a vulnerability, has become fashionable."

"So, what... you want to declare open season on humans?"

"And on ourselves. The human's greatest

strength is his numbers. What is a lion among a pack of wolves? No offense meant. There are not meant to be this many of us, Regnum. Our numbers were controlled by the fact that so few could survive the change and that we were as much the prey of humanity as we were their predator."

"But Hadrian is your father. Can't you guys be born?"

"It is extremely rare. No, like most of the so-called sons or daughters of our world, I was simply turned. It is a strong bond."

"A bond that you are willing to toss out so that you can hunt humans, humans who have just as much right to live as..."

"They gave up that right!" His face went hard, his body rigid as he stood. "Tell me, what have they done?"

"This! All of this," I said, indicating the beautiful church we were standing in. They have built and grown and lived..."

"They forgot how to live long ago. But we can remind them, Wolfgang." His eyes narrowed as he whispered the last few words. "How is it that I am standing here in this great beacon of religious power?"

"There isn't any power here. It's a building. It's beautiful, but still just a building." I said looking away as I spoke.

"But there are structures much humbler than this into which I cannot set foot." His eyes searched every corner of my face, reading my thoughts in the lines of the expression. "They are few and far between, and getting fewer and fewer every day, but they are out there."

"So, what makes this one so different?"

"The simplicity of the answer is outweighed only by the complexity of its existence." He paused for effect, and it was working. "Faith."

"In God?" I asked.

"Does it matter?"

"It sure as hell does to me."

"I do not profess to know of the existence or nonexistence of any one deity or many. What I do know is that there are things that we know and things that we don't. If the people in this building know that I can't come in, then I can't."

"So, these people don't know that," I said, smelling more bullshit.

"No, they are too busy searching for others they can point at and say, 'they worship the wrong way,' or 'they say the prayer the wrong way,' or 'they interpret scripture the wrong way.' They don't see that none of it matters."

"And what does?"

"Belief I suppose," he said, shrugging his shoulders. "I don't really know how it works, but I can tell you that when they knew of our existence, there was not a church, mosque, or synagogue that I could step into. It did not matter what God they served or what faith they subscribed to. There was purpose in their actions, power in their belief, not like what you see now, the mechanical mantras

131

performed more out of habit than belief. Worship for many has become a gathering of social interest, so one could say they were there and look down their noses at those who were not. They have turned to killing each other in religious wars, Crusades, Jihads and Caliphates, when there are things much more dangerous. So, you see, Detective, I am trying to help us all. By knowing of our existence, they will be better. We are the cure to their indifference."

"We are a mistake, a genetic screw up that can't do anything but kill and destroy!"

"Then are we not just like them?" He said, looking pleased with himself.

"They do more than that," I said, knowing that I was losing ground.

"Enlighten me."

"They heal, they create." I was losing my patience.

"We create," he said, almost daring me to argue. "And as for healing, just because we do not need the skill does not limit our worth." He waited, knowing I had nothing to say before continuing. "Ask yourself this, Wolfgang. What if we are the ones made in the image of God?"

CHAPTER 25

I spent the night tossing and turning with less than restful sleep in between. Markku was clearly insane, but I needed to figure out what he wanted with me and why he chose to share his vision of a "brave new world" with me. Was he warning me or trying to recruit me?

Feeling more tired than when I went to sleep, I dragged myself out of bed, showered, and headed to the office, hoping for but not expecting a quiet day. Sure enough, Ramirez was waiting for me. He sat on the edge of my desk nervously tapping a pencil on a notepad looking from side to side like he was making sure no one noticed that he was looking around to make sure no one noticed.

"Damn Jo, it's way too early for you to have your nuts in a knot." Roll call was in ten minutes, and I had only had two cups of coffee, so I was not in the mood to make anyone else feel better while I still felt miserable.

"Asshole," he said, standing up and flipping through pages of his notebook. He was obviously looking for something, or at least pretending to. "You leave to talk to some psycho, you don't answer your phone, and then you expect me to be happy to see you when you finally show up? Fuck off."

Joaquin Ramirez rarely used language that strong despite his military background. I knew I had messed up and owed him an apology; I just had to figure out what I needed to apologize for. "Alright, alright," I said, holding my hands up in surrender. "Markku is a bad dude and I do not have the best relationship with him; I should have called to let you know I was good."

"I'm not your mother, Wolf, but damn it all, I am kind of responsible for you." Ramirez stopped flipping pages; either having found what he was looking for or done with the charade. "So, what did he want?"

"Huh?"

"I asked you what he wanted to talk to you about. And while you're at it, who the hell was the werewolf chick that delivered the message last night?"

"Best I can tell she is Hadrian's security, or at least a big part of it," I said, hoping to avoid the subject of Markku's ravings. "She is the muscle of the operation, and with good reason."

There was nothing shady about what Markku said; I just didn't know what to make of it and I didn't want the extra noise of Ramirez's opinion before I could even formulate my own. "So, what do you think our... I mean my next move should be on the 'juicer' case?"

"What about that guy last night? The guy

who was staring at you in the bar."

"Oh yeah, him," I said as the entire scene rolled through my mind. "I don't know what to make of him other than the fact that he creeped me out."

"Creeped you out? Why? I saw you talk to him on the way out so...who is he?" he asked intently.

"I'm pretty sure he wasn't human, but more importantly, he knew what I was. Hell, he could've been the paper boy for all I know," I said with a little less tact than I had intended.

"Well, don't you think that might be someone you may have wanted to get a little more than just the creeps from?" He said, matching my less than cordial tone.

"I was a bit preoccupied with some wolf bitch escorting me to a meeting with a guy who kicked the shit out of me a couple days back," I said, squaring off to face him. "Why don't you ask your séance girl with the big mouth?"

Ramirez looked down and tucked his lips between his teeth. "She left a little after you did," he said, his voice tinged with regret.

"Oh...is she okay?" The concern I heard in my own voice was much more than I expected. Milagro couldn't have thrown more insults at me when we first met if she tried, and still I found myself worrying after her.

"I think she'll be okay," he said, sounding less than convincing. "She knows things, you know but, she hasn't seen things, at least not the things in our world." He turned away, slowly walking toward the briefing room. "Watching you change that night messed her up a little."

"Watching me change?"

"Yeah," he said slowly, now staring at the floor. "She shouldn't have been there. She didn't need to see that."

"Hey," I said, placing my hand on his shoulder. "No she didn't, but that wasn't your fault. It was mine. You were just doing your job, I'm the one who lost it. So let's follow up on whatever you got in that little notebook and keep doing the job... Okay?"

Ramirez nodded and offered me what passed for a smile with him, which I returned. "So what else can you remember about the guy from the bar?"

"Oh, you mean Blinky." I said trying to inject humor into the sappy moment. "He did say something strange though. When I told him I was a police officer, he said he knew exactly what I was."

"Well, you're right. It sounds like he might be one of us."

"And something else," I said, remembering. "The guy had no scent."

"What?" he looked at me as if I had just smacked him.

"I couldn't smell him."

"We have to get back to that bar."

CHAPTER 26

Ramirez wouldn't go into what had him on edge about the lack of smell thing, and I had to get to roll all. He just told me to call him as soon as I wrapped up whatever I had to at the station. Basically, he was asking me to take a day's worth of work and cram it into a couple hours. No big deal. If that weren't enough, at roll call, the sergeant announced that another body had turned up in the same state as those from the hotel two days ago. Was our Succubus at it again? Was it the kid?

After about ten minutes the sergeant finished up the morning's assignments and announcements. We began shuffling out of the room when I saw Officer Shepherd walk straight toward me. *Damn!* I thought, realizing that I had completely forgotten about the bludgeoning case. The image of the little boy Isaac talking about monsters and his mother formed in my mind, and I was immediately hit by a wave of guilt. How could I have forgotten about him?

"My desk," I said, loud enough to carry over the grumbling cops making their way out of the tiny room. Officer Shepherd nodded his head and changed direction accordingly.

Determined not to forget again, I made my way through the crowd to get the latest from Officer Shepherd. It was painfully obvious that I was lousy at multitasking, but if I was to pick what was more important to me, helping a little human boy was head and shoulders above trying to track down some demon so that a bunch of freaks could save face. Then I remembered that she was killing people; she was killing humans. How do you choose which lives are more important when they were all victims?

"It has to be the same perpetrator," he said as he dropped a manila folder on my desk. "The pattern is right there for anyone looking for it."

"Remind me," I said, opening the manila folder and scanning the contents.

"Blunt force trauma to the head."

"What else?"

"Approximately the same time of death."

"What else?"

"Detective!"

"Look, Officer Shepherd—"

"Shep."

"Fine, Shep," I said, closing the manila folder. "The lieutenant is not my biggest fan, so if I want to have any chance at all of taking over the investigation, I need to have as much information as possible."

He stared at me for a moment, then his eyes widened a bit as though he had just recalled something. "Hold on a sec," he said, reaching for the file and flipping through it until he came to the photos. "Here," he said as he placed a photograph of the kitchen on my desk. "Do you remember the last house, the dishwasher?"

"Yeah," I said, searching the photo for the point he was trying to make.

"And you remember the dish drainer at the first house?"

"Yeah... the same thing, a frying pan, plate, knife and one fork sitting in the dish drainer right next to the sink." The image wasn't strange in and of itself, but combined with the filth of the first crime scene kitchen and the stark contrast of the same items staged so neatly, it was eerie. "It's weird but it might not be enough to---"

"Now listen to this," he continued, pulling out his cell phone. "I didn't think much of it at the time, but in the fridge at the first crime scene there were three items." He tapped on the screen of his phone as he spoke. "A loaf of bread, a carton of eggs, and a half gallon of orange juice."

"Okay," I said. "I'll bite." I stopped short realizing that I no longer liked that particular expression. "You got me. What's the big deal about those items?"

"Well, they caught my attention because, just like the dishes in the drainer, they were neatly placed. Almost as if, you know, someone with OCD or something," he said, still tapping. "And this," he said as he swiped furiously at his screen. "This is what the inside of the second crime scene fridge had in it."

He handed me the cell phone and I could see he had pulled up a photo of the inside of a refrigerator. On the top shelf, precisely placed next to each other but not touching were a loaf of bread, a carton of eggs, and a half gallon of orange juice. Not only were they not touching, they seemed to be spaced evenly apart, as if whoever placed them there had used a ruler. "Okay, I admit that's freaky but—"

"Swipe to the next picture," he said, interrupting my protestations.

I did as he asked, and the image of a different refrigerator slid onto the screen. The shelves were covered with various colored spills that had hardened into what appeared to be gelatins. There were half-open bags of heat-and-eat type meals, sodas, and cheap beer. Then I saw them. Every other item on the top shelf had been shoved aside, and in their place was the bread, eggs, and juice laid out with the same care as in the other image. "Jeez!"

"Yup, and did you notice that whoever did it even cleaned the area of the shelf before placing the items on it?"

"Yeah, and it looks like they might even be the exact same brands," I said, swiping back and forth between the two images.

"They are, and not just that," he said, crossing his arms. "All three grocery items are missing the same amount."

"What do you mean, the same amount?"

"I mean that the bread in both crime scenes is missing two pieces, there are two eggs missing from each, and as for the juice, you would have to break out a scale to confirm, but just eyeballing it, looks like about the same amount was poured out of each one."

"Aw, man!"

"What? You can't tell me this is not enough to go—"

"It's enough," I said, hanging my head. "I'm just trying to wrap my head around how I'm supposed to convince the lieutenant to give me this case with what amounts to a breakfast order."

"Yup," he agreed. "And the thing is, that is exactly what I think this killer is doing." Shep stood there for a moment and began shaking his head. It seemed that even he was having a hard time believing what he was about to say. "I think this guy is walking in, killing someone, then making breakfast, sitting down to eat it then washing up."

"Jesus H...I mean... What the hell are we supposed to make of... Thanks, Shep," I said finally. "Now let's just hope the lieutenant buys it."

CHAPTER 27

"Are you out of your fucking mind?!" Lieutenant Bowman exploded out of his chair.

"Sir, there is definitely a connection between these two cases. If you need me to dig for more, I can —"

"What?!" He said, not bothering to hide his contempt for me. "Of course, there is a connection. You think I'm an idiot?"

"Okay, so I can run lead on the—"

"Hell no!" He leaned over onto his desk, resting his considerable weight on his fists. "Like I said, are you out of your fucking mind?" He stressed every syllable, never blinking and continued staring as if his question were anything but rhetorical.

"Sir, you assigned me this case," I said, indicating the file I had brought with me. "And now there is another murder that mirrors, almost identically, the details of that case. It only makes sense that those investigations be coordinated."

"Not only does it make sense, Detective, it's also standard procedure." He sat down spreading out his arms in a gesture of what he must have thought exuded absolute power. "Which is why you will be turning over all of your files and notes to Detective Abrahms by the end of the day."

"What?"

"Detective Abrahms investigated the second crime scene and will take over the first case as well." The lieutenant folded his hands and placed them on his desk. I didn't know that man well enough to be sure, but it looked like he was smirking at me, enjoying his dominion over me.

"Sir," I said, keeping my frustration at bay. "Why not just let me continue my investigation? I have at least a day's head start on finding the assailant, and I have made significant progress."

"Progress that I am sure Detective Abrahms would be more than happy to read about in your reports."

"Sir!" I said, much louder than I should have. "I have already interviewed witnesses as well as the first victim's son, and I have clearly dug deep enough to find the connection between the two cases. It makes absolutely no sense—"

"What doesn't make sense is you being here at all!" he said, rising slowly from his chair, his face reddening as his volume increased. "What doesn't make sense is you investigating cases in this department! What doesn't make sense, boy, is you being a detective on my force!" He was at full volume now, hatred dripping from every word. "You were assigned what was supposed to be a simple violent crime. Now it turns out we might have a serial killer out there. So, I'll be damned if I have some half-assed freak of nature playing cops and robbers embarrass me, this precinct, or this department just because some other freak of nature with money thought it was a good idea to use this police force to cover up your filth!"

"I found out," I said through clenched teeth.

"What?"

"I said, I found out. Not we, I found out that this could be the work of a serial killer," I said holding up the file again. "And maybe that is what is really pissing you off."

"Excuse me."

"Your pal Abrahms didn't put this together. You didn't catch it. I walked into your office and dropped this little nugget on your plate, and now you're up in arms not wanting me to continue on a case you gave me."

"Careful, boy," he growled.

"You thought this was just some crackwhore getting her brains bashed out by her boyfriend or something, didn't you?"

"You need to leave," he said, pointing toward the door.

"That's what you want isn't it? Me gone?"

"I wouldn't shed a fucking tear if you did."

"Fine, give me this case and let me screw it up."

"Say again?" He arched an eyebrow, seemingly unsure of what was happening.

"Let me run this case. If I screw it up like you think I will, you get to fire me and save face with the city and the freaks of nature."

Lieutenant Bowman leaned back in his seat, wrapping his lips tightly around his teeth, his eyes narrowing but never looking away. "Alright, Regnum," he said finally, "you got it." He picked up the folder and offered it to me. "This is the big dance, boy. You fuck it up and you're gone."

"Will I have the full cooperation of this precinct?"

"Yup."

"And if I make this case, are you going to get off my back?"

"I will treat you like I treat everybody else I don't like, and if you don't like it you can quit."

Realizing this was the best I was going to get from him, I took the folder and walked out.

CHAPTER 28

"Well, what the hell did you go and do that for?" Ramirez said.

"Because the man is an asshole."

We were standing in front of the Medical Examiner's building on East Jackson Street.

"Look, we get treated like that all the time. It's their fear of us that brings out the worst in them."

"Just because it happens doesn't mean we let it keep happening. I mean, I am not about to jump up and down claiming to be offended, but I'll be damned if I let someone take something I care about away from me."

"Since when did you start caring?" he asked, then continued without waiting for an answer. "Since when did you actually start giving a shit about anything but how miserable you are? I'd have thought you would have done cartwheels at the prospect of losing the case."

"Yeah? Well maybe the prospect of a kid having to grow up alone because someone bashed his mother's head in got me a little more invested!" We were both shouting; passersby were staring, but neither of us cared.

"You don't get it!" he said in a whisper but without losing any of his intensity. He looked around, then stepped away from the building indicating that I should follow. "You can't gamble with this job, Wolf."

"What are you talking about?"

"You can't quit, you can't offer to be fired, you can't refuse a transfer or promotion, none of that." Ramirez was pleading with his eyes, and I was getting nervous. What had I done?

"But wait," I said, struggling to understand what Ramirez was trying to tell me. "I was offered a job and I accepted it. So, that being the case I sure as hell can leave it… Right?"

"No, you can't," he said looking around then stepping a little closer. "This thing we are into, this organization, it's big alright. I don't know how big, but I can tell you that I have not found anything of significance that they are not plugged into. Politics, business, organized crime, you name it, someone from our world is pulling strings in some way."

"So what?" I asked more out of reflex than actually wanting to know.

"Well, here's where it gets sticky. All of these connections have to stay as secret as possible with the human players knowing as little about what we are as possible."

"And?"

"And law enforcement is an especially nasty bag of tricks because at least a few humans need to know exactly what we are so that, collectively, we can cover up crimes committed by people like us. Now, the fewer the better, but every time they place one of us in a department there is at least one more human that learns about us… in this case your favorite Lieutenant."

"Aw hell!"

"Yeah."

"That's why he hates me!"

"You're different, he fears you, and you're taking a job away from one of his kind. Oh, and I am sure your charming personality isn't helping the matter either," he said, trying to lighten the mood.

"Damn it!"

"This organization takes a risk every time they place someone like us on the force or in any other authority position. That's why they don't really get into the whole worker's rights thing."

"What would they do to me?"

"I have no idea, but I can guess it wouldn't be a scratch behind the ear and a nice belly rub."

"Piss off," I said, smiling at the joke in spite of myself. "Damn."

"What?"

"I think I am starting to realize how royally screwed I am."

"Hey…Wolf," he said, trying to sound reassuring. "Let's just do our jobs and do them right. When we solve this thing, you can focus on finding whatever piece of shit killed that kid's mom and no one will get themselves unmade. Okay?"

"Yeah."

"Okay, now let's go inside and see what we can find out."

We made our way into the building and down the various hallways flashing our badges where needed and making sure to sign in where required. The autopsy had not yet been performed, so we were just there to get a preliminary look at the victim and decide if it was connected.

One of the assistant medical examiners walked us down to the coolers and found the correct drawer. She was young, plainly dressed and all business. Her professionalism made her all the more formidable which made her all the more attractive despite her lack of trying to be so. Pulling open the drawer, she looked at us both as if to make sure we were prepared. In truth, I had never been to this part of the morgue, and I was a bit unnerved already, but I nodded my head just as Ramirez did. She slowly unzipped the bag and walked out of the room, leaving us to our investigation.

"She does damn near three in one night and then starts a one per night pattern?" Ramirez asked incredulously as we stared at the body. The body was shriveled just like the victims from the hotel. "I thought you said she only did about two, maybe three and then disappeared?"

"That's what Speaker Man told me," I said, studying the corpse in front of me,and trying to find some detail that might help.

"Zuñiga."

"What?"

"His name's Zuñiga," Ramirez said the name slowly. "Antonio Miguel De Badia y Zuñiga."

"All that crap you just said was a name?"

"Yeah," Ramirez said unsuccessfully trying to stifle a laugh.

"One of yours?" I asked before my couth filter could kick in and stop me.

"One of mine?" Ramirez asked, raising a chastising eyebrow. "No Wolfgang, the name is from old Spain. Mine are from South America.

I sensed that I had struck a nerve, so I moved on trying to make it seem like a smooth transition. "Anyway, that's what he said."

"Well, she's way off script on this one."

"They haven't been identified yet, right?" I asked, looking at the body of what I guessed, based on her hunting patterns, to be a twenty-five- to thirty-five-year-old man that looked more like he was eighty.

"So far nothing on the first two from the hotel. Their fingerprints didn't match anything state or federal, so we were lucky there. Both are still listed as a John Doe, but sooner or later they're going to get around to dental records. The results for this guy haven't come back yet. Looks like these were good guys, no criminal records."

"Or guys that didn't get caught," I said.

"True," he said, leaning over the body to study the victim's neck. "What do you make of these?" Ramirez pointed to what looked like a faint blue stripe on the left side of the victim's neck. As we looked closer, there was a crescent shaped cut at the end of the blue stripe.

"A bruise?"

"Maybe," he said, looking at the right side of the neck. "Uh... yup. Looks like that is the thumb because I got four fingers on this side." Ramirez walked around the open drawer to the other side of the corpse, allowing me a better view of the whole picture. "You see?"

I did see. The bruises were narrower, as would be the case with a thumb and fingers of a human hand, and at the end of each were those same crescent shaped cuts. "Do you think those are nail marks?" I was looking closer at the cuts.

"Or claw marks," he said looking closer as well. "The thickness of the nail is a bit more than would be normal for a human." Ramirez straightened up, crossing his arms and looked to be putting something together in his mind.

"I thought a succubus put some kind of whammy on her victims so that they gave themselves up willingly," I said, straightening up as well.

"That's right," he said, still contemplating. "It doesn't really make sense."

"Maybe she was just pissed," I said lamely.

"Succubi are bad enough normally. I don't think I want to see one who is mad at the world."

CHAPTER 29

We left the morgue and started heading back to the bar where we saw the guy with no smell. Once again, we had more questions than answers and, it seemed it was getting to be a habit with this case. We both figured we weren't going to learn much at the Medical Examiner's office, so we zipped up the body and checked out with the assistant. The autopsy was not going to be ready for another day or so and it felt like all we could do was move on to the next step. It was as if we were saying to the corpse in front of us, 'sorry for ya, we're doing what we can'.

I drove as Ramirez read through some books he had brought along. He was checking into some theories he had about the no scent guy. He was flipping through the pages looking for some bit of information that was obviously very important, judging by the frown he sported on his normally less than cheery face.

We pulled up to the place just after eleven, so the lunch crowd had not arrived in full force yet. The waitress directed us to the manager but only after the requisite badge flashing. After a few minutes the manager came out of the kitchen area, caught sight of us and headed our way. Just a few long strides put her near enough for me to see that her eyebrows were pushed so close together they made a nice 'v' in between them.

"Can I help you gentlemen?"

"We just need a bit of information," I said before Ramirez had a chance to be his charming self. He didn't do well with people he had just met.

"Yes?"

"Last night around eight o'clock, there was a guy sitting at that table over there." I pointed, and she followed my hand with her eyes.

"Okay."

"We need to know anything you can tell us about him."

"Well, no one who worked last night is in, so I don't know what---"

"Look lady, we don't have time---" Ramirez started loud enough for everyone in the bar to hear before I could put a hand on his arm.

"Anything you might be able to look up or check on," I said with my best puppy dog eyes, no pun intended. "Please," I indicated Ramirez with my eyes, warning her that he might make a scene.

"If he paid with a credit card, I might be able to find something. What table did you say he sat at?"

I pointed the table out again, and she went off to find what she could. "You have a knack for rubbing people the wrong way, you know that?" I said to Ramirez after the manager was out of earshot.

"I just want people to do their jobs. Is that too much to ask?"

"You have no idea what her job is. Maybe we should have asked some regional manager or something," I said facetiously.

"We're the police and her job right now is to help us find out as much as we can about this guy!"

Even for Ramirez, this was intense. Something was in his head, making him jumpier than usual. The manager came back before I could push him to tell me what it was.

"This is kind of strange," she said walking back, flipping through a printout of some kind. "Are you sure about the table?"

"This one right over here," I said walking over to it so as to head off any confusion.

"As far as I can tell, nobody sat there."

"What do you mean?" I asked.

"There aren't any tickets for that table, cash or otherwise after seven forty-five," she looked at both of us, and I could see that she was as confused as we were. "It didn't seem right, so I called one of the waitresses who worked last night, and she said that no one wanted to sit there. It was like the table had something wrong with it."

"That just doesn't make any sense. He was sitting right there when I left," I said, shaking my head, staring at the place where he sat. "Wait a minute, he didn't have a glass in front of him when I spoke to him. Maybe he just didn't order anything?"

"No one comes into a bar to just sit. Even if he

did, the server would have stayed on him to order something. She said that there was no one there."

I glanced at Ramirez, hoping to see some sign that he knew what was going on. He was looking down at nothing, his left arm crossed and holding his right elbow as he chewed on his thumbnail.

"Do you know what this is about?" I asked.

He shook his head.

We walked out of the bar with even more unanswered questions. This was turning into a red-letter day. Ramirez, and what was left of his thumb, had both hands in his pockets and was still staring at the ground without really looking at it. He shook his head every so often as though he was discarding an idea or thought that just didn't fit.

It was almost noon, and the sidewalks were getting a bit crowded with people looking for their lunches. I was looking up and down the street, not wanting to interrupt his thoughts when I spotted someone standing there about ten yards from us and he was staring at me.

"Jo," I whispered. "Looks like blinky has a brother."

"What?" he said, still half lost in thought. "Wait, where are you ..." He must have seen where I was headed because he rendered an opinion real quick. "Wolf, stop! You don't want to screw around with—"

"Hey!" I could no longer hear Ramirez over the sound of the city and my own voice. "Where's your boy at?" The man didn't speak, but the resemblance was eerie. Except for slightly darker hair, they could have been twins.

He kept staring at me as I approached, his expression never changing. "You guys have a serious rudeness issue, you know that?" I was five steps away. "Where's the other guy?" Two steps. "And why do you guys--" I raised my hand to point at him. There was a movement too fast to see, and then it was dark.

CHAPTER 30

I woke up to the smell of beer and the sound of Ramirez calling me a dumbass. I blinked a few times and looked around to find myself back inside the bar with the phantom table.

"You sure you don't want me to call an ambulance?" said the manager.

"He'll be fine, low blood sugar. You know?" Ramirez said, obviously making up reasons for having to drag me back into the bar with my lights out.

"Okay... let me know if you need anything." She hesitated a moment, nodded and walked away. The other onlookers, following her lead, drifted away from the booth.

"What the hell do you think you were doing?" Ramirez was helping me to sit up as he chastised. "You take off and go screwing with things you don't understand, and you're going to take care of your immortal problem real quick."

"Jesus, will you shut up," I said pressing on the sides of my head, trying to keep it from exploding from the pain. "You don't see me holding my head here?"

Ramirez was visibly shaken, and I decided to soften my tone, remembering his last partner. "We had nothing to go on. The kid hasn't turned up and tweedle dee dee and tweedle dee stupid are watching us like they have a concern. So, I figured a conversation was in order."

"Yea, well these guys aren't really known as talkers."

"Well, what the hell are they known for?"

"Well, if I'm right... let's see; Sodom and Gomorrah, Passover, firstborn children, that sort of thing."

"What?"

"They're kind of like messengers, or delivery and recovery guys."

"Great, I got supernatural leg-breakers on my case now? What did he do to me anyway?" I said, trying to shake the pain out of my head and only making it worse.

"I have no idea. I didn't see him until I got to you."

"How could you not see him when I walked right up to him? And how could you not see what he did? It feels like he hit me with a bat."

"Wolf, I'm pretty sure you just got your ass kicked by an angel."

"What did you... An angel?" I let my hands fall slowly to the table and looked hard at Ramirez, waiting for the punch line of a joke I was not in the mood for.

"The no smell thing pointed me in the right

direction, and when I saw you tear off after something that wasn't there? It's the only thing that makes sense." He started in on his thumb again, thinking and muttering to himself.

"You've gotta give me more than that," I said, hoping that whatever he said wouldn't confuse me more than I already was.

"Right, listen. Angels are for the most part incorporeal, and only---"

"You mean they have no bodies?"

"Yes, corpus means body, Jesus, don't you read?"

"Don't you have a point?!"

"Whatever," he said, shaking his head and resuming his explanation. "They are only visible when they want to be and to who they want to be or when they touch someone."

"Well, he sure as hell touched me," I said, grabbing my head again.

"But here's the thing," Ramirez said, looking at the floor and shaking his head. "What the hell are they doing here?"

"Yeah, that's a good question," I said, beginning to feel more myself and therefore getting more and more pissed off. "You work on that one while I try wrapping my head around the fact that you just said there are angels in Richmond fucking Virginia."

"Wolf…"

"Oh wait, wait, I have a few more questions on my list like, why in the hell would an angel walk into a bar. Jeez! Sounds like a bad joke!"

"I know it's a lot, but you have to try and keep —"

"A lot?! Jo, did you just say a lot?!"

"If you will keep quiet and let me—"

"It's another fucking universe, Jo! We left the world of 'A Lot' back in freak town with vampires and werewolves. You got me dancing with the angels now, Jo! How are you going to sit there and expect me to keep it together when you just dropped that little nugget on me!"

"You done?" Ramirez sat back and crossed his arms.

I nodded my head not knowing what else to do. This world had become so much more than I had ever imagined, and I had been thrown into it. "I'm sorry," I said. "I just... what am I supposed to do here?"

"Look man," Ramirez said, leaning toward me, his eyes softening. "If it helps, 'angel' is just what we call them, what we have called them for millennia." Ramirez raised his arms from the table, palms up and looked to the ceiling as if searching for the words there. "This place is called Legends, right?"

"Yeah," I answered, wondering where he was going.

"So, all good legends are based on something true, something that probably happened in some way, a long time ago. These angels or creatures, or hell, aliens if you want, they were seen or felt or witnessed a long time ago. The people that saw them had a certain belief system. Now, a

mortal's tiny brain cannot just accept things. They have to explain them, label them, even if they are completely wrong. They don't care, they just need to feel safe, and nothing that is strange is safe in their minds."

"So, you're saying that whatever these things are, humans called them angels because they didn't know what else to call them?"

"A name is just a name," he said, shrugging his shoulders. "You've got to start with something. And back then, who knows, maybe that was the only name to explain what those things could do."

"Fine," I said. I was still very unsure of everything, but I was getting used to that feeling. "So, what the hell are they doing here?"

CHAPTER 31

It was getting to be too much; angels, demons, vampires, werewolves, and who knew what other monsters were out there. Of course, it was not like the humans needed any help in that department; they had monsters of their own. The latest version was the one going around bashing people's heads in for no apparent reason.

Sitting at my desk, I stared at the files in front of me. I had no idea where to start. After dropping Ramirez off at his car so that he could do more research on what usually brought angels out to play, I headed back to the precinct. I was trying to piece together something, anything, on the bludgeoning case, but I couldn't focus. There was just too much going on, not the least of which was a wager with the lieutenant that amounted to my job or a solved case. A few days ago, I would not have cared one way or the other, but Ramirez was pretty clear about any future prospects I might have if I lost the bet. Again, a few days ago, I probably would not have cared but, this kid, Isaac, he deserved something. What that something was, I had no idea, but he deserved something.

What the hell was I thinking? What possibly could replace the kid's mother? What could I possibly do that would take away this kid's pain? The woman was no saint, and she didn't really take care of him all that well, but he loved her.

Looking at the clock on the wall, I realized that I had been sitting there for over an hour. All that time and I hadn't come up with a single idea or even a thought that would help me solve the case. Taking a deep breath, I tried to refocus on the files. Both case files were spread out on my desk, comparing them page by page, line by line. I was trying to find some connection between the two victims; if this was a serial killer, then there had to be a reason he chose these two specific people.

Both victims were women, and for all intents and purposes, single moms. Okay, now that I had the tough calls out of the way, I could try and find something useful. The victims looked nothing alike, they worked different jobs, and they weren't members of any civic or social groups together. Hell, they weren't even in the same tax bracket.

Turning the page, I saw the section of the file that was supposed to contain the statements of relevant witnesses. Flipping pages in the second file, I found the same section and there was nothing. There were no relevant witnesses in either case. In the second victim's more affluent neighborhood, everyone was at work, except for the victim of course, who worked from home. In the poorer neighborhood that Isaac's mom called home, no one saw anything because everyone minds their own business. Every interview that was conducted contained some form of "I don't know nothing."

Suddenly, the image of Lieutenant Bowman standing in his Peter Pan pose popped into my head, and I couldn't help but think he assigned this case to me specifically because after two or three days no one, not even the newspapers, would care that some poor drug addicted woman was killed in the crappy part of town. Between that and the fact that no one sees anything down here, he must have figured that if he was going to waste someone's time, it might as well be mine. Well, the joke was on him, because everyone was paying attention now.

Looking further down the page at Detective Abrahms's interview with the child of the second victim, I knew he was better than I was. Why didn't I let him take the case? What was I thinking? Comparing the two interviews, his and mine with Isaac, it was clear that I was out of my league. Abrahms had somehow been able to get all the information I had gotten from Isaac and so much more, even down to his last set of grades. I couldn't figure out why that was even relevant, but then I saw it, a short note in the margin.

Sliding Isaac's interview closer, I flipped back a page and confirmed it. It wasn't much but it was more than I had before. The kids went to the same school. I shook my head thinking that this was going to lead nowhere and picked up the phone. I used the landline so that the caller ID on the other end would show that I was who I said I was.

"Chimborazo Elementary School. How may I help you?"

"Hi, my name is Detective Regnum, and I want to set up a time when I can interview some of your teachers in connection with a case I am investigating. How would I—"

"You're talking about those poor boys whose mothers were killed, aren't you?" I couldn't help but think she sounded a bit excited at the prospect.

"Ma'am, I really can't go into that right now. If you will just let me know what I have to do to make this happen I would really appreciate it."

"Well... you would have to give me the students' names. You know, so that I could be sure that the teachers you need are all here," she said with a bit too much satisfaction in her tone. Some detective I was.

"Fine," I said and gave her the names.

She politely told me that she would call me back with a date and time once she confirmed with all the teachers involved. I thanked her genuinely and hung up.

I sat there staring at the files in front of me, and I couldn't help but feel like I was losing. I was failing miserably and still asking myself why I was so adamant about keeping the case. Then, right in front of me I saw the reason, a small photo, like the ones done every year at school. Isaac was smiling his best smile and I could feel my heart breaking. I picked up the phone and dialed another number.

"Child Protective Services, Pamela speaking, how may I direct your call?"

"Ms. Evans please."

"Certainly, and may I say who is calling?" Her voice was pleasant but tired sounding.

"Detective Regnum of the Richmond PD."

"One moment please," she said and placed me on hold. At first, I was surprised at her lack of reaction to the police calling, but then I realized that a place like this would almost certainly get calls from the police all the time. The thought made me feel even more like crap.

"Detective?" I recognized Ms. Evans's voice. "What can I do for you?"

"I was wondering how Isaac was doing," I said, sounding uncertain even to myself. "You know, how he's holding up and all."

"As well as can be expected, I suppose. He wasn't too happy when he was placed, but that is typical of—"

"Placed?"

"Yes Detective, placed in foster care."

"What?" My mind started whirling.

"Detective, you have to know that we can't keep these children for very long," she said softly. "All we can do with the limited resources we have is make sure the children are stable and find them the best home we can."

"But foster care? I mean, haven't you found anyone? A family member, long lost aunt, anything?"

"I'm sorry, Detective. We tried but unfortunately, we found no one," she said sadly.

"Okay... So, this foster home. How is it?"

"Detective, I really can't say."

"What do you mean, you can't say," I said frustration getting the better of me.

"Look, they're certified and inspected regularly."

"What does that even mean?!"

"It means Detective, that Isaac is getting the best we can give him!" Her voice had grown angry, but I also heard what sounded like regret. She cared for these kids, all of them. She was doing everything she could, but even she knew it was not enough.

"I'm sorry Ms. Evans. I didn't mean to imply anything."

"It's alright. You seem to care very much for Isaac—"

"I do," I said before thinking.

"It is not something we see very much from the authorities. I suppose you all have to harden yourselves or you wouldn't be able to do your jobs for very long." She was talking now like a mother, maybe even a grandmother, someone who knew what it meant to care for a child at home and not just an institution. "Hold on to that as long as you can, Detective." She was apologizing! The pain in her voice was almost seeping through the phone and making me hurt even more. "These foster homes, most of them are good, run by good people who give of themselves to help kids who are otherwise helpless. Of course, there are the others, not many but they are out there. The ones who run their homes like a business." I could hear the anger creeping back in when she spoke of the business types. "Still, chances are Isaac went to a caring place with people who will do their best but..."

"But what?"

"Detective, even the most caring foster home is still a foster home, and the longer it takes for us to find a family to adopt him, the harder it is going to be for Isaac to ever feel normal again."

Not to feel normal again. I knew what that was like, and I wouldn't wish it on anyone.

"Thank you, Ms. Evans," I said.

"Thank you, Detective."

The phone felt heavy in my hand. The click on the other end of the line was clear but I just kept on holding it. I pulled it away from my ear and stared at it as my mind counted the number of ways this kid was screwed. Then I started counting the number of leads I had in the case. The math was not good.

Laughter a few desks away yanked me out of my own head. Officers and detectives were getting ready to head home for the day, or to any number of after work hang outs to brag or bitch about their days. So, what was I going to do?

The ache in my belly was still there and I realized I needed help. I hung up the phone, tapped on my keyboard to wake up my computer and opened a search window. Finding the city tax assessor's website, I started typing and before long I had the address I was looking for. Punching it into my phone's GPS, I started for the doors. It was all I could think to do. I just hoped it was going to be worth it.

CHAPTER 32

The John Marshall building was just north of the Coliseum, its name displayed on the roof with giant black letters attached to metal framing. It was a beautiful building right in the middle of downtown Richmond, but it had seen better days. Stepping out of my car, I made my way to the enormous entryway doors. Once inside, I noticed the freshly polished, marble tile in the foyer, the elegant steps that led to the main lobby, the high ceilings, all of which reminded me that this building had history.

The elevator took me to the top floor and the apartment I wanted. As I approached the door, I heard the latch click and the door eased open. I froze, my senses taking in everything, because no one knew I was coming. Then I smelled the blood. What had I walked into?

"Whatever you brought in, you may set it on the table to your left and leave." His voice came from inside the apartment. "I will send your tip down promptly."

Was he slurring? Slowly, I pushed the door open and stepped inside. As I stood in the doorway,

I looked to my left and saw the aforementioned table. The smell of blood was stronger now; it filled the entire room but there was no sign of it anywhere. Cautiously, I stepped inside, closing the door behind me. Heavy curtains were drawn across every window, blocking out most of the light, but there was more than enough for me to see the entire room clearly.

The high ceilings, typical of the more historic buildings in the area, were elegant, with ornate crown molding bordering them. There was very little furniture, a leather sofa with matching armchair and chaise lounge as well as end tables flanking each one. There was no television, and the furnishings were arranged so that the occupants faced each other. Crossing further into the open concept living space -bad choice of words- I passed the kitchen area. Every appliance gleamed, which made perfect sense considering he probably had never used them.

The smell grew stronger as I approached the large French doors that I assumed led to the bedroom suite. Without making a sound, I crept closer. I could hear the rustle of silk sheets and pillows being moved. He was getting out of bed. Quickly covering the last few yards to the bedroom doors hoping to surprise him, I stepped through. The surprise was mutual.

"Oh. Wolfgang. What could you possibly want?" Markku sat in the center of an enormous bed looking at me with weary eyes. He had been in the process of untangling himself from the crisscrossed limbs of three nude women when I stepped in. The women, otherwise beautiful, were motionless and covered in blood. Recovering from the initial shock, Markku sighed then continued the process of extricating himself from the mass of bodies.

"What the hell did you do?!"

"Wolfgang, please," he said as he got to the edge of the bed. "Remember that this is rather early for me."

"I don't give a damn about how early it is for you." I was beside myself. "What the hell was I thinking?"

"What were you thinking?"

"That maybe you could help me."

"And perhaps I can, but could you come back around eight-ish?"

"I can't accept anything from you, you sick bastard."

"And why is that?" he said, standing and turning to face me.

"Because you're a murderer!"

"Oh? Is that what has been stopping you? Really?"

The question threw me off. His entire demeanor confused me, as though I was missing the question that everyone else had already answered. Add to that the fact that he was standing there naked as the day was long, staring at me like I was the one out of place; his indifference probably stemmed from the fact that he was magnificent, like something the Ancient Romans would have chiseled out of marble. I could appreciate the human form, male, or female as much as anyone, but it was a different thing altogether to try and have a conversation with one at the same time.

Not knowing what else to say, I turned to leave.

"Wolfgang."

"What?" I said, turning back around.

"They are not dead." He reached down onto the bed, took hold of one of the more voluptuous legs, lifted it from the blood-stained sheets and let it fall. The woman to whom it was attached moaned then shifted position. "They are here by choice," he said, stepping toward me. "Just like you."

He was halfway from the bed to me when he thankfully grabbed a black silk robe from the valet stand and put it on before standing directly in front of me. "Now what do you want?"

"What is... this?" I tried focusing on what I had just walked into since I still couldn't quite wrap my head around why I was really there in the first place.

"I think the modern-day parlance would be," he paused as though searching for the word, "pre-gaming," he said, moving past me into the main living space. I stood staring at the three women still on the bed, still unmoving. All three were gorgeous in different ways. One was slender and petite, exuding youth and promise. The second was strong and athletic, almost feline in her virility. The third was the one who moaned when Markku dropped her leg, voluptuous and inviting. The lines of her body gentle, the curves perfectly balanced between gravity and firmness. Heavier than the other two, she had the thick ankles and calves of a dancer. Just like the rest of her, she was soft in all the right places and firm everywhere else.

Markku stepped back into my line of sight slowly pushing the doors closed as he spoke. "Please Wolfgang, we wouldn't want you getting overwhelmed and making a mess. I am rather fond of these three."

"Why are they bleeding?"

"As I said earlier, by choice."

"Who would choose to be bled like a... hell I don't know what, but who would want that?"

"Some mortals have discovered the absurdity of their own existence," he said, dropping onto the chaise lounge. His movements were uncharacteristically graceless. "Now, having discovered that absurdity, some choose to find fulfillment in life by way of experiences; some albeit, seemingly bizarre to the rest of the mindless herd you call humanity."

"What does that even mean?"

Markku slammed his right hand on the end table, shattering it. "Life has no meaning Wolfgang! Nothing! There is no purpose, no grand scheme, no ultimate goal." Markku let his head hang a little as he let out a sigh. Having regained his composure once more, he eased his body back onto the lounge. "The sooner you learn that, the less of a miserable, self-loathing bore you will be. You will still be miserable of course, but at least you will not be dripping it metaphorically, all over my rug." Once again, I could hear a slurring of words.

"What's wrong with you?"

"Wrong," he said, chuckling. I had never heard Markku chuckle, and it was unnerving. "Whatever could be wrong?"

"I don't know but, you almost staggered over to that lounge, you're slurring and compared to our last meeting you seem a little...less..."

"I am not aware of what it is you speak."

"Fine, I shouldn't have come here anyway," I said, turning to leave.

"And why not?"

"What?" I turned to look back at him. He was laying on his side staring at me. Propped up on his elbow and wearing the silk robe, he might have been posing for a portrait.

"Why should you not have come?"

"Because I am a cop and I have no business coming to a killer for help."

"They are not dead," Markku said, waving a dismissive hand in the direction of the bedroom.

"Maybe not them, but you have killed."

"Not since we met."

"Excuse me?" I didn't know what to make of what I had just heard. I stepped closer to him, hanging on every word, expecting some trick or misdirection.

"At our last meeting, I offered you my help to which you replied that you would not accept help from a killer. I sincerely wish to help you, and in that sincerity, I have abstained from any extracurricular activities."

"And why do you want to help me?"

"I do not know." The words hung there like a bra on a clothesline, no one wanting to acknowledge that it's there but unable to look away. Finally, he broke the silence, "and in answer to your question, the girls take certain uh, chemicals into their bloodstreams so that when I drink from them - they do this voluntarily I would remind you- I receive an interesting drug and blood cocktail that... well let's just say, dull all of my senses. I think you refer to it as going on a bender." He sat up slowly and swung his legs over the side of the lounge, placing his feet firmly on the ground as though to stop the room spinning. "Now, what do you want my help with?"

I had no real reason not to ask for his help and more than a few reasons why I needed it. Looking around the room at nothing, my eyes settled back on Markku. As if he could feel my indecision, he motioned for me to take the armchair opposite him, and I did.

"I am screwing up these cases," I said, slumping into the chair.

"You refer to the Succubus and...?

"There were a couple of bludgeonings in my precinct. Originally, I was assigned to what was thought to be an isolated case of domestic violence or some minor drug thing, but now there's another one and they are definitely connected."

"Why do you care?" His tone was not sarcastic or dismissive in any way. He was truly curious.

"Normally I wouldn't care about some demon running around except that she's killing people."

"And you still feel a kinship with them where you have not developed one with your own..." Markku caught himself and reworded. "You have not found a connection to this new world you have been forced into."

"Yeah," I said, acknowledging his efforts. "Anyway, as for the murders, there is this kid. He's got nothing... no family, no home. His mother gets killed through no fault of his own, and now he is shoved into foster care until he gets adopted." I shifted uncomfortably in the armchair. "And what do you think the chances are of a school-aged kid with trauma getting adopted?" Just then I began to realize how much Isaac was becoming a factor. Somehow, I needed to help him.

"Well, it would seem that I am indeed in a position to help," he said rising.

"Okay, how?"

"Well," he said grandly, making his way to the kitchen. "I am conducting my own inquiry into the Succubus that has come to our fair city, and I believe I may have some insight into your problem." He opened the refrigerator door and pulled out a container of orange juice. "However, that will require all my faculties and so we should meet again once I... well let's just say I have more playtime planned." Markku opened up one of his cabinets and pulled down three pill bottles and what looked like some multivitamins. "As for your bludgeoner, I suggest you use your other talents."

"What talents?"

"Wolfgang," he said as he tapped out a few pills from each bottle onto a saucer. "Whether you consider your new abilities a gift or a curse, you have them nonetheless. This killer and all who have seen him, or her, are only human." He finished putting away bottles and orange juice before turning to me. "You are so much more than them. Use that, use your enhanced senses and track this killer down."

CHAPTER 33

My little chat with Markku had lasted long enough that traffic leaving the downtown area of Richmond had eased down to a mild annoyance instead of the normal rage incubator. Turning right on Broad Street, I started for the first crime scene. The crime scene was already two days old, but it was all I had, and I was running out of time. I figured that I had until the next bludgeoning took place before Lieutenant Bowman pulled me off the case and, considering all the trash-talking I did at our last meeting, I really had no leg to stand on. If that happened, Ramirez had made it clear that I was not going to have a good day. Hell, I might not live through the day after the powers that be found out what I had done.

Crime scene tape crisscrossed the banisters on either side of the porch steps. The sun had already gone down but the light from the streetlamps bounced brightly off the yellow and black plastic. The place looked different at night, or perhaps I had just not been looking that hard the last time I was here. Being so nervous about my first crime scene I had likely missed a whole lot of detail.

Fear had sort of locked me up and may have cost me precious time, or worse the life of the second victim. What if I missed something that would have solved this thing before anyone else had to die?

I shook my head as if trying to rattle the thoughts out, then opened my car door and stepped out onto the street. As I made my way up the stairs, I somehow felt very alone. There were no flashing lights, no buzz of voices, the bustle or closeness of people coming in and out of the place trying to do their part to help piece together what had happened that led to a woman losing her life. Instead, there was only the sound of the street.

Stepping through the front door, I found myself in a different world altogether. The stillness was like something you could touch, as though the air was somehow thicker, having to be pushed aside before you could take a step forward. All the rhythms, the noises from outside, barely penetrated the silence of the place and the loneliness grew deeper. Nothing moved because there was nothing to move. There was no life in the place, not even the ticking of a clock to break up the deafening quiet that threatened to suffocate any who stayed too long.

The now all too familiar feeling of dread came over me. Dread of all that was, all that had been, and all that was to come. I was not here by choice, and that left me with only two other possibilities. Either I was meant to be here, which led me to question what sadistic mind had decided this was where I needed to be, and then of course, why? Or was it all some random set of circumstances, some cosmic accident that put us all on this rock, made us scurry about like bugs in a clear jar, with only a vision of a reason to be where one was but no real way to walk through and take it, no way to seize and hold even a strand of purpose?

I remembered when I was attacked... when I was changed. I felt fear at that moment. The fury of what had attacked me, all teeth, fur, and eyes, was overwhelming, and I fought it, tore at it with all I could, not with bravery but for lack of knowing what else to do. In that moment I felt a fear previously unknown to me. But this was not fear. This was dread, and I was not sure if I could take another step. Why was I here? What could I possibly do to make anything worthwhile out of this madness? How could I break through the glass wall of the jar and catch my breath? I was running out of air, and I wasn't moving.

'Use your gifts', he had said to me. It was all I had left and so I closed my eyes and inhaled deeply, opening my mouth, filling my lungs before slowly exhaling. I felt my heart quicken slightly with the renewal of oxygen now entering my bloodstream before it settled into a natural, steady rhythm. I took another breath, anchoring what little sanity I had to the noises outside the tomb-like room in which I stood and slowly opened my eyes.

I scanned my surroundings, taking in every detail as though I were seeing it for the first time.

I had not bothered to turn on the lights; I didn't need them. I saw everything in the room even more clearly than I had in broad daylight when I first arrived. I moved from room to room, slowly taking in every detail but finding nothing. I could see every contour, every shape, every corner, and every curve but there was not one new detail, not one thing that took me any closer to an answer. My insides began to tighten again with angst. I had no idea what great revelation I was supposed to have this time around. Everything was the same, from the overflowing ashtrays to the refuse covered floors that smelled of...

I stopped walking. Closing my eyes once again, I slowly smelled the air around me. Images filled my brain, images that coincided with every scent that now filled my nose, various food stuff rotting away, the dog, the people who had trampled through the home searching for what I might have just found, and blood. I could smell the blood of the victim and then... something else. I smelled Isaac and my heart began to ache.

The mental image of Isaac, teary-eyed and wondering why he was now an orphan drew me out of the euphoric heights of discovery and refocused my attention on the task at hand. The key was to isolate some scent that might help me get to the answers I needed. My mind started churning out ideas, none of which seemed useful until I started imagining what the killer might have done while in the house.

I walked back out to the kitchen area and stood in front of the kitchen table. If Shep was right, the killer had made himself breakfast, sat down and eaten it after killing Isaac's mother. The table was a simple, circular wooden piece, in dire need of a paint job. There were two chairs, one on either side, basic metal frames with worn cushions. I bent over at the waist so that my nose hovered inches from the table.

It became disgustingly obvious that the table had not been well cleaned in a while. I could smell cheap macaroni and cheese, milk gone sour, peanut butter and jelly, but no eggs, no orange juice. The killer must have been extremely neat, avoiding any spillage which was probably why I could not smell any of what we theorized he had eaten.

Giving up on the table, I looked over at the chair. There was definitely something there so I moved closer. Along the chair back I mostly smelled Isaac, but as I moved lower to the cracked and faded cushion that was the seat, I smelled the killer. It was strong, as though whoever it was had only just left the chair. The smell was probably as faint as could be, but to my animal senses it was as though I had a face full of gym shorts and there was no mistaking that it was a man.

My cell phone rang, and in the silence of the crime scene, it was like a klaxon making me jump. After giving myself some time for my heart to stop pounding, I pulled the phone out of my pocket, looked at the name on the screen and touched the answer button.

"Hey Jo," I said.

"Where are you?"

"I'm fine thanks, and how are you?"

"Looks like our girl took another one," Ramirez said, ignoring my sarcasm. "The body has been sent to the morgue. I'll meet you there and then we can figure out a way to get a look at the crime scene."

"I can be there in about fifteen minutes," I said as I walked toward the front door.

"Alright. I'll be right behind you."

I hit the end button just as I closed the door behind me and started down the steps toward my car. My mind was going like a gerbil on crack with all I had learned at the crime scene. Finally, I could say I had made progress, just not enough. But now, I had to step back into the land of the freaks.

Yanking open the car door, I sat and went to grab my keys when I realized my cell phone was still in my hand. Before I could think too long about it, I punched in the number then typed out a text message. I stared at it for what felt like forever and then touched the send button. *Too late now*, I thought to myself.

CHAPTER 34

"None of this makes any sense Jo," I said, watching him come through the main doors of the city morgue.

"Look man, you were the one that said this was going to be over after two or three victims," he said while performing the appropriate gesticulations for 'I don't know what to tell you'.

Our conversation was put on hold as we walked up to a very bored looking security guard. We didn't speak a word until we finished signing in at the desk and had walked through the next set of double doors.

"Well, that's what I was told by the boss man," I said, opening the next set of doors then following him inside. "I am definitely not the expert here considering that two years ago, I didn't even know things like me existed."

"Good point," he said, checking the hallways to be sure we were alone before moving to the drawer assigned to our newest victim. Pulling open the drawer, the smell was enough that Ramirez took a step back. I was stock-still because despite the stench, I was smelling something else, and I was hoping that I had not made a huge mistake. Jo stood up ramrod straight then began looking around, almost panicked.

"Easy, Jo," I said.

"Wolf, we gotta go!" He spoke in a whisper so loud that people on the next block over could have heard.

"I'm not here for you, Detective Ramirez," Markku said as he stepped into the light from around the end of the row of coolers. Jo stood his ground, but I could see his right hand hovering near his sidearm. I placed my hand gently on his shoulder hoping to let him know that this was expected, sort of. I had sent the text but I had no idea if he was done with his playthings yet, and therefore had no idea if he would show. "Oh no, that is definitely not her work," he continued, stopping right next to Jo, close enough to make me uncomfortable.

"How do you know? Have you seen her victims before?" I asked, trying to regain control of the situation.

"No, I have not."

"Then how can you be sure?"

"I may not have seen *her* victims before, but I have seen victims like this before."

"Like what?" Ramirez asked now, more curious than scared.

"Show me one of the victims from the hotel, your first set of victims please."

Jo and I looked at each other, and like a bad comedy, we both shrugged our shoulders at the same time and went to it. We found the drawer holding the salesman from the conference at the hotel. After we pulled open the drawer ,Markku walked over slowly to inspect, like someone looking for something they already knew was there. "Look closely at the skin, detectives."

We bent over the body in unison, looking hard even though we had no idea what we were looking for.

"Notice the brittle texture," he said, touching the area where the pectoral muscle would have been had there been any form whatsoever to the dried-up husk. Jo and I both recoiled at the sight but not before noticing that the skin almost cracked under the pressure of Markku's touch. We leaned in a bit more to examine more closely. The skin was shriveled just like the other, but it was hard with small cracks you could only see when you were so close your nose was nearly touching. "Now let us go back to your latest victim."

Markku walked briskly to the first table and asked us to look again as he performed the same touch test. The skin moved like the loose skin over your elbow. "This one has simply been exsanguinated while that one," he motioned to the cracking corpse, "has had the life sucked out of him."

"Jesus Chr…"

"Please, Wolfgang," Markku said. "You may not be a believer, but it is still rude."

"Your office is a church!"

"Point taken."

"So why did she do it like this?" Jo said, trying to get us back on task.

"Do what?"

"Kill him."

"As I said before, Detective Ramirez, she didn't."

"Well, how do you know that?" I asked.

"Because this is the work of a vampire," Markku said with pride.

It was like the air had been sucked out of the room. Ramirez was staring at Markku and all I could do was to mentally scramble for some question to ask, some intelligible thought that might begin to make sense of what I had just heard.

"Close your mouth, Wolfgang, you will look more intelligent."

Looking at Markku, I realized that I was slack-jawed.

Markku smirked as he continued. "See the bite marks?" he asked as he indicated a spot on the inside of the left thigh. "Now for a vampire to do this to a human, it would take time, especially considering it was done with only one bite."

"Why would a vampire bite his victim there?" I asked, staring at the body.

"Two reasons. Any guesses?"

Ramirez looked hard at Markku for a moment before shaking his head and speaking. "Because the femoral artery is there. If his victim was standing up or held up maybe you could drain him more completely."

"Very good Detective, and if we are to believe our eyes, we must assume that was his intention."

"You lost me after the femoral...thing," I said, getting frustrated at once again being the only one in the room that did not understand the conversation.

"The femoral artery is a major blood vessel that runs along the inside of the thigh." The words were spoken as though Markku were holding a class.

"When you slaughter a pig, you hang it by its hind legs and slit its throat to drain out the blood," Ramirez added without taking his eyes off the body.

"And the second reason?" I asked.

"Because he or she wanted to conceal the wound in order to cast blame on the Succubus," said Markku.

"Well, why the hell did it want us to think that?" I asked.

"I think you will have to ask them when you find them."

"Look, Markku," Ramirez said evenly as if he did not want to catch anything by speaking to him. "For a vampire to do this, they would have to be pretty strong right?"

"Yes, they would," Markku said, looking at Jo with a newfound respect.

"So, if that's the case then the vampire would have to be pretty old, right?"

"Again, correct."

"About as old as you?" I asked, searching Markku's face for a reaction.

"Lucky for you or, unlucky as the case may be, whoever did this would be older and stronger than I. For that matter, I can tell you that I would have no desire to do anything like this." Markku turned to look at me. "Wolfgang is very familiar with my tastes." Now it was his turn to look for my reaction. He smiled at me when our eyes met, and I could see he was enjoying making me uncomfortable.

"If you two are done making googly eyes at each other, I would like to point out that we now have two serial killers running around Richmond, one of which—"

"Three," I said, still staring at Markku.

"What?" Jo said, leaning over between Markku and me.

"I said three." I kept my gaze on Markku for a moment longer, then focused on Jo. "We have three serial killers, remember? I got that little situation where someone bashed a couple innocent ladies' heads." Out of the corner of my eye I could see Markku's smile broaden.

"Right," Jo said. "Well, as I was saying, one of which we have no idea as to a motive, and the other may have already skipped town."

"Not to mention," Markku chimed in, "that you seem to have a pair of angels gallivanting around your precious city and, if you will forgive the pun, heaven knows why."

"How the hell do you know about that?" Jo, obviously no longer intimidated, squared off on Markku.

"How the hell?" Markku raised his eyebrows in mock surprise. "How apropos."

"Just tell me how you know about that," Jo continued, unphased.

"I have people watching the city same as you, Detective," Markku said, spreading his hands wide, palms up. "I would think you would welcome the assistance, considering the two of you are woefully outmatched in all of these matters, save perhaps the aforementioned bludgeoner that Wolfgang seems particularly vexed with."

"You know what?" Jo's face was reddening. "When we want your help, we'll ask for it! Okay?"

Markku smiled menacingly before looking over at me.

"He did."

CHAPTER 35

The night had been too short and the sleep was too little. I was sitting in a parking lot with the ignition off, staring out of the windshield. After all the revelations at the morgue last night, I could not get my mind to stop whirling around every possible explanation for the complete trash taco that my chances of solving any of the cases had turned into. So, I was just sitting in my car, staring at the building in front of me.

The elementary school was in what was called the East End, and it looked like every other elementary school: single story cinder block construction with rectangular windows and a playground complete with monkey bars and swing set. It was the beginning of the day, so the parking lot was full. I found a spot near the swing sets and, after checking my watch to confirm the hour had come, I got out and began making my way to the main entrance.

It struck me as ironic that last night I was looking at life, recently ended and here I was where life was just beginning, at least for some. The cynicism of death as a common, even mundane occurrence versus the wonder of discovery and infinite possibility could not be more diametrically opposed. But somehow, we all get from here to there, all of us. We find a way to leave all our wonder, all our hope, all of the possibility that we discover in places like this as we traverse through our lives, closing door after door behind us until there is only one door left. It is a door we all eventually walk through... Well, not all of us apparently, some of us have found a sort of extension, and some of us didn't want it.

The bell rang just as I walked through the main doors. Little people were scattering about getting to their respective classes. There was laughter and friendly chatter, 'hellos' and 'goodbyes', smiles and just a few groans bouncing off the tile floors and brick walls. I found myself hoping these children would hold on to that simplicity for as long as they could, but I knew some of them would not. Isaac's life had been given a violent shove out of that youthful innocence into a very painful reality.

I found the small plaque that read 'Main Office' just as the last doors were closing, leaving the hall and main lobby in relative silence. I walked over, opened the door, stepped into the room, and was immediately greeted by a large mature woman who asked if she could help me in a tone that made me feel like I was reporting for detention instead of conducting an investigation.

"My name is Detective Regnum with the---"

"May I see your badge and identification please?" she said while stepping over to an open binder laid out on the counter. She picked up the pen that was connected to it with one of those metal lines made up of tiny metal balls and looked at me expectantly.

I pulled out my wallet and flipped it open like they did in the movies. I had always wanted to do that, but after seeing her less than impressed expression, I slowly folded it so the badge would show and tucked it into the breast pocket of my sport coat with much less flair. "We have you in Conference Room One-Eleven," she continued, still filling out a row in the binder.

"Thank you I appreciate the---"

"Please sign here, Detective," she said, spinning the binder around, pushing it toward me and offering me the pen. I signed, gave her a slight nod, and stepped out of the office. I had no idea where Conference Room 111 was, but I was not about to ask someone who's major in college was obviously not Theoretical Cuddling with a minor in Good Feeling Engineering. So, I started walking down the hallway on my left trying to look like I knew what I was doing. After walking about half a football field, I bumped into a very friendly janitor who pointed me in the direction I had just come from.

Quaint could be a word used to describe the conference room, I thought it was just plain cramped. The table took up most of the room while the four chairs around it pretty much took up the rest. The bookshelves lining the lower half of the walls were stocked with various items from unmarked binders to wooden blocks, probably for some type of therapy to help with motor skills. In the center of the table there was a clipboard. I moved to the chair furthest from the door so I could see anyone coming in and took a closer look at the clipboard. On it was a sheet of paper with names written on it. Next to each name was a school subject. Maybe Ms. Warm-and-Fuzzy at the main office was nicer than I thought, or maybe she was just efficient. She had apparently prepared a list of all the teachers I would be speaking with and the order in which I would see them.

One by one the teachers came in, sat, and told me how shocked and sorry they were. All of them described Isaac as a model student despite his disadvantages. When I asked what they meant by disadvantages, each one told me that they suspected it was an abusive household and that the other kids would pick on him because his clothes often smelled a bit moldy or musty. My heart ached for Isaac. It was a hard life all around for him and as of yet, I wasn't helping any.

None of the teachers were able to give me any thoughts on who the killer might be, and my list was getting shorter and shorter. One of the teachers even had a hard time remembering who Isaac was, but as he got up to leave, he opened the door and my head snapped up. The air that was drawn in from the hallway carried with it a scent; the scent of the man now standing in the doorway. He stepped out of the way, allowing his colleague to exit before stepping in. Greeting me with a broad warm smile, he extended his hand. I took the hand in mine out of habit, looking at the man now sitting across from me, inhaling deeply, my nasal passages opening wider, becoming more sensitive. There was no doubt. The man smiling at me, sitting in the chair opposite mine had recently sat in another chair...the one in Isaac's house.

CHAPTER 36

"Detective?"

My mind raced in different directions, processing what I had just discovered, questioning every conclusion before it had even fully formed in my head. This man had sat in the chair, the chair in the kitchen, the kitchen where he bludgeoned Isaac's mother to death. Then, for some sick reason, he casually made himself breakfast, sat down and ate it while she either bled out or suffered brain death due to massive blunt force trauma.

"Detective?"

Wait, I thought to myself. It was the middle of the day, he should have been at work, here in the school. Did he call in sick? Why did she let him in? Did she know him?

"Detective! Are you alright?"

"What?" My head snapped up once I realized I was staring at the table in front of me. I looked at the man across from me, truly seeing him for the first time. "Yeah, I'm fine. Sorry, I just spaced out there for a second."

"That's alright. I just wanted to be sure I was in the right place. The principal didn't tell us what this was about so, I had no idea what—"

"I asked her not to say," I said while trying to find out how to ask what I was already certain of.

"Okay… Can you tell me what this is all about, Detective?"

The man was in all ways average. Brown hair topped his head and brown eyes interrupted the space between forehead and nose. He was slimly built, not tall or short, not handsome or plain; he was someone you could walk by a thousand times and not remember what he looked like. The most striking thing about him was his open and warm smile. He truly looked to be a friendly person.

"Sure, I'm Detective Regnum and—"

"The king."

"Excuse me?" I asked, taken aback.

"Your last name, it's Latin from the root 'Rex'. It means 'the king' or 'of kingly station' depending on how it is used in the sentence."

"You speak Latin?"

"Not fluently but I learned quite a bit as I studied music. Many of the madrigals have lyrics that are in Latin. Even some of the—"

"Got it. So, I take it you're the music teacher."

"Yes."

"Mister…." I looked down at the list in front of me trying to gather my thoughts.

"Langston," he said.

"What?"

"My name is Greg Langston," he said, smiling and extending his hand again.

"Is one of your students Isaac Reardon?" I asked without taking it.

"Oh my God! Is this about Isaac?"

"Yes," I said, feeling a bit more in control. "As well as Timothy Smaltz. He was one of your students as well, wasn't he?"

"Uh… yeah." He looked down at the table, and I could not tell if he was trying to look surprised or if he was figuring out what to say next. "I mean of course, all of us thought it might be about the boys. You know, a detective coming to the school and all but…"

"But what?"

"It just… it still hits you. You know?"

"No."

"Excuse me?"

"I said no, I don't know how it hits you. Could you tell me about it?" I was losing my temper without even knowing it. I could see his face scrunch up in confusion. I just hoped I had not tipped him off to the fact that I knew what he had done. "What I mean to say is that I am still working on all of the relationships the boys had, so I'm not quite sure how you feel."

"Oh, uh… sure," he said, still looking at me as though he did not know what to expect.

"Did you know both boys well?"

"I suppose."

"What do you mean?" I was trying not to push too hard, but I had to get him talking again.

"I mean, how well can you know a kid you

only spend a couple hours a week with, right?"

"Yeah, I guess you have a point there," I said, trying to find anything I could use, anything that would tell me what his motives might have been.

"They were good boys; I can tell you that."

"Oh, why do you say that, Mr. Langston?"

"Call me Greg."

"Okay."

"I don't know, I guess I mean they..."

"Yes?"

"In spite of what they went through... well, Isaac more than Timmy I guess."

"What did Isaac go through?"

"None of the other teachers told you?"

"It's usually better if there are corroborating stories... you know...details," I said hoping that he had not caught on to the fact that I was calling him a liar.

"He was picked on a lot."

"Why?"

"Well, neither boy was very popular but... Isaac often had an odor the other kids would smell and... well you know kids, they are vicious when it comes to stuff like that."

"Was Isaac, you know, not a clean child?"

"Oh no, he was very clean, very neat but..."

"But what?"

Greg Langston, music teacher, bludgeoner, serial killer, was squirming in his seat. "I guess it was..."

"Yes," I said, pressing him.

"His clothes. His mother would send him to school in dirty clothes, and when she did wash them, she must have left them damp because he would then smell of mold. To be completely honest I think he would try to wash them himself and just didn't know any better."

"And the other kids would—"

"Cruel doesn't even come close!" Langston was ramping up. "They were like a pack of hyenas!" I could see his face getting redder and redder as he continued. "Laughing, teasing, even beating him sometimes!"

"That's terrible."

"No matter what I did, they wouldn't let up. I sent them to the principal's office in droves until the office started blaming me and hinting at firing me for some kind of lack of control ridiculousness!"

"But what about Timothy? What was his—"

"Timmy?"

"Yes, what happened to—"

"Well, I guess once the little darlings lost their collective punching bag after Isaac was transferred, they couldn't resist finding a new target."

"What do you mean?" I asked. Could it really be this basic?

"One day, Timmy comes to me in tears, and I mean sobbing, Detective."

"Okay."

"It seems that Timmy's mom had woken up late and in the ensuing craziness was rushing him out the door after getting him up late. He told me she had some kind of conference call that she couldn't be late for; she works from home by the way." He was almost yelling by this point.

"So, when Timmy asked if he could use the bathroom before heading out to the bus she just stuffed a granola bar in his hand and told him he could use the bathroom at school! At school?! Can you believe that?"

"How long is the trip from—"

"It's over twenty minutes!"

"Oh man," I said, realizing exactly what had put this guy over the edge.

"Yeah, 'oh man' is right. He pissed himself right there on the bus, right in front of those same sadistic... I'm sorry, Detective." Langston took a breath and looked at me nervously. "It's a difficult thing for me to just sit there and watch."

"Yeah," I said in agreement.

"I mean it would be for anybody, right?"

"Yes it would, Mr. Langston."

CHAPTER 37

"What do you mean, you know he did it?" Officer Shepherd was standing next to my desk, his hands waving around in frustration then dropping to his thighs making a slapping sound.

"I just do," I said, clicking through page after page of documents on my computer screen. I had to find something I could use to push the investigation further in the direction of Mr. Greg Langston.

"Look Detective, we can't be seen as fixating on someone at the expense of our other leads based on nothing more than 'you just know'," Shep said in a tone I am sure he meant to be calming but struck me as condescending and annoying.

"Well, thanks for that. I was thinking I could just use the old charm along with my dashing smile to get a conviction."

"Detective, I didn't mean to tell you how to do —"

"You don't think he'll use the 'Not It' defense, do you?" I was being a first-class dick, but I couldn't help myself. How could I explain how I knew what I knew? How could I tell anyone, let alone prove that this guy was the killer without saying I knew it because my super schnoz told me so? I would just end up in a custom fitted white jacket designed for self-hugging while Mr. Langston sat up at night aching for his next order of eggs over easy.

"I'm sorry I bothered you, Detective," Shep said finally and turned to walk away.

"Hey man, I'm sorry. I'm just really frustrated right now," I said, pushing my chair back and away from my desk. I spun slightly so that I could make direct eye contact with him. Shep turned around and looked back at me expectantly. He was listening but not quite ready to put his head back in the lion's mouth. I have got to stop using animal metaphors.

What the hell was I going to say that would make sense. "Let's call it a hunch, alright?"

"A hunch…" He crossed his arms, still not looking even a bit convinced.

"Listen, I used the wrong words, okay? I didn't mean to say that I knew he did it."

"Okay," he said. "But what do you care what I think? I'm just a uniform."

"Hey, you're the one that came up to my desk snooping around," I said jokingly, trying to lighten the mood.

"Yeah, and all I did was ask you why you were digging into some music teacher's life."

"Okay, okay, you're right. I didn't mean to bite your head off." Wow, I have to stop using that expression too. "Just, hear me out, okay?"

"Alright," he said, sitting down in the desk chair next to mine.

"I was asking him the standard questions. You know, the same thing I asked every one of the other teachers. Right?"

"Right," he said, nodding for me to go on.

"So, I get to the part about 'how did he know the kids were good kids' and he starts getting into how the kids got picked on."

"Okay," he said, leaning in a bit closer.

"Then he went nuts, ranting about both the kids' mothers. I mean, he just lost it, blaming the kids' mothers for all the bad that happened to those kids."

"So?" Shep was not buying it so far. He was listening, but I obviously did not have enough.

"So, he was talking about them like he hated them," I said, searching for more. "Now, I know that's not enough, but it is more than what we had when this day started, and I think it's at least worth looking into. Don't you?"

He hesitated for a moment before nodding slowly. "Yeah," he said finally. "But… you still haven't answered my question."

"What question?"

"Why do you care what I think?"

"Because you seem to be the only one around here who isn't all team Abrahms!" I had not intended to say that. Truth be told, I had not even really formulated those thoughts in any kind of rational order, but I felt them. "Look, the lieutenant is not my biggest fan and he—"

"Why?"

205

"Why what?" I asked, mildly annoyed at the interruption during my naked self-pity.

"Why does the lieutenant have it in for you?"

"Jeez man, he doesn't think I have put in the time to have been made a detective. Alright?"

"I don't think you have put the time in either."

"Yeah, well, at least you don't go around acting like it," I said, surprised, but still able to appreciate the guy's honesty. "Anyway, he wants to give the case to Abrahms."

"Okay," he said, looking a bit confused.

"Look, I opened my big mouth and told the lieutenant that I would bring an arrest on the case, or he could have my badge."

"Holy shit, man." Shep slouched back in his seat, looking at me and shaking his head. "What is it with this case that has you all twisted up?"

"It's the kid, Shep," I said. "The first victim's kid. I can't get him out of my head. He was just… broken. You know?"

"Yeah," he said softly. "I know."

Officer Shepherd was looking at the floor and, from the way his eyebrows were all knotted up I could tell he was thinking hard. "Well," he said, still staring at the floor. "Looks like I'm going to be digging into anything that connects the music teacher with the crime scenes."

"Yeah?"

"Yeah."

"Good, because I need the help."

"Yeah, you do," he said, standing up.

"You going to tell me why?"

"Well, at first it was because of professional curiosity."

"And now?"

"Well, it ain't your charming personality that's for sure," he said, smiling unconvincingly. "It's because you actually give a shit, and most of us here do. But Abrahms? That guy is just an asshole looking to get promoted."

"I really appreciate it man," I said, relieved. "Thanks for betting on the underdog." Damn it! I did it again. "I mean... just... thanks."

"Don't read too much into it, Detective," he said, walking away. "It's not my ass on the line if we don't deliver." He was right, of course, but I needed all the help I could get, even the kind that is grudgingly given.

My cell phone rang. I snatched it off my desk, checked the number and answered. "What's up, Jo?"

"Meet me at the kid's apartment."

"What kid?"

"The brain surgeon from the first set of killings. You know the chowderhead we took to see Milagro?"

"Now?" I looked at my watch, then at the screen with Mr. Langston's information.

"You got something better going on?"

"As a matter of fact," I said, growing irritated, "I got a lead on the bludgeoner case and I—"

"What kind of lead?"

"The kind where I know exactly who did it.

Now, I just have to figure out how to prove it," I said too loudly.

"Does the killer know you know?"

"No but—"

"Then he isn't going anywhere," Ramirez said. I could hear traffic in the background, so I assumed he was driving.

"Are you on the way there now?"

"Yes," he said. "I just left Milagro's place. She remembered something she saw in the kid's head."

"Oh yeah? What?"

"The kid gave her his name before she bugged out," he said.

"So?"

"She could have tracked him down to his place. You know, to finish the job," he said as if I should have arrived at this conclusion already. "Not only that, but if he was her last victim, maybe we can figure out why he was important enough for her to go back after him specifically instead of just picking someone else off."

I checked my watch again. I was not looking forward to the trip. Jo had been edgy since we learned that a vampire was responsible for the killings we were finding now. Apparently, one horny demon girl was okay, but add a bloodsucker and that was a step too far. I suppose you have to draw the line somewhere.

"Fine," I said. "I'll be there in twenty minutes."

CHAPTER 38

I drove straight down Venable Street, crossed over, using 17th Street to Broad, then jumped on I-95 to get over to the other side of the James River. After a few minutes I got off at exit 73 and found myself in the area of Richmond commonly referred to as Southside. It was a former industrial area of the city but now, many of the old factories had been converted to loft-style housing. There was an open parking space across from one of the newer buildings.

Once out of the car, I started looking around for Ramirez. If the kid was the reason that our homicidal nympho had stopped, then Ramirez was right. We needed to know everything we could about him. After all was said and done, we had nothing else, and now that there was a second killer trying to look like the first, we couldn't afford to overlook any detail if we were going to tell the difference and figure out who our new walking juicer was.

Poking his head out of a set of glass doors Ramirez waved me over before ducking back inside the main lobby. The frosted glass door closed behind him, and I could see one of those key card readers, like the ones they have in the hotels, on the side of the door frame. When I got to the door it pulled open so I could only assume it was an after-hours security measure. Still, it was better than nothing.

"How do you know who did it?" said Ramirez as he pushed the up button on the elevator.

"Did what?"

"Killed the two moms." Stepping into the elevator, he punched the floor number and continued. "You sounded pretty sure about who your cookware killer was when we talked on the phone."

"It's the music teacher from the school where both boys went," I said, following him.

"How can you be so sure?"

"I went back to the scene alone and..." I didn't know how to describe what I did to figure things out without sounding like a freak with a fetish, or at the very least come off like a dork. "I went back and literally sniffed around." When in doubt, always use a puppy pun.

"You did what?"

"I used my enhanced sense of smell to check the place out when there wasn't so much outside distraction and background noise," I said, trying to explain it logically once my comedic chops failed me.

"Aw shit," he said, stepping out of the elevator.

"What?"

"You weren't doing that the entire time?"

"No! How the hell was I supposed to know to do that?" I was feeling defensive, following him down the hallway and explaining myself like a child.

"We really have to come up with some kind of Monster School for guys like you."

"Yeah? And why don't you just kiss my—"

"Here it is," he said, stepping up to the door.

Putting a key into the deadbolt, turning it, and then doing the same to the knob lock he pushed open the door. The door opened easily, and he stepped inside. Still feeling a bit on the cranky side, I followed him in. There was nothing special about the place, nothing that made you stop or stare. As a matter of fact, he was kind of neat to a fault; everything was in its place and in some logical order. You did not have to know the logic behind it to know that there was a purpose for everything in every room. One thing was obvious, he lived alone.

Ramirez and I looked through the kitchen, and when there was nothing of interest there, we went into the smaller of the two bedrooms which obviously served as the kid's office. We searched through the desk and the drawers of a small filing cabinet, but neither of us found anything out of the ordinary. Everything you would think would be in a home office was there, from personal documents to utility bills and lease documents. The feeling of futility was starting to creep into my head when we moved into the other bedroom. Once again, we found nothing out of the ordinary. The bed was made, and clothes were folded neatly in the drawers or hung with precision in the closet.

The sound of a key in the deadbolt stopped us in our tracks. We heard the lock being worked back and forth, and Ramirez took tentative steps backward until he was in the master bathroom drawing his sidearm as he did. Instinct and involuntary bodily functions I still did not fully control took over.

"Wolf!" came a harsh whisper from the bathroom doorway. Ramirez was looking at me, half in awe, and half panicked.

As I looked back at him, I caught my reflection in the mirror and finally understood why he was trying to get my attention. My ears were pulled back slightly, my lips curled into a snarl, and I was growling! It was a low terrible sound I didn't know I was capable of.

Regaining control, I stifled the growl and slowly backed into the closet as I heard the door open.

The scent drifted into the room like an invisible mist; it was not Todd's. Gently, it entered the range of my senses, my subconscious trying to identify the source. Then it enveloped my world, drawing me into a place without shape but full of sensation. I felt my stomach tighten and my skin tingle.

Step by step, the source of the aroma moved through the main room just out of sight, cautiously at first and then with more and more purpose. The sound of a drawer opening and papers being rustled could be heard and I immediately thought of the end table in the living room or the desk in the home office. Whoever was in the apartment with us was looking for something. The sound of the drawer being closed hard came from the doorway followed by steps approaching the bedroom where we hid. I crouched even lower, not daring to check on Ramirez for fear of making unnecessary noise, but I hoped he had found sufficient cover.

It was her. It had to be. She was gorgeous! Every movement, though quick and purposeful as she searched, exuded a sensuous mastery of every inch of her body. There was grace in her and beauty, an aura of lust and sensuality but with a sense of power that demanded adoration. I almost called out to her against my own will.

She came into the kid's bedroom, and I moved deeper into the closet but craned my neck in order to keep even a sliver of her in line of sight. I saw her at his dresser. 'Was she robbing him?' I asked myself. Rifling through his drawers tossing aside everything as though she were looking for something,she did not seem to know I was there. She began pulling out stacks of clothes and placing them on the bed. Drawer after drawer she continued until she closed the last one and turned to the bed. Reaching underneath the bed she pulled out a suitcase, placed it on the bed and started to place the clothing from the dresser into the suitcase.

She was packing his things, which meant that after the dresser she was going to move to the—

Just as the thought entered my mind, I saw her begin to turn in my direction and that's when I knew it was over.

"Freeze!" I yelled exploding out of the closet, weapon drawn and aimed at center mass. For just an instant I saw the demon beneath the beauty. Her eyes glowed red and her sharp white teeth shone behind her blood red lips while the skin of her face turned the color of ash. "Where's the kid?" I asked, trying not to look shaken after what I had just seen.

Quickly recovering, her heart stopping beauty once again in place, she relaxed into a graceful even languid stance eyeing me inquisitively. Her lip curled into a smile, and I almost saw the words she spoke as though they emanated from her body. It was a sound like a soft hum, but one that aroused more than warned, and though only her lips moved, it felt as though her entire being was speaking to me.

"What is your name?"

"Lady, we know what you are, and we are not trying to have any trouble. We just want the kid. Okay?"

Her voice was like cool hands caressing my face and I found myself unable to speak. "You are not human, are you?" She took a small step toward me. "If I had to guess you are one of the Vigiles. Tell me your name."

I felt my mouth starting to move but no sound was made. My arms had begun to tremble, either from the weight of the gun in my hand or my body aching to go to her. "You are not very good at this, are you?" It was a statement more than a question. Her smile broadened. "Which means that you are either very new at this or very weak."

Another step towards me, and I began to lower my weapon.

"Man, she's trying to put the mojo on you. Snap out of it!" I heard Ramirez's voice somewhere in the distance before I saw a shadow of him standing at the doorway of the bathroom out of the corner of my eye, his weapon pointed at the woman in front of me. Part of me wanted to listen but I was too far gone. Part of me wanted to step in front of his gun so I could shield her from harm. I could feel every inch of me vibrating, and for every instant I had denied myself an emotion for fear of where it might take me, I was now assaulted with a flood of them, ten times stronger than I had ever felt. "Wake up man!" Ramirez was screaming now. "Wolf!"

"Are you really?" She laughed a sound like a warm bath and my legs gave way. I felt my mind start to swim and all my thoughts were of her and my desire for her. "The Vigiles sent a wolf to me?" She asked, laughing again. "Oh, you poor boy, they must not like you very much. And it seems that you have done nothing with yourself for quite some time. Just look at how you tremble, and all that I have exposed you to is my voice and my scent." She took another step, but hesitated as she looked over my shoulder at Ramirez. "Everything I am is exactly what you desire. I can manipulate my voice and manner and yes even my appearance into whatever my chosen prey yearns for."

I saw her shape change slightly but her scent was like a drug, and I could not move. "But with you, I need not bother. I do not even have to hide my intent. I will sink my claws into your chest and pull out your heart as I suck out your soul, because you are so weakened by me and by the lust that you are trying so mightily to control. Now, Knight of the Vigiles, you will die." She took another step forward and I saw her change again.

"Yeah bitch, keep changing!" I heard Ramirez in the distance again. "I know what you are, and you won't get me with that mojo shit. Where's the kid?"

Her eyes flashed red once again and her voice changed.

"You will never see him again. He is mine!"

She lunged at me, but my eyes were already closing. Then I felt something hit me hard.

CHAPTER 39

"Get the hell off me," I said when my head cleared enough for me to see that Ramirez was laying on top of me.

"Relax Romeo, this is no picnic for me either, but it was that or let her fly right through you as she headed out the window."

"Nobody told me she could fly!"

"What the hell did you think the wings were for?" Ramirez was dramatically slapping dust off his pant legs that was not really there. "And it's not like you were going to stop her anyway. Hell, she could have walked out the front door, and you would have stood there staring at her."

It pissed me off, but he was right. I was completely at her mercy with no strength to do anything. I would have let her kill me, and though I had no strong opinions on whether I lived or died, I sure as hell had an opinion about how I lived or died.

"Alright," said Ramirez, now pacing the room like a mad man. "We have to get organized. This is huge, it changes everything."

"What the hell are you talking about, man?"

"This has to be Lilith!" Ramirez stared at me

like I was the one that was crazy. "The angels! The angels! We've got to report this," he said, as if he just realized it. He was staring at the floor, and I could almost see the gears in his head turning red as he was piecing things together.

"Jo, what are you—"

"You go in and report," he said as he ran toward the door. "And I'll research this, and we'll meet back at the bar."

"What bar? And who the hell is Lilith?" I was yelling out the questions in the hopes to break through his stream of consciousness ramblings, but the door was already shut. I had never seen him act like that, so where I usually would have argued against going to see my favorite Speaker Man, whatever it was that had just happened seemed to rattle him, and I liked that a lot less. Besides, maybe he would be able to tell me who this Lilith was.

*****

"She was Adam's first wife. She came before Eve."

"Adam? Eve? You mean like in the Bible Adam and Eve?"

"The very same." Speaker Man sat down in the same chair he occupied just a few days ago, and the look on his face did not give me the warm fuzzies.

"Made from dirt, fig leaf, talk to animals, Garden of Eden Adam and Eve?"

He nodded despite my 'that is ridiculous' expression. I started to laugh more out of anger than anything else.

"Though I sometimes find your ignorance amusing, if not annoying, I am curious as to what you find funny." He said, now completely back in his arrogant prick persona.

"A few years ago, I was stomping around upstate New York wondering if anything meant anything, and that, if there was a God, what I did to piss him off. Now here I am listening to you tell me that the lead suspect of my investigation is a woman of biblical times who was not even in the Bible!"

"Perhaps you should read the so-called Good Book again, Wolfgang." He spoke slowly, adding to the condescension in his tone. "She is spoken of in the Talmud but is more like rabbinical folklore actually." He stood and made his way to one of the bookshelves that lined every wall of the room.

He closed the old book he had been reading and placed it back precisely on the shelf looking at me the entire time. "Even in your precious King James version of the Bible, there is evidence. In some translations she is even named outright, in the book of Isaiah I believe."

"I may not be a theology major but I read most of the Adam and Eve story in Sunday School, just like everyone else who has a pulse, and I don't remember anything about a divorce."

"Not everyone reads the Bible, Detective," he said looking at me with one eyebrow raised.

"Yeah? Well, I am sorry if I insulted the Hindus, Muslims or whoever else is out there but—"

"Detective, the sooner you accept the fact that

your understanding of the world may not be the most accurate, the sooner you will cease to reject your current situation."

"I do reject my current situation!"

"That is obvious."

"Then stop jerking me around!" My temper was getting the better of me and I did not care. "When you say Adam and Eve, you're talking about the Bible so if we can just get back to—"

"Are you aware that the Jewish Torah is, in essence, the Old Testament of your precious Bible?"

"It's not my Bible!" I was not getting anywhere. Speaker Man seemed unable to stop himself from poking holes in whatever I said. "What I'm trying to say is that I don't even know what I believe myself. So, I am not the guy to tell someone else their beliefs are wrong."

"I see," he said moving back to sit in the chair. He set his elbow on the arm rest then raised his hand to the side of his head, thumb to cheek bone and first two fingers at his temple. He looked at me for what seemed like a half hour before finally sitting up and saying, "While you may be far from enlightened, that last statement is at least a start."

"Thank you... I think. Now can we please get back to who this Lilith is? As far as I know there is nothing about a first wife in the Bible."

Then why are there two places where creation of man is mentioned?"

"What?" My jaw hung open until I realized it and closed my mouth.

"Common thought among those that subscribe to this theory," he continued as he rose again from his chair and headed back to the library, "is that the first mention of creation was a bit different from what is taught in your Sunday School." He pulled another book from the shelf and flipped it open. "Here it is," he said, running his finger down the page as he read aloud. "In the image of God created He him, male and female created He them." He looked up at me. "That, it is believed, is where Adam was created and Lilith along with him." Speaker Man paused here. I guess he was trying to make sure I was following him. "The important distinction is that many believe that they were created in the same manner since they are both created in the same verse and no differentiations made as to the process. Do you understand?" He looked at me again. "If the scripture is to be taken literally, then they were both created from the dust of the earth. Only in the following chapter does it go into the story of Adam being lonely and God taking his rib and making Eve." Placing the Bible back on the shelf, he strode slowly back to his chair but did not sit. "The story goes that after Adam and Lilith were made, Adam insisted that Lilith lie beneath him to make love. She said that they should lay side by side as equals. They argued and she left. Adam cried out to God that he had been left alone and God sent angels to bring her back."

"Angels?" I sat bolt upright.

"Yes?"

"I've bumped into two of those guys in as many days," I said, finally making at least part of a connection in this ridiculous story I was being told.

"Have you really?"

"Yeah, and one of them put me on my ass."

"You are rather fortunate that is all he did. Typically, a visit from an angel does not end that well."

"Maybe I'm tougher than I look," I said, not liking the realization that, despite having been made into a superhuman creature, I was still getting my clock cleaned on a regular basis.

"I think it is more likely that you are not what they are looking for."

"Gee, thanks again," I said, slumping back into my seat. "What you're telling me is that all of it is true."

"To which truth do you refer?"

"Angels, you know harps and halos and all that."

"Once again the depth of your ignorance astounds," he said, rubbing his temples with both hands. "I do not endorse any particular school of thought. Angels are called angels because that is the word agreed upon by a group of mammals that did not recognize or understand what they were seeing." He stepped in front of the chair now and spoke as though he were explaining long division to a stubborn ten-year old. "I do not pretend to know whether these creatures come from some divine being with an ultimate plan or if they are from the cosmos checking in on an experiment begun just to see if it would work. That being said, I fail to see the relevance our ontological existence has on the current situation. I think we should focus on the task at hand, don't you?"

"Yeah, sure," I said, taking my scolding like a good dog.

"Thank you," he said, finally sitting in the chair he had been hovering around. "The angels found her in the sea, but when they ordered her back, she refused. So, they cursed her to be the mother of all demons; to steal the seed of men and give birth to demons. Her vengeance is that she murders her victims and, legend has it, takes babies in their sleep. Even to this day, Jewish mothers hang the symbols of these angels over the cribs of their newborn babes to keep away the demon that is Lilith."

"So, you're saying that our Succubus is really this Lilith, *the* Lilith?"

"Yes, and it was the angels you saw that are the most compelling evidence. You say you saw two?" I nodded in affirmation "Well then, there is one more you haven't seen yet."

CHAPTER 40

The contrast of the dark refuge of my vampire boss and the bright sunshine of midday made my eyes hurt as I stepped out. With some effort, I found my way back to my car and sat down to try and get my head together. It seemed that with every new revelation, my day was just getting worse. I was literally dealing with an issue of Biblical proportions. Here I thought I was well on the way to becoming an agnostic.

Just as I started the engine and pulled out into traffic, my cell phone rang. Checking the number on the screen I saw that it was from a landline back at the precinct. Tapping the answer button on my dashboard touch screen I said, "hello."

"Hey Detective, it's Shep."

"Hi," I said, hoping for some sort of light at the end of my tunnel of a day. "Please, tell me something good".

"I wish I could, sir."

"Seriously?" I said then pulled the phone away from ear to say a few words under my breath that should not be said to anyone.

"We can't place Mr. Langston at the scene."

Shep spoke in a way that conveyed just fact but there was a hint of disappointment. I could tell that he really did try.

"Why not?" I said with more angst than I intended.

"Well for one thing, there were no official appointments in his schedule or with the school for his alleged visits to the victims."

"Ok, but what about—"

"And," he said loudly, continuing his thought process, obviously confident he was about to answer my next question before I asked it. "On the day of the murders, no one saw him leave the school."

"How in the hell could no one notice a guy was missing for at least an hour from a building with over a hundred people walking around?"

"I was thinking the same thing, so I paid a visit to the school and asked around a bit. The guy literally eats at his desk every day, alone."

"So, no one would know if he actually stayed in the building or not," I said, trying to piece together a way to prove what I already knew to be true.

"And, if he had a free period before or after lunch, he would easily be able to be gone for nearly two hours without anyone knowing."

"What about the receipts for the eggs and all that?"

"No good."

"What? Why?" The desperation in my voice was clear, even to my own ears. I was running out of options.

"He paid cash, and before you ask me, the answer is yes, I went to the store. While I was there, I showed everyone I could find a photo I took from the school's webpage."

"And?"

"And nothing," he said, frustration creeping into his tone. "Sure, people had seen him, but they couldn't tell you when and where. Even if I suggested dates, their best answers were different versions of maybe."

It was all going sideways, and I could not for the life of me find a way to get back on track. My options were being chipped away with every word he said, but I still had one; I had an option that would take care of Mr. Langston for good. My phone beeped telling me there was another call coming in. I checked the number and saw that it was Ramirez. "Shep, I gotta take this call."

"Oh yeah? You got something more important to talk about, man? In case you forgot, you were the one that told me your job was on the line if you didn't close this case soon."

"I know, I know," I said, sounding like a 12 year old arguing with his father. "I may have to come at this another way but right now I have to go."

"Alright, but you better hurry. Word is already spreading that you're gone by the end of the week."

"What day is it?"

"Wednesday," he said and hung up.

I touched the answer button on my phone,

still digesting what I had just learned about the future, or non-future of my job and maybe even my life. "Yeah Jo, what's up."

"Where are you?"

"Parked outside of the boss man's place," I said looking back at the neat little row house that housed a being that was probably three times as old.

"Legends, meet me there in twenty."

"Ok but..." The phone beeped again, and I realized I was talking to myself. Tossing my phone on the passenger seat, I started the car, shifted into drive and in less than the allotted twenty minutes, I was walking through the doors.

I spotted him toward the back and began making my way through the mostly empty tables. One of the few people in the place got up from a table just in front of Ramirez and I saw her sitting with him just as I caught her scent. Milagro was watching me as I approached with what looked like pity in her eyes. I could not decide definitively, but I was pretty certain that I preferred her hatred.

"Did he confirm it?" Ramirez said before I even had the chance to sit down. His face showed a mix of intense curiosity about the possibility and deep-seated hope that it was not. "Could it be her?"

I nodded my head and then motioned to get one of the server's attention. I needed a drink. A spritely blonde came over to take my order, and in less than a minute there was a beer in front of me.

"*The* Lilith..." Ramirez continued, his eyes glassy.

"Am I the only person alive who never heard of this chick?"

"She was Adam's first..."

"Yes, I know who she is now!" I said irritated at once again being the dunce of the group.

"This is big. I mean a Succubus was bad enough, but this is the mother of all demons." He leaned back in his seat running both hands across the sides of his head staring at nothing as he spoke. "She is older and more powerful than any of us, more powerful than anything we have ever gone up against."

"I got the picture; now, how do we find her?"

"Find her? You don't find Lilith!" he said loud enough to elicit glances from a couple of guys at the bar. "You get the hell out of her way! What the hell are you going to do to her if you do find her?" Ramirez leaned forward, lacing his fingers together on the table, his eyebrows lifted in mock interest.

"Hell, I don't know," I said, leaning back. "Try and find out what she did with the kid? Stop her somehow?"

"Stop her? Her biggest strength is lust! You go up against her and it will be like...like a pyromaniac trying to fight a forest fire!"

"Alright," I said in low tones, more to myself than anyone else.

"Stupid son of a..." he said, jabbing his finger in my direction, apparently too frustrated to finish the curse, then slumping back in his chair again. "You don't educate yourself, and I mean fast, you're gonna get yourself unmade with a quickness!"

"I said alright!"

All eyes in the bar were on me now, from the two barflies and bartender to the greeter and patrons at the tables all the way across the room. I made a timid gesture of apology and turned back to the drink that was in front of me. I could almost feel the eyes lingering until Milagro thankfully broke the silence.

"So, what now?"

"According to everything we know she's as good as gone," I said thinking of Todd, wondering if there was any chance he might still be alive.

"And even if she isn't," Ramirez said leaning forward conspiratorially, "how do you track a demon?"

"How do you track any of your kind?" There was no insult or malice in her tone. Milagro had been pulled into this kicking and screaming, but it seemed she had accepted it and truly wanted to help.

"For all intents and purposes, supernatural beings still think and react like regular men and women," Ramirez said, sitting up a bit straighter as he explained. "The behaviors are pretty much the same. The only thing that is different, really, are the methods. If you insult us, we get offended."

"I guess I didn't think about it that way," she said, looking at Jo and I apologetically. "It makes sense though, it's just," she paused, searching for the words. "It gets into your head, you know. The idea that with these strange powers, or gifts, whatever you call them, you would be somehow different."

Listening to her speak, I realized I had the same preconceived notions but as I heard them spoken out loud, I felt the beginnings of a thought.

"I suppose for those of us that live long lives," Ramirez continued, "experience begins to play a part. That can seem like some sort of higher level of being."

"But..." I said, the idea taking shape in mind, "when it comes down to it an asshole is an asshole whether he is supernatural or not."

"Not exactly how I would put it but, yes," said Ramirez. "We have pretty much the same motivations. If you hurt us, we want vengeance. If you stroke our egos, we are more likely to give you what you want. Our non-human gifts only change the way the thing is done but-"

"But..." I interrupted, having decided what I had to do next, "murder is still murder"

CHAPTER 41

Frustration can sometimes be a more compelling emotion than anger. Whether you feel helpless, lost, or incapable, the feeling builds and builds until any action, even the wrong one, creates the illusion of progress. It's like being in a traffic jam and taking the alternate route knowing that it will take just as long as sitting in it, but at least you feel like you're moving. I was moving now, and I really didn't know how it was going to turn out.

I was playing cards with a whole lot of people, and I was refusing to show my hand to any of them. I had not told Speaker Man about Milagro or the vision she had, or the copycat vampire killing the humans and making it look like it was Lilith. I did not tell Ramirez about the kill club Markku had so kindly showed me, more to protect him than anything else I supposed. I figured information like that could get someone killed. And I sure as hell had not told anyone on the force how I figured out who was running around bludgeoning mothers in their homes. There was never a time in my human life when I had to keep so much from so many. If Ramirez was to be believed and this was a kind of gift, it was the very definition of the gift that kept on giving.

I had left Milagro and Ramirez back at Legends, making excuses about having to check in with Officer Shepherd about my bludgeoning case; and whereas I was thinking about how to deal with Langston, I realized that if I was going to stop him, I needed to go see someone.

*****

"I need to see him."

The same pretty, well-spoken receptionist was staring at me wide-eyed as I burst into the lobby.

"He's not avail---"

"Now!"

I smelled her before I saw the blur out of the corner of my eye, just in time to dodge it. Jumping backward and landing in a crouch at the entranceway, I saw Inyoni's clawed hand slash viciously at the spot where I had just been. The sleek form of her body belied her lethality. Poised and ready to strike, she had not fully changed but her left arm was covered in golden fur, and the claws were as deadly as they were beautiful. The skill it took to control her change to just one part of her body intimidated and fascinated me, but I was not to be stopped.

The human receptionist sat back down and calmly hit a button on the side of her desk, sending her and the chair she occupied into a recess as a door closed in front of her, protecting her from what was about to happen.

"Tread carefully, Regnum." My name came out her mouth more like a growl than an actual word.

"I need to see him, and if I have to go through you to do it then I will."

"You cannot get past me, boy. I have been gifted since birth, which is more than twice as long as you have been alive. Leave and this need not go any further."

"You might be right, but we are about to find out."

I had only been in two fights since my change. The first was a draw because neither one of us knew what we were doing. Of course, Markku had thoroughly mopped the floor with me, but I had recently fed, my senses were sharp, and I was at my strongest. Now I just had to hope that I was scared or pissed off enough to change before she called my bluff.

"You are more important than you know," she said without advancing.

I could not process it. Her eyes were pleading as her left hand flexed with hungry claws exposed. "Walk out of here. Please," she continued. There was no fury or anger in her voice which told me two things. First, she really was about to kick my ass and second, she really didn't want to.

"Inyoni!" His booming, doubling voice was unmistakable. Hadrian stood in the hallway. I saw genuine relief on Inyoni's face as she lowered her hand, the claws now retracting, fur receding and the bones realigning into a beautiful and completely human hand.

"One day you are going to have to tell me how you do that," I said, looking at her hand as I walked past her.

Hadrian turned and strode into his office, as I followed. He turned abruptly and spoke in a menacing voice.

"Detective, you are making the often terminal transition from amusing to annoying." He stood feet firmly planted shoulder width apart, hands hanging loosely at his sides. I could see his hazel eyes turning black until his eyes looked as lifeless as a doll's and as dangerous as a shark's.

"Are you threatening me?" I asked without thinking.

"Does it matter?" He smiled with the corner of his mouth as he spoke, exposing one of his elongated canines. I saw his right hand flex slightly and I knew he was ready for whatever I thought of next. He saw the hesitation in my eyes as much as I saw contempt in his, and his smile grew broader. I was losing again and this time it looked fatal.

"How does it work?" The question fell out of my mouth as soon as I opened it. I had no real plan on how I was going to handle Hadrian, so I plunged ahead without thinking.

"What?" Hadrian was obviously taken aback.

"How does it work?" Seeing the chink in his armor I pressed him. "When you want someone taken out, how does it work?"

"You are out of your depth, Detective. We do

not, as you say, take people out and if we did, I would certainly not tell you." Hadrian said, regaining his composure.

"Let's assume I don't believe you... because I don't. So, I will be specific. I want to make someone go away. Will I have cover?"

"You are a police officer. I would think you have all the cover you need behind that shiny little badge of yours."

"I'm not that kind of cop," I said reflexively. Later, I would wonder why I instinctively protected a profession I didn't want to be a part of in the first place.

"Then what kind of... cop are you, Detective? From what I understand, you seem to be doing rather poorly on your very first assignment."

"How the hell do you—"

"In fact, I hear you may be looking for a new line of work in the near future. Of course, that is if we assume your days on this plane do not end along with your tenure at the Richmond Police Department."

"If you care so much about my career, then why won't you tell me what I want to know?"

"What is it you think I will tell you, Detective, how to kill with impunity? How to destroy one's enemy without conscience? Or do you seek to know how to avenge the death of a young boy's mother?"

"He bashed her head in!" The blood rushed in my veins, and I felt the throbbing in my temples.

"And now you would end his life," said

Hadrian as though he were citing statistics and not discussing premeditated murder. "That does not become an officer of the law, Detective, nor does it stand with your position as Vigiles."

"I don't even know what that means, and I don't really—"

"It means," he said loud enough to stop me speaking, "that you are a watcher of the night. It means that you protect our world and our way of life, such as it is."

"And who are you to say what I do? Aren't you the reason this Vee-hee whatever was made in the first place?"

"No," he said, and as he said it, I saw something flicker in his eyes... Could it be regret? "I was there when the Vigiles were formed, Detective Regnum. When Caesar Augustus formed the first Cohort of Vigiles to protect the streets of Rome during the night, I was there."

"You talk about it like you admire us," I said watching him. He glared at me as though I had wounded him before regaining his expressionless composure. "So, why are you now the number one bad guy? From what I know you are the main thing we night watchers watch."

"This world needs balance, Detective," he said, and again I saw that flash of regret in his eyes.

"Balance?"

"You are a relative child in this world, Detective."

"A child?" Somewhere in the back of my head,

I knew what he said was true, but my pride still got the better of me.

"You are ignorant about many things," he said. Then, if I was to believe my eyes, he actually smiled. His eyes were focused somewhere in the distance, but he was smiling. "Perhaps, if you live long enough you will learn why we do the things we do."

"Ignorant?" I was getting tired of being dismissed. Then I did what I often do when tact is called for, I spoke before thinking. "How's this for ignorant? You knew that Lilith was coming!"

"Lilith?" The smile faded and I saw my opening, but it was obvious that he knew nothing about her.

"You lied when I asked if you knew there was something going down. I could smell it on you." I saw his eyes widen slightly. "Now we have some kind of blood-sucking freak of nature copycat killer trying to pin even more killings on our little naughty nympho who, by the way, doesn't really need any help in that department! But that's ok because I'm gonna kill her too!"

Even as the words were spilling out of my mouth, I knew I was pushing too far, but rage and frustration had taken hold of me, and I did not care what happened next. "And you know what else? I really can't think of anyone I like more as this copycat than you!" I watched as the surprise flashed across his face and it enraged me even more. "So, you need to decide if you are gonna help me take care of

my little problem or I might just add you to my list!"
Then it happened. His eyes narrowed and filled with
a fury that made my blood run cold.

"Listen very carefully, mongrel!" The strange
double voice reverberation echoed through the
room. "Your life may depend on it." He walked
slowly toward me as he spoke, his chest heaving,
his lips quivering as though he were struggling to
contain his wrath. I braced myself trying not to look
like I was doing it. "I knew nothing of the demon
or any demon. Furthermore, I choose when and if I
allow you to know whatever I do or do not know,
and I choose to allow you this. If you challenge
Lilith, you will likely die." He stopped so close to me
that his nose almost touched mine. "But threaten
me again and you certainly will." The hungry smile
was back. "What do you smell now, boy?"

CHAPTER 42

"It would appear that you annoy my father almost as much as I do." Markku's too-smooth voice came through my cell phone and felt as though it was oozing into my ear.

"What do you want?" I really had no desire to speak to him but when my phone rang, I was too busy leaning on the side of my car trying not to vomit while slowing my heart rate enough to check the caller ID. Hadrian had stepped within striking distance and for some ridiculous reason, I had not stepped away. In such close proximity, if he had wanted, I would have been dead before I hit the floor. I knew there was no way he hadn't smelled the fear on me. At the time I guess I just hoped that staying in the batter's box with a ninety-nine mile per hour fastball coming at your head counted for something in his book.

"Inyoni said she could hear you both from down the hall."

"She's a wolf; she could have heard us from down the block if we were thinking too hard," I said not hiding my irritation.

"You are half right at least."

"What do you want?"

"My, you are on edge, aren't you?" His laughter was warm yet somehow not at all inviting. "As I hear it, you need to come see me."

"And why the hell do I need to do that?"

"Because you are talking about committing murder and suicide in the same breath, and I do not think you understand which is which."

"Are you going to help me?" The idea of one more person telling me what I could or couldn't do was not something I was in the mood for. "Or are you just planning on hearing yourself talk some more while I pretend to be interested?"

"Carpenter Theater, I am arriving now. Go to the balcony, center section, and you should have no difficulty finding me."

"The Carpenter? Why would I want to—"?

"Go to 'Will Call', they will have a ticket for you. Just give them your name."

"This cloak and dagger crap is..." Realizing that he was no longer there, I stopped talking and fought the urge to throw my phone into the river.

The idea of dropping everything and scampering across town just because Markku snapped his fingers did not sit well with me, so I decided to occupy myself with other things until I felt good and ready to sit down for some half-assed Yoda speech from a guy who, just a few nights ago, had me bleeding and pinned against the fender of his shiny Aston Martin. I pulled out my cell, got into my car and settled in for some follow up calls and serious time-wasting.

"This is Shepherd," his tenor voice came from over the phone.

"Shep, it's Regnum."

"What's up, Detective," he said, giving me his full attention.

"What about phone records? There was no forced entry so maybe we should assume he went over there for some sort of parent-teacher conference thing." I was reaching, but just in case Markku was not willing to help me kill this guy, I needed to keep working on the legitimate side of the law as much as possible.

"Way ahead of you, Boss," he said with not a little pride in his voice. "It took a while to get through the red tape, but I got mixed news. He called the first victim but not the second. If he had an appointment with her, he was careful not to get it on any record."

"Damn!" My head was starting to hurt. It was a long shot, I knew, but I had made the mistake of hoping.

"Maybe if we can go through the victim's calendars, plus any of the grocery store employees that may have seen him buy the eggs, O. J., and bread, we might just have enough for an arrest."

"Maybe," I said, not really believing I had a chance.

"Oh, before I forget, the morgue guy was looking for you."

"The morgue guy? You mean the medical

examiner?"

"Yeah, that guy."

"Wonder what he wants," I said, more to myself than to Shep. "I'll give him a call."

"Cool. Talk later." And with that, Shep hung up.

I stared at the phone for a few seconds before tapping the screen to access my contacts then tapped on the number I needed. The phone at the Medical Examiner's office rang about five times before going to voicemail. I left a message, looked at my watch and decided I had burned enough time so that it would not seem like I jumped at Markku's request. I started the car and headed out.

* * * *

I spotted the marquee a block away from the theater, right on the corner of 6th and Grace Street. As I got closer, I could see the words 'LA TRAVIATA' spelled out in bright lights. I didn't know what it meant, but I was pretty sure I was going to hate it.

Entering the main lobby, I was immediately struck by the apparent age of the place. It was obvious that many renovations had been done, but the feel of the place was still very much there. The dark colors, graceful curves, and filigree -just shy of being garish- completed the picture and made me feel like I should be in a tuxedo instead of khakis and a sport coat.

The lobby and passageways were pretty much empty. I had taken my time getting to the theater so, just about everyone who was here to see the performance was already in their seats. Stepping up to the ticket window marked 'Will Call', I put on my best smile. The elderly woman behind the glass was not buying.

"Hi, my name is Detective—"

"You certainly took your time."

"I hadn't planned on being here."

"Apparently not," she said as she reached under the counter, produced a ticket, and slid it under the little opening. "Intermission just concluded so, please try to be quiet when you enter the theater."

"Thanks, I will do my—"

"I assume you can find your way, Detective?"

"Actually, I could use a little—"

"Read your ticket and follow the signs." With that she turned and passed through a small door at the rear of the booth. I kept looking at the spot where she had been standing, not sure about what had just happened. After figuring that she really was not going to help, I read my ticket and followed the signs.

After climbing a set of stairs, I found a set of double doors marked Balcony Center. As I opened the doors, I was almost knocked back a step by the combined voices of a tenor and soprano in duet. The sound was not unpleasant, but the sheer power behind the voices was jarring. Recovering, I stepped into the relative darkness of the theater.

Markku was right; it was not hard to find him. He was the only person in the entire balcony; center, left or right. Making my way down to the row closest to the edge of the balcony, I eased myself into the seat next to him.

"Good evening, Wolfgang."

"Markku," I said, matching his hushed tone. "You know, no one really calls me that."

"Am I no one?"

"Never mind," I said, knowing he was not going to stop doing it. Instead of arguing further, I took another look around the balcony section. "I take it this is not a very popular show."

"Why do you say that?" Markku had not taken his eyes off the stage or the singers on it.

"There's no one here," I said, motioning to the rest of the balcony. "I mean, they filled up the section down there," I pointed to the seats below us, "but that's only about half the tickets, right?"

"I bought out the entire balcony," he said absently, still very much focused on the stage.

"Oh…"

"I prefer solitude when I partake of the arts," he said.

"Any particular reason why?" I was not sure I cared but it seemed like the next logical question in the little verbal game we seemed to be playing.

"In the event I feel the urge to cry."

The statement caught me off guard. I looked at Markku but could only see his profile, his eyes still riveted to the stage, unblinking.

"But… vampires can't cry…your bodies don't generate tears."

"Very good Wolfgang," he said, nodding his approval. "But we *can* cry, just not in the conventional way. Similar to how the human function of perspiration manifests in us, our water-based bodily excretions are replaced by what we consume." He paused for a moment, maybe to let me digest what he had just said. "We cry blood."

"Oh," I said, feeling at once revulsion and pity. His tone was flat, but I could still hear a touch of sadness in his voice.

"So, you see, it would be rather inconvenient if I were to allow myself to feel anything in front of..."

"Yeah, I do," I said, feeling uncomfortable, but not for any of the reasons I thought I would. "You can only cry when you're alone."

"And since when we are with others is when we most often feel most alone..." There was a slight tremble in his voice. "I come here to cry."

"Then why am I here?"

"Because," he said, turning away from the stage to look at me for the first time since I arrived, "we need to talk." He looked at me a moment longer, the flecks of brown against the ice blue of his hazel eyes taking nothing away from the effect. "But, in a moment." He turned gracefully and looked back at the stage. I followed suit.

The stage was beautiful, the set spectacular, and as I watched I found the music arresting. I had only heard opera on the radio whenever I accidentally ran across a classical music station as I scanned for classic rock. Apparently, the speakers in my car weren't designed for it because whenever I did, it would sound like cats with their tails in a vice. I was therefore, surprised to find myself listening, truly listening to the music in a place that was actually designed for the sound.

The tenor I had heard upon entering had been replaced by a baritone, but the soprano was the same. The emotion on the performers' faces was drawing me in, and I found a sense of their words despite them being in Italian. Above the stage, there was a screen with -what I guessed was- the rough translation of what was being sung and I began to follow the story.

"Looks like they're arguing," I said, indicating the two singers on the stage.

"They are. His name is Germont, and she is Violetta. Germont is of the aristocracy, as is his son. The son has, against his father's wishes, fallen in love with the courtesan, Violetta."

"Courtesan?"

"For lack of better words, a woman of questionable virtue. Germont is asking her to let his son go so as not to embarrass the family and ruin his daughter's chances of a good marriage."

"Now it looks like... Is she crying?"

"Yes, she is, she has agreed to leave the love of her life and, since she has tuberculosis -though none but she knows it- she will die alone and very soon. Do you ever wonder what that will feel like?"

"What do you mean?"

"In this life, or non-life that we lead, we will

almost certainly die alone, Wolfgang."

The voices were beautiful, the baritone voice of Germont weaving effortlessly with Violetta's clear, bright soprano. Out of the corner of my eye, I could still see Markku's profile and there it was, a tear of blood.

"The name of the duet is Dite Alla Giovine, *Tell the Young Girl*." Markku began translating as the singers continued, even as the blood tear from his eye was joined by another. "Violetta sings 'Tell the young girl, innocent and pure, that there is one who has been a victim of disgrace, one with only a ray of hope for happiness but, for her, she will sacrifice that hope and die'."

The powerful baritone began the next verse and Markku continued. "Cry, cry in your miserable sadness. Cry, cry I see the immense sacrifice you make. I feel your pain in my soul. Take solace in the nobility of your heart."

We watched the rest of the opera in silence and more tears fell.

CHAPTER 43

The curtain slowly lowered as the singers took their final bows to the roaring applause and shouts of 'BRAVA' and 'BRAVO'. As the patrons began making their way into the aisles, the lights came up and Markku stood. He pulled out a small mirror and handkerchief then began wiping the blood from his face. Strangely, I was not horrified or disgusted; I was almost glad for him, glad he'd found at least some catharsis.

"You went to see my father in order to learn how to surreptitiously kill a man."

The conversational whiplash could have been worse, but I was getting used to Markku's abrupt subject changes. "What else do I have?"

"I told you to use your senses," he said, putting the mirror away and folding the now blood-stained handkerchief.

"I did but it turns out I can't list my sense of smell as evidence in a murder investigation."

"How unfortunate." He put the handkerchief in his coat pocket and made his way to the front of the balcony.

"Yeah, it really sucks," I said, joining him at

the railing. We both looked down at the people milling about below us, their inane conversations returning to the banal subjects of work and the next social gathering.

"Even if you kill him without being discovered, your lieutenant will still fire you for not solving the case."

"Yeah, but at least no more kids will have to live without their mothers."

"And if you lose your position with the Richmond Police Department, you will be of no use to the Vigiles which, in all probability, will result in your being eliminated."

"I don't see how I can avoid it," I said, realizing that I had resigned myself to that end.

"There are other ways, Wolfgang, but not if you also insist on facing Lilith."

"That too? Look, I don't know all this history or bible crap ok. What I do know is that she killed a bunch of people, and nobody seems to want to stop her." I stepped away from the railing and stormed halfway up the aisle.

"What about the other killer? You don't seem too concerned with the vampire that has begun killing in your precious city."

"If I stop Lilith, he won't have anyone to copy, and while we are at it, I am pretty sure it's your dad."

"It is not."

"Really? He's powerful enough, and he has plenty of enemies. And he's damn sure not up for citizen of the year."

"The victims were human."

"Your father slaughters humans in those kill clubs all the time."

"He kills no one," he said, turning from the railing to face me.

"What?"

"He facilitates the killing of humans for those that would kill them anyway," he said moving toward me with his arms outstretched demonstrating sincerity. "In this way he can control a darker element of our kind that would otherwise endanger our secrecy."

"You don't want secrecy. You want us all exposed."

"I do, but he does not." Markku let his arms fall to his sides. He looked around the theater as though he were searching for his next words. "I believe in balance, yes, and I have no love lost for my father, but the truth is he is not capable of what you accuse him of."

"And why is that?"

"If you live long enough you may find out."

"That is the second time I've heard that today," I said with growing frustration. "What the hell are you talking about?"

"Another time perhaps," he said, his eyes returning to mine.

"Fine, how do I beat her?"

"Lilith?" he allowed himself a laugh. "You don't."

"Nothing is invulnerable. What is her

weakness?"

"She has one, but you are not it. She is both complex and simple at the same time. She feels all that we do, only more deeply. She has been walking this earth since it took form and has felt more pain than any of us can possibly imagine." He sat in one of the chairs and stared out at the ornate ceiling of the theater. "She has also facilitated more deaths than every immortal walking combined."

"You said she has a weakness."

"You are not listening. There is no defeating her. Do not throw away your life when you know there is nothing you can do."

"What is it?"

"Why would you do this?" Markku turned in his chair to look at me.

"You're the one not paying attention," I said. "I do not want this!" I spit out every word slowly. "This life, this immortality, this gift, this curse, whatever the hell you want to call it. I don't want it!"

"So, you will just kill yourself."

"I'm not killing myself, but I damn sure am not going to just sit by and watch some billion-year-old demon chick keep on killing guys without trying something, anything."

"Then you will die."

"And I am not in the least bit worried about it."

"I was wondering when you would finally admit that to yourself."

"Admit what?"

"That you hate your own existence."

"Fuck off!"

"You hate yourself and you think it is because of what you have become but, you hated yourself long before you were changed. You were just too stupid to realize it."

"You're full of shit!" My protestation rang hollow even to my own ears.

"And you think that if you find a cure you will somehow start to like what you have hated for all this time? You actually believe that if you cure yourself that you will be any less miserable than you are right now?" Markku's brow furrowed as though a new idea had just entered his mind. "That is what he promised you, is it not? Is that not why you joined the Vigiles?"

"This is not natural. It's not right."

"What is right?" He leaned into me with a look of earnest pleading in his eyes. "Is it not right to try and live, to squeeze every drop of joy out of whatever pitiful existence is given us?" He spread his arms indicating all around him. "Life is pain. There is no rhyme or reason, no profound meaning. It is pain, and we who have the strength to face that truth either fight for fighting's sake or we wither and die. Human and gifted alike cling to some hope or dream that we might get to a place in life where the pain stops. Those beliefs comfort us, allow us to keep living despite all that we see. But, in the end they are just lies we tell ourselves to keep the inevitable at bay. There is nothing but pain." He looked hard at me searching for comprehension "You were made this.

Whether it be by accident or fate, you are what you are, and you must accept it or, cure or no cure, you will not survive your own misery."

"How do I beat her?"

"You can't," he said, turning away as if in surrender.

"I kept your little secret from daddy, now tell me! You owe me."

"You do not honestly believe that I made no contingency plans in the event you told him of our meeting?" Markku leaned on the railing again, staring out at the few stragglers still milling about the theater. "You think I just blindly let you into my world without protecting myself? I owe you nothing."

"Then tell me to get me out of your hair." I had one last card to play. "End me. Tell me what to do or I will be a pain in your ass for eternity."

"What makes you believe that this is a worthy excuse to die?"

"She killed at least two men and maybe a third."

"Maybe?"

"We haven't found his body."

"How do you know she is involved?"

"She attacked a kid in the middle of a hotel conference room but let him live. Now he's gone missing, and I have to assume she went back to finish the job."

"She let him live." It was neither a question, nor a statement. He stared at nothing for a moment then turned to me and leaned in close again. "If I tell you, and by some miracle you survive your encounter, you will owe me."

"Owe you what?"

"The witch," he said, stepping past me and walking up the aisle to leave.

"What?"

"Go see your little witch," he said over his shoulder. "She touched his mind and Lilith has touched him as well. If the man is still alive, your little witch may be connected to the mind of Lilith."

"Touched his mind?" I turned to look at him, but Markku had already passed through the double doors. "You mean the kid?" There was no answer.

*****

The parking lot was mostly empty by the time I walked out the lobby doors and crossed Grace Street to get there. Pulling out my phone to check the time, I saw that it was a little after ten. Too late to call Milagro. I also saw that I had a missed call, a voicemail, and a text all from the same number. Somewhere in the back of my mind a little flag went up and then I remembered my conversation with Shep. The assistant chief medical examiner was looking for me, and if the rest of my day was any indication, it was not going to be good news.

I tapped the call button and Doctor Harrison Fairchild-Palmer answered on the first ring.

"Detective Regnum?"

"Yeah, it's me. Shepherd said you needed to talk to me."

"Right," I could hear a combination of excitement and uncertainty in his voice. "Are you anywhere near the morgue? I want to show you something."

"I can be there in about twenty minutes," I said, wondering what I was going to be walking into. "That work for you?"

"Perfect, I'll be here."

CHAPTER 44

There was way too much enthusiasm in Doctor Palmer's voice for me to feel anything but dread as I got into my car and headed out to see him. For all I knew, he had just figured out that the cause of death for the victims I brought him was not exactly natural.

As I pulled onto I-95 I pulled out my phone and dialed up Ramirez. It may have been too late to call Milagro, but I was pretty sure that he didn't sleep. Coupled with the fact that, at this point I really didn't care much, it seemed like the perfect time to catch each o ther up. The phone rang three times and I started to think that he might be asleep after all. He picked up just before I hit the end button.

"Yeah?"

"Do you know anything about some kind of link that Milagro might have with the chowderhead's mind after... you know, reading it like she did?" I was not sure if I was using the proper supernatural terminology, but the silence on the other end of the line was a pretty good indicator that Ramirez knew what I was talking about.

"She might not be strong enough to do it."

"What do you mean?"

"How do you know about that part of her gift?" His tone shifted, and I felt like I was on the wrong side of an interrogation.

"Markku," I said, hoping he wouldn't push for more. I did not want to lie, but I really did not want to get into why I was talking to Markku in the first place.

Ramirez was quiet for what seemed like forever. I knew the line was still good because I heard him sigh. "You're going after her, aren't you?"

"Yes, I am," I said without hesitation. "I just need to know how to find her."

"Don't force her to do it."

"Force her?"

"Ask her, but if she doesn't think she's ready for it, don't push it. She only discovered her gifts a few months ago. Hell, she might not even know she has that ability, so don't push."

"I won't."

"You're gonna die, man. You know that right?" Ramirez said it in such a way that told me he cared, but knew he was not going to be able to convince me otherwise.

"I'll do my best not to."

"I don't believe you," he said and hung up.

*****

Most of the lights were out in the building when I arrived. It might have been a little creepy if I hadn't been there a few dozen times already, and the ability to see just about everything, even in the dark, came in handy as well. The sound of my shoes hitting the tile floor sounded like gunshots to my sensitive ears, but according to Ramirez, I needed to make an effort to be louder to keep humans from getting suspicious. So, there I was stomping down an empty hallway to see a dead body and trying to look and sound normal.

Doctor Palmer was flipping through pages of a file he had open on a desk in front of him when I walked in. He almost jumped out of his seat the instant I stepped in front of him. So much for making enough noise.

"Detective, you startled me."

No kidding, I thought to myself. "Sorry about that. You wanted to talk to me?" I really wanted him to get to the point as soon as possible, if only to keep my head from exploding with all the possible things that could go wrong. The guy did have more than a few victims of supernatural death and at least two otherwise immortal corpses in his coolers. Now there was a contradiction in terms: immortal corpse. I seriously considered coining that one.

"Yes, of course," he said, picking up the file he had been reading before making his way to the wall of coolers. "We've made some progress."

"Great," I said, feeling anything but thrilled. I was sure progress was the thing most detectives wanted to hear from guys like Doctor Palmer, but from where I stood, anything he learned was bad for me and my new little freakish community. "What did you find, Doc?"

"Well, I've made two positive identifications. The first ID is for one of the two bodies you brought me last week, and I was also able to identify one of the latest victims you brought in. Ironically, there seems to have been a connection between the two."

"You I.D.'d them?" My hands started to shake. A positive identification meant the clock had started. I had to close the case fast, and make sure that nothing pointed to anything unnatural.

"Yes, but that is not the most interesting thing I found."

"No?" Things were going south fast, and I had no way of stopping it.

"Here, take a look." Doctor Palmer pulled open drawer after drawer, then proceeded to unzip every bag until I was staring at four bodies, none of which looked at all at peace.

"What am I looking for, Doc?" My strategy was simple: get the Doctor to tell me what he had discovered without letting him know that the bogeyman might actually be real.

"There is a difference in the cause of death of the last group of victims you brought me. Now, that wouldn't be super interesting on its own except that both are extremely strange; like I've never seen it before kind of strange." He started flipping pages again as he talked.

"What difference?"

"Ah, here it is. You see, these guys over here," he said, stepping toward one of the victims from the hotel where Lilith had done the damage. "Well, I don't even know how it's possible, and mind you I have to get a cellular biologist involved on this one, still…" He paused, then looked at me, and I could see the wheels in his head turning like he was figuring out how to explain something to a moron. "You know that the human body has a charge, right?" He kept looking at me. I could only guess that he was waiting for the light bulb to appear over my head. "An electrical charge, to put it simply. Well, it looks like these guys had every volt taken out of every cell of their body at the same time! Like they were demagnetized or something!"

"You're serious," I said, trying to sound doubtful, but knowing full well that he was not only serious but most likely exactly right. My mind was making connections, filling in the blanks of how Lilith, or any succubus killed, how they sucked the life out of a body.

"There is nothing that I have ever read or seen that would lead me to believe that I should be but… Yeah, I am." Doctor Palmer stared at me for a few seconds then moved over to the other two. "These guys, on the other hand, are a little less fantastic but still really, really strange."

"How so?"

"They've been exsanguinated," he said, staring down at one of the victims. "Every single drop of their blood has been removed. And this one," he said, flipping through more pages in the file. "This is the one we identified. His name is Justin Taber. And we identified him…" Doctor

Palmer turned and walked to the other side of the room, pulled open another drawer, unzipped and stepped back. "...because he had an assault charge for shoving this guy down a short flight of stairs a few years back."

"That's a weird coincidence." And, I thought to myself, the last thing I needed. The body we were standing over was Simon's creation. The vampire that Simon had created and then been forced to kill, losing his own life in the fight.

"His name was Andrew Carver, and he was a local artist."

"Wow, again that's just weird." My mind was racing, bouncing between trying to absorb everything the doctor was saying while trying desperately to come up with counter stories.

"Nope, the weird thing is that Mr. Carver here was a paraplegic. He had been in a wheelchair his entire life due to malformed knees and ankles. Do you see anything wrong with his legs?"

"No," I said, still not knowing how I was going to cover up the fact that, when Andrew was turned into a vampire, his body healed and was made whole. "How did we identify him?"

"Same as Justin Taber, DNA. We got Justin's because he was charged with assault and, though it took a bit longer, we had Mr. Carver's because of the medical records from the emergency room after the charges were filed."

"Okay," I said as calmly as I could. "I'm going to start cross-checking any other assault charges I can find involving these two—"

"We're not done yet," he said, looking at me apologetically.

"What do you mean?"

"After we started cross-checking Mr. Carver's DNA, a string of other killings and assaults popped up. Since his samples were taken as a victim, we didn't put it together."

"Put what together, Doc?"

"Looks like Mr. Carver killed or assaulted about seven or eight people over the last month before he was himself killed. But..."

"But what? Spill it, Doc," I said, getting more and more worried.

"His DNA," he said.

"What about it?"

"Andrew Carver's DNA matched the killings but it was... somehow different." Doctor Palmer looked at me with an expression that was equal parts fascination and horror.

"Different how?" I knew what he was going to say but I had to hear it to know how royally screwed I was.

"It wasn't human."

CHAPTER 45

"Slow down, Wolf," Ramirez said. This time it did sound like I had woken him up. "You're saying the M.E. has identified one of the victims that our copycat did and that he also identified the guy that Simon turned?"

"Yes! What are we supposed to do when this happens?" I tried to slow down my speech and my speed as I drove through the residential area of Chimborazo where I lived.

"First of all, I thought it wasn't your problem anymore since you have a date with a dirt nap tomorrow." His sarcasm was palpable even over the phone. He was angry. "But if you're curious, it doesn't sound like we need to do anything."

"What?"

"Look man, the kid that Simon turned was still in his normal life span, so when the records show that he was 20 something years old it will all line up."

"But what about his legs and—"

"Any tests they run will be inconclusive or won't make any sense, so they will just chalk it up to some outside factors they don't know about. The other guy died of blood loss, so they won't make anything of that other than just a crazy way to go."

"And what if they identify Simon somehow?"

"They won't. He was too old to have any DNA in the system and even if he had been a young vampire, once it's determined that a vampire has survived the change, we have people who go through and erase any evidence he or she ever existed."

"Yeah," I said. "They obviously did a bang-up job with this Andrew Carver kid."

"He had only been turned for a few months, Wolf. Hell, sometimes it takes that long to figure out if the new creation is going to survive the change."

"Apparently, he wasn't doing too well adjusting, since it looks like he went on a killing spree. What the hell was that about, Jo?"

"I don't know, but it looks like I'll be figuring that out alone." The phone beeped and Ramirez was gone.

Tossing the phone onto the passenger seat I turned left and parked on the street just shy of the intersection. Getting out I walked the rest of the way to the intersection, turned right and walked up the front steps. The night was hot and sticky, like every other night, but I hardly noticed; my head was full of other things.

I could not figure out why everyone seemed so concerned about how I died. Ramirez made it pretty clear that I was a dead man just for lining myself up to get fired from the Richmond Police force. I had no good ideas about how to turn what I knew about Langston's connection to the murdered women into anything actionable, and that meant the lieutenant would have my badge in a little over a day. So what did it matter if I tried to stop Lilith and got killed in the process? At least I was trying something. It just didn't seem good enough for Ramirez. Apparently, I was supposed to just grind it out and let someone else decide when or if I died. And, what the hell did Markku care what happened to me? At least his dad had a valid reason, or at least what looked like one. He just wanted to be sure that I didn't leave freak blood or evidence of our world everywhere when I kicked the bucket.

I took a deep breath, looked up and saw that I was standing at my front door with my keys in my hands. Putting the key in the lock, I turned the knob and let myself in.

"Wolfgang, I presume."

Spinning on the ball of my right foot, I fell into a shallow crouch facing the direction the voice had come from. In a millisecond I heard, processed, and knew that I did not recognize her voice, but I had smelled her before somewhere, perhaps mixed with other smells or other emotions.

"My," she continued, "you are yummy looking."

"Who the hell are you?" Her shape was clear to me in the dark, and I knew exactly where she sat in the far kitchen table chair. She had one foot on the floor, the other swinging back and forth at the end of a leg draped languidly over the table creating a very open position that, were it not for the breaking and entering, would have looked like an invitation. Yet, though I could see all that, I could not see her face.

Watching her closely, and still very much on guard, I saw her reach slowly up to the light switch on the wall. Light flooded the room and there she was, Dr. Bag Lady from the kill club. She smiled at me as she lowered her arm slowly until it rested on her ample thigh. Slowly, I came out of my crouch, closing the door behind me as I did. "Who are you?" I asked again, taking a step towards her.

"As I hear it, you know exactly who I am."

"Forgive me for wanting introductions when it comes to a home invasion," I said.

"Of course, my name is Leigh. Oh, and just to be clear, I meant yummy as in I wouldn't mind breaking some furniture with you, not as in the midnight snack kind of way." She was looking me up and down smiling as she spoke. "Though, if I had my wish, a little of each would go a long way. For both of us I think."

"What are you doing in my apartment?"

"Markku thought I could be of some help."

"Markku? And what does he think I need help with?"

"It seems," she said, swinging her leg off of the table and standing ever so gracefully, "that you have not had a good..." She took a step toward me. Red high heels, black skintight jeans, and a black silk button-down blouse might have been cliché in any other situation but combined with her amber-red hair and jade green eyes, the image was delicious. "Let's just say, you look like you could use a bit of stress relief."

"Stress relief?" I stood up a bit straighter hoping to look as though she were not affecting me.

"Yes, the furniture breaking kind."

"Look, lady I—"

"Leigh."

"Leigh," I said, taking a half step back. "I assume you know what I am."

"Oh, sweetie, I am counting on what you are."

"Then you know this is probably not a good idea."

"You're right, it isn't," she said, her hands coming up to her blouse and unbuttoning the few buttons that were still fastened. "I haven't had a wolf in a very long time."

"Excuse me?"

"That," she said as she continued walking toward me, "makes it a great idea." Stepping closer and closer, her blouse hung open, exposing perfect - almost too large- breasts that needed no bra to hold them in defiance of gravity.

Her dancer's body moved with a slow, predatory grace: powerful, beautiful, strong and supple. I could hear my breath quicken. I could feel my heart racing, the blood pulsing through my veins. I clenched my teeth, willing myself not to change.

"Don't fight it," she said. "You won't hurt me.

Even if I was not older and stronger than you, I can promise you that whatever form you take, you will want me." Her hand caressed my face. Her touch was electric, and my eyes rolled back into my skull. I smelled her, and it was intoxicating. "You will need me," she said as her hand ran down the front of my torso, then to the front of my hips and between my thighs, gripping me. "I will let you have me, and you will have no choice but to take me."

My head lolled to one side, and I felt the haze coming over my consciousness. Then the first wave of pain hit me. My entire body tensed.

"Do not fight it!" She took hold of my jacket and shook me.

I remember growling and writhing, the pain and pleasure warring with each other, lust and fear tearing at my mind and body.

"Let go, Wolf. Let it happen," she said looking into my eyes. I could see her intensity change to excitement before closing my eyes again. "As you wish." She shoved me backwards as though I weighed less than a child. I flew through the air and slammed hard against the wall. The shock of her strength slowed the change for an instant. My eyes opened just as she slammed into me, her hand around my throat even as it grew with my changing.

"I will just have to take you!" It was that last thing I heard her say. I felt myself being thrown, slamming into the opposite wall before landing on the bed, then she was on top of me, her right hand finding my throat once again as her left pinned my right arm to the mattress. I reached for her with my left wanting to pull her close to me. Then I saw my hand. It was changing, I was changing, and I could not stop it.

CHAPTER 46

The scent of sweat and sex filled my nostrils, and something else, blood. My eyes snapped open, and I jarred awake before the pain hit. The glass in my joints, the fire in my chest.

"Shhhhh," she said, her voice calming and soft. "You're okay."

I felt her hand brush back the hair from my forehead. Her soothing voice hushed away the pain and fear. I tried to rise but a hand, not forceful but firm, held me in place then caressed my bare flesh.

"What happened?" My voice sounded like it came from outside of my body.

"Everything," she said with a low husky laugh. "Just lay still, let the blood flow to your extremities for a moment."

"What are you—"

"Lay still for just a bit and the pain won't be as intense. Let your body adjust to its new shape before you try to use it."

I did as she asked. Lying motionless face down on my bed, I used the only thing I knew would not cause me pain other than my sense of smell, my eyes. Slowly, I scanned the parts of the room

I could see without moving my head. There was a human-sized dent in the drywall where I must have hit before she threw me onto the bed. There were five long gouges in the wall near where my head now lay, and then I saw the blood. They were small spatters, but they were everywhere, and there was no mistaking the sight of it or the smell.

"Yeah... you may want to have someone clean up a bit before you ask for your deposit back," she said, obviously following my eyes with hers.

"What happened?"

"Let's just say we were both a bit enthusiastic."

"Oh God," I said, stirring until her hand stopped me. "Did I hurt you?"

She laughed loudly, a deep laugh, confident and alluring. "I was going to ask you the same thing. Have you seen your walls?"

Slowly, I began opening and closing my hands, testing for the pain. Extending my neck and rolling my head back and forth I felt discomfort, but not the searing pain I had expected. Carefully I rose to a seated position to try and get a look at the rest of the room. I did not get past the bed. Leigh had been sitting just behind me, close enough to keep a hand on me and comfort me through the transition. Once I turned around there she was, and I was dumbfounded. Leigh was stunning when clothed and a goddess when she was not.

No longer needing to keep me still, she had lain back against the pillows wedged in the corner at the head of the bed. The pillows were arranged in such a way as to make a kind of armchair for her, and she filled it perfectly. She looked straight into my eyes, daring me to look away, making no effort to cover herself with sheets, a pillow or even a shy thought. She simply laid there as if displaying herself, knowing that she was breathtaking. Reclining there on my cheap sheets, in my less than pristine apartment, she still looked like an Amazonian queen. Her right leg was bent at the knee and supported by her shapely foot, while the left lay flat on the bed. They were positioned far enough apart to expose everything one would have wondered about otherwise. Her skin was the color of magnolia petals contrasting with the green of her eyes, the red of her lips and the rose-colored buds at the tips of her breasts. From the top of her head where her hair cascaded evenly over both shoulders just long enough to pool at the crest of each of her perfect breasts, to her curvaceous legs, she was perfection. I devoured her with my gaze, my eyes dancing all over her body until finally they returned to hers. She looked at me with eyes like a doll's, big and round, giving away no sense of what she was feeling. She was the enigma, the question I needed answered. I didn't know if I was overcome with lust, stunned by beauty, or in the grip of some unknown magic, but I could not stop looking into those eyes.

Without a word she swung her legs over the side of the bed and began gathering her things.

"You were letting me look at you," I said, wondering if I was being played.

"Yes," she said, smiling over her shoulder at me.

"Why?"

"I was hoping to leave you with an image you would want to come back to."

"What do you mean?"

"Think of it as extra motivation for you to live through the day," she said, buttoning up her blouse. "Markku thought that if you were sexually sated, then maybe you might stand a chance with Lilith... for more than a second or two at least." She finished buttoning her blouse and began looking around the room. "But all that aside, I kind of like you. So, if you manage to survive, I am really hoping we can do this again." Finding her shoes on either side of the room she picked them up then turned to me. Standing there in nothing but her blouse and holding her shoes in one hand I felt the urges rising in me again. "Do you have a pair of sweatpants or something I can borrow?"

"What? Why?"

A sly smile crept across her lips. "You kind of shredded my jeans."

CHAPTER 47

I stared at the door for a while after Leigh had closed it behind her on her way out. I don't know exactly for how long, it could have been a few seconds or minutes, my mind swimming from thought to thought, beautiful image to beautiful image, and all about her. I had completely dismissed the idea of it but now, it seemed possible; possible to have a relationship with someone, even being what I am. Yet strangest of all was the fact that having been with her then watching her leave, I felt lonelier than I ever had before.

Pushing the thought out of my head I willed myself out of the bed. There would be no relationships for me. There would be no happily ever after. With the day I had planned, there would be no after at all. I looked around the room for what was left of my clothes and began digging through the shreds for my cell phone. I punched in Milagro's number and waited for the ringing to begin.

"Hey," she said, her voice low and cautious.

"Hi," I said, my normal eloquence failing me. "I was wondering if you had some time for me. I have a favor to ask."

"What is it?"

"I think it might be easier in person." The truth was I wanted to see her face when I asked. I wanted to be sure that if she agreed, it was because she knew she could do it.

"Okay... I'm home if you---"

"I have to make a stop first. Will you be there in a half hour?"

"Sure."

*****

The morning rush was over, so the traffic heading out to Glen Allen was almost nonexistent. Ms. Evans had given me the address.

The houses were nice, not too big, with nice yards and plenty of room. After a few minutes maneuvering through the neighborhood, the voice on my GPS let me know that I had arrived at the correct house. I pulled into the driveway. My foot had barely touched the top of the porch stairs when the door opened.

"Hi, you must be Detective Regnum." The woman at the door was in her early thirties with dark hair and the most genuine smile I had ever seen. Her eyes were sharp and intelligent, taking everything in at once without judgment.

"Yes ma'am."

"My name is Kelly Branch. Please come in."

The home was neat and welcoming, decorated with intent and well thought out. It was obvious that Kelly was good at what she did and, between the wonderful smells coming from the kitchen and the perpetual gleam in her eyes, it was very clear that she enjoyed what had to be this thankless work.

"So, you're Isaac's foster mom?"

"Yeah," she said smiling, but with a touch of sadness. "He is a great kid, it's just..."

"What?"

"It's hard to know if he's going to come out of this okay. He's in so much pain and he's so scared."

"Of what?"

"Everything." She stepped further into the living area, her head held just a bit lower. "I mean, I know it takes time, and I know he will adjust. I just... You can feel the pain emanating off him like a kind of cloud and all I want to do is hold him until it goes away." She turned to look at me, gathering herself. "I'm sorry, I guess I just wanted you to know his current state before you talked to him. He's told me a lot about you, you know?"

"Really?" I was genuinely surprised.

"Yeah, I can tell he likes you." She was smiling again but then, "just be gentle, okay? I know you're here to do a job but---"

"Actually, I was just here to visit."

"Really?" Her eyes brightened.

"Yeah, I just wanted to say hi and see how he's holding up."

"Oh, this is so great!"

Before I knew it, Kelly had me in the friendliest version of a bear hug I had ever experienced. "Oh, I am so sorry," she said, releasing me and taking an apologetic step back. "It just means so much that you would do this for him."

After the awkwardness of the moment passed Kelly took me upstairs. She pointed out each room naming the foster children that occupied each. She let me know that the others were in school and assured me that Isaac and I would not be disturbed.

"Hey champ," I said as I stepped into the room.

"Hello." Isaac looked almost exactly as he did when I saw him last. He sat at a desk writing in a notebook, and he was still, understandably, not smiling.

"How are you holding up?" I said taking another step. The desk was on the opposite side of the room facing a window out to the backyard. As I stepped closer, I could see that Isaac was not writing; he was drawing. "What are you working on?"

"Nothing."

"Looks pretty good for nothing. In fact, it looks like you're making a pretty good likeness of that tree on the other side of the yard."

"I guess."

He was so small, so closed off from everything around him. The all-too-familiar ache was back, but this time, I just let it come. This is why I was going to track Langston down and end him. I would learn what I could from Milagro, take out Langston, and then finish with Lilith.

"Hey champ, can I talk to you for a sec?"

Isaac looked up at me for a moment before putting his pencil down. "Okay."

"I wanted to come by and..." Suddenly, I was feeling nervous. What did I actually come here to say? "Well, I suppose I just wanted to let you know I was thinking about you."

"I... I guess I was thinking about you too," he said, and I felt him opening up, if only just.

"Really? Like, what about?" I could see him hesitate, like he was unsure of what to say or how to say it.

"Nothing, I guess." He turned and went back to his drawing.

"Okay champ, it's alright. It's enough that I got to see you." He was done or so it seemed, so I stood up and got ready to leave. "If I don't see you again just know that I'm going to make this right for you." I turned to go, but his voice stopped me.

"Why wouldn't you see me again?" His voice was small and scared again.

"I have some things to do that might... take me out of the area but, it will be for the best."

"But if it didn't..."

"If it didn't what?"

"Take you out of the area... Would you visit me again?"

Why did it hurt so bad? Why could I not breathe? "I sure would, champ." I had to leave, or this kid was going to see my heart break, and he had suffered enough. "I gotta go."

"What I was going to say before..."

His words stopped me at the door. "Yeah?"

"It was about how your dad called you champ."

"He did."

"He was a good dad."

"Thanks."

"I think you would be too."

CHAPTER 48

Walking up the familiar stairs to Milagro's apartment, It occurred to me that the last time I was here she had tried to blow my brains out with a pretty big gun. It seemed so long ago, even though it had only been a few days. She was different now after seeing me change. I was not sure what it was or if it was more than just one thing. Did she still hate me? That didn't seem right, especially after she agreed to meet me alone. Did she fear me? Maybe, but not enough to prevent her from seeing me. Did she feel sorry for me? That made more sense than anything else I had come up with, and I realized that I almost preferred her hating me.

"Hey..." she said then stopped. She had opened the door as I reached the end of the hall, but now she just stood there, seemingly unsure. "I'm not really sure what to call you. I guess I have never had to call you by name."

"I always introduce myself as Ray," I said after a moment. "You know, basically a version of the first couple of letters from my last name."

"Right."

"But it never takes."

"Why?" She cocked her head to one side and her perfect little brown eyebrows knitted together in an adorable little question.

"Let's just say…" I thought for a moment. "Just call me Wolf," I said smiling.

"Ok," she said, and I could hear the relief in her voice as well as see the smile on her face. She opened the door wide and motioned for me to step through and I did. "I suppose Dog Chow isn't exactly a pet name," she said as she led me down the hall then immediately gasped, turning to look at my face. "Oh God, I meant…"

We looked at each other for a moment, me confused and her embarrassed until I finally got the double pun. I burst out in laughter and after a moment, Milagro joined me. We made our way into the living area and sat in the same chairs we had the first day we met. "So, what is it you needed me for?"

"I need to find her, Milagro," I said.

"Yeah, I figured that's what this was about."

"What do you mean?"

"Joaquin called me."

"Jo?"

"Yeah, he let me know what you are trying to do." Her eyes searched mine as she spoke.

"And what's wrong with what I'm trying to do," I said, standing up in frustration and pacing the room. "I'm trying to stop a killer from killing more--"

"What you're trying to do is get yourself killed, so don't bullshit me, cabrón!" She stood and actually squared off, getting right in my face. So much for being scared of me. "Go ahead, Wolf," she said, ironically almost barking out my name in what I could see was genuine anger. "Tell me I'm wrong."

"What does it matter?" I said, sitting back down again.

"That's a dumb ass question!" Milagro strode up to me like a gangster in a Spike Lee film until she was looking down at me. "That's a question that some weak ass little bitch would ask. Are you a weak ass little bitch?" Her right arm was slinging her index finger up and down so that it came inches away from the left side of my face in classic street intimidation style, jabbing at me on very specific syllables like 'bitch' and 'you' "But that doesn't make sense because what I saw the night before last was someone fighting what he was changing into, knowing that all he was doing was making it worse!"

The slinging pointer finger stopped, and her arms extended out to her sides in a conciliatory pose. "I get that you hate what you are. I get that you hate this gift or curse or whatever, but if you were willing to fight that change, why won't you keep fighting until you figure it out? You aren't the only wolf so obviously, other people are handling it. But, no, not you." The finger slinging began again "Maybe you are a little bitch! Maybe you are just Dog Chow!" She was raging, her chest rising and falling with every furious breath she took. But this time her fury did not come from hate as it did just a few days ago. She cared, she cared what was going to happen to me.

"So you won't help?"

"You think!" She was still standing over me, no hint of fear or even mild concern. "You fight the change because you don't want to hurt anybody, right? Tell me I'm wrong." I didn't, which apparently gave her license to continue. "So maybe if you pulled your head out of your ass long enough to take a breath, you might get some oxygen in that brain of yours and figure out how to help people with what you can do instead of whining about how unfair it all is!"

She stood over me for a few more seconds then turned abruptly and threw herself into the seat from which she had just exploded.

"Dog Chow," I said, looking at her from under arched eyebrows.

"Yeah? What about it?" She locked eyes with me, daring me to challenge her.

"I think I'm more of a cat person."

She tried to keep it together, but my sincere expression got the better of her and we both laughed. We laughed hard. Back and forth we continued the volley of laughing; she would look at me out of breath and see me still guffawing and a fresh wave of laughing would take hold of her. I would catch my breath, but the moment I saw her double over still giggling I would rear back in the chair and continue as well.

After we calmed ourselves and dried our tears, she finally spoke. "I want to help, Wolf; I really do.

But I just can't do this for you, knowing what's gonna happen."

"Oh," said a voice from the far corner of the room. "I think you will."

Milagro and I jumped out of our chairs; instinctively, I placed myself between her and the voice. And there he stood, shoulder-length black hair, slacks, and a black T-shirt. I didn't recognize the face, but I did know one thing. He had no scent!

CHAPTER 49

"Who the hell are you?" Milagro's voice was loud and fierce. "And what the fuck are you doing in my house?" She had obviously gotten over the initial shock and was back in pissed off mode.

"The wolf knows me, I am sure, but you may call me Sam." He stood motionless; even his mouth moved almost imperceptibly.

"Something tells me that is not your real name," I said, recovering a bit slower than Milagro.

"Semangelof is my true name," he said, still not moving.

"Sema what?" Milagro was trying to get past me to confront the angel, and it was all I could do to hold her back. "Listen Cinnamon," she continued, the slinging pointer finger beginning again with renewed fervor. "I don't care what your name is. Get the hell out of my house before I—"

"---You got to back off here," I said to Milagro over my shoulder, my arms fanned out behind me like a human guardrail.

"What?" She looked at me in angry shock. "You think I'm afraid of Salami over there?"

"The wolf is merely trying to protect you," he

said, looking at her his expression blank. "He has already met my associates and is very familiar with our talents."

"Associates," I said, still struggling to hold Milagro back. "You mean the twins."

"Senoi and Sansenoi, and yes they are brothers," he said.

"Oh yeah?" Milagro slipped out from behind me, and I had to grab her by the arm to keep her from getting any closer. "Well, Semolina," she said, pointer finger slinging away and adding what I like to call the swivel neck for good measure. "Why don't you go get your little punk ass bitches Sonny and Cher, find yourself a stage somewhere and go into a production of Fuck Off, the Musical!"

"Where is Lilith?" he said, taking a step forward.

With some effort, I pulled Milagro back and stepped back in front of her. "Look friend, your associate said he knew what I was, so I'm guessing you do too." Positioning myself protectively in front of Milagro. This time she didn't struggle, apparently realizing that this was not just some guy. "Let's not do this."

"The child must tell where we will find Lilith," he said, looking at me with the same flat eyes.

"Child?" Milagro may not have been struggling, but she was obviously not afraid. "I wasn't going to do it for him, so I sure as hell ain't doing it for you."

"Choice," he said, still looking at me.

"Choice?" Milagro and I both repeated what the angel had said.

"The child will choose to help me or not," he said, indicating Milagro with a slow, almost robotic gesture but still not looking at her. "If she chooses the latter, then the burden of choice falls to us."

"How so?" I was pretty sure I was not going to like the rest of the speech, but I had to go along for now.

"I will choose whether or not to force her to help me, and you will choose whether or not to try and stop me."

"For my part," I said, planting my feet firmly, "it's not really a choice."

"And if you choose to try and stop me you may or may not choose to change. If you do, then you may survive; you may even be a mild annoyance to me, but you lack control." He took another step forward and then looked at Milagro. "The child would most certainly die."

The silence in the room seemed endless. The angel watched me, I watched the angel, and Milagro seethed like an angry Doberman on a short leash behind me. I kept looking at him, searching for some hint of what he would do but saw nothing that would tell. What I did see, now that words were done and only the choices left to be made remained, were his eyes. They were eyes that appeared as though they had been open for millennia. Eyes that, though they showed no emotion, spoke what could only be described as the purest truth. No passion, no anger, or sadness. What I saw in those eyes was the present, the past, and the future without bias or prejudice, without acceptance or resignation, simply all that was.

Knowing in my heart and mind that the angel was without malice, I turned slowly to look at Milagro. Gently, I took hold of both her hands and when her eyes came up to meet mine, I nodded slowly. The look on my face must have made an impression because without a word spoken between us, she nodded back and made her way to the same chair that Todd was sitting in just days ago when Milagro entered his mind. She sat, closed her eyes, made some adjustments to her posture and took a few deep breaths before opening her eyes and looking at the angel.

"I will do what I can, but you have to allow for the fact that I've never done this before."

"I do," was all he said.

I reached for Milagro's hand, hoping to at least provide comfort.

"No," she said. "You can't touch me or talk to me while I do this."

"What exactly are you going to do?"

"The closest I can come to describing it is..." She thought for a moment. "Think of it as REM sleep."

"Rapid Eye Movement?"

"Yes," she said, smiling at me. "I have to get myself just under fully conscious, but still aware of what I am doing."

"I'm not following," I said, confused.

"Have you ever had that weird sensation of falling just as you fall asleep and then jerk awake?"

"Yeah," I said. "It always freaks me out."

"Well, that is a step too far," she continued still smiling but, it was a scared smile. "I need to stay in the place where I know I am not really falling."

"Then what?"

"Then I can reach out to Todd and find him, if he's still alive."

"And what if he's not?"

"What, alive?"

"Yeah," I said, sensing that the other shoe was about to drop, and it was a size fourteen.

"I could get lost."

"What?!"

"I could get lost, Wolf. Time is not the same in the subconscious. If he's there I'll find him almost instantly. But if not, it will feel like a few seconds to you out here, but it would be hours for me."

"Then I just wake you up after about... I don't know... Sixty seconds?"

"Thirty. Hopefully I will find him before then, but I don't want to stay in there any longer than that."

"Wait, why not? Why don't you want to stay any longer?" My mind was whirling.

"Because it's a place for the human subconscious," she said putting on a brave face, but I could see the fear growing behind her eyes. "And, if someone goes in there still holding on to their consciousness, there are things in that place that will... Just get me out, okay?"

CHAPTER 50

The hard part was sitting there watching her. Milagro was laying back in the big chair, her feet planted on the floor, her arms at her sides. She was breathing in a slow but precise rhythm like a ticking clock on the wall, as if anyone still had one of those in the house. I was sitting just a few feet away in a wooden chair I had grabbed out of the kitchen. I needed to watch her for some sign that she was in, or crossed over, or whatever you call half dreaming half awake, because as soon as she did the clock started. Thirty seconds was the cutoff but I was not sure when to start the countdown.

I looked over my shoulder and saw Semangelof standing on the other side of the room. He was motionless, those unblinking eyes focused on Milagro but somehow seeing everything in the room all at once. His expression was still blank, a face without emotion but he had made himself pretty clear, it was this or a fight, and a fight meant collateral damage. I figured as long as the job got done, what difference did it make who got to Lilith, but Milagro, Ramirez and even Markku were right. I had other reasons for tracking her down myself. I just wasn't so sure anymore.

In a move so fast that I barely saw it, Semangelof was suddenly staring directly at me. He turned his face back to look at Milagro in such a deliberate way that I quickly turned my attention back to the task at hand. Her eyes were darting back and forth from beneath her eyelids. Damn it,' I thought to myself. How long had she been under while I was daydreaming? I had to play it safe after Milagro's warning, so I assumed five seconds had passed and started my countdown.

Every moment was excruciating. I really didn't know how long she had been under, and though I kept the count, time felt like it had stopped. There was no way I could really know when to pull her out if she couldn't find Todd, and I was starting to think I was counting too slowly.

Twenty-four seconds and I was done. I reached for her arm, but before I got to her my own arm was locked in Semangelof's grip. I snapped my head round to look at him, getting ready to take a swing no matter how ineffective it would be when I saw him raise his other hand and hold up five fingers. He then folded in his thumb, and then his index finger and I realized he had been keeping count.

With two fingers left, a sharp gasp came from Milagro as she jerked awake. Semangelof let go of my arm and I was at her side an instant later, moving thick black locks of hair from her face.

"I got him," she said.

"He's still alive?" It was more a statement of surprise than an actual question.

"Where?" Semangelof was already heading to the door.

"I, uh," she was stammering, still seemingly not fully conscious.

"Where?" He turned to face her. He stood at the threshold of the hallway which led to the front door. "You will honor your word, child."

"Fine," she said, defiance returning to her eyes. "He's at Shiplock Park."

"You are certain," he said without inflection or feeling.

"I saw the damn locks through his eyes. He's there, asshole!"

"You just going to go kill her?" I was not sure why I cared, but the question just came out.

"I will find Senoi and Sansenoi, then order her to return or destroy her," he said, turning to go down the hall.

"Yeah? Well just be careful the kid doesn't get hurt," I said, helping Milagro to her feet.

"If he is with her, he must be destroyed as well."

"What?!" I was already heading after him, but the door closed before I was even in the hallway. "Damn it!" I turned and looked at Milagro with pleading eyes.

"Go," she said sadly, understanding exactly what had to be done.

"Thanks," I said, turning to leave.

"Wait!" Her voice sounded as though something were wrong. "There's something off about this."

"What do you mean?"

"The kid, Todd."

"What about him?"

"He wasn't hurt," she said, looking at the floor as though she were piecing together her thoughts. "He wasn't even scared."

"What does that matter?"

"I don't know, but it doesn't make sense."

"Maybe not but if I'm going to beat the three stooges, I gotta—"

"Go, but be careful," she said to my back. Then just as the door was closing behind me, she called out, "You don't have to die today, Wolf!"

I ran down the stairs, keys already in hand and headed straight for the car. The engine roared to life, and I slammed the gear shift into drive. The tires screeched as the car jumped forward into traffic, leaving angry yells and horn honks in its wake. Blue lights exploded from behind the radiator grill and back window of the Dodge Charger when I flipped the switch on the dash. The siren screamed, bouncing off the buildings and other cars around me, echoing loudly and letting everything within earshot know to get the hell out of my way.

I pulled out my phone and hit the speed dial for Ramirez.

"Aren't you dead yet?"

"Jo, listen to me! The angels, they're after the

kid!"

"What?"

"They're gonna kill Todd if they catch him with Lilith."

"How the hell do you know that?"

"Because I asked one of them politely. What difference does it make?" I was screaming into the phone now. I had no time for this. "He said it and I believe him."

"Alright, alright, I hear you got your sirens going. Do you know where the kid is?"

"Yea, he's at Shiplock Park. I'm headed there now."

"Ok, I'm on my way but listen for a second."

"What man?"

"After I got off the phone with you last night, I visited the morgue and then went to see Zuñiga."

"Speaker Man?" I was still not used to using the guy's real name, and I didn't care to start now.

"Yeah, whatever. I read the journal again and there is something really weird."

"Not really the time for this, Jo!"

"Shut the fuck up for one second! I am at Andrew Carver's apartment, and yes, the kid was not right in the head. He was working off a hit list, taking out people that had screwed with him when he was still a paraplegic."

"So?"

"He was doing revenge killings, Wolf! And Simon found out about it."

"I still don't see what this has to do with

anything." I turned off the interstate, nearly clipping a city bus as I jumped on to 24th St.

"Bottom line is, I think…" The phone went silent.

I looked at the screen on my phone and saw that the call had ended. I thought about calling him back but quickly decided against it. Ramirez knew where I was going and was probably on his way too. I had too much else to worry about: three angels to outrun, a demon to kill and some kid I barely knew to save.

CHAPTER 51

Great Shiplock Park was at the far end of Shockoe Bottom. The Richmond City Canal ran along Dock Street, providing water access for all the goods that were once manufactured or brought here for shipping to all the factories and warehouses in Shockoe. The big metal walls that made up the locks at the mouth of the canal were designed to give ships access to the James without having to fight with strong currents and changing water levels. The ships would approach the locks, enter from the canal side, then the metal walls would close, and water would be pumped in. With each lock the water level would be raised higher and eventually match the rivers' levels. Then the ship could now safely enter the James and continue downriver to deliver the goods anywhere along the Eastern Seaboard and sometimes across the Atlantic.

All of it was abandoned when the mill stopped producing, and in an effort to gentrify the area, the City of Richmond decided to doll the place up and make it a park. That's where Milagro said he would be, alone. If he stayed that way, I thought, things might not end badly after all.

I parked the car and got out slowly, searching the area for any sign of Lilith. It was mid-morning, so most humans were at their jobs, oblivious to what was about to go down. Todd was nowhere to be seen, but I could smell him.

Closing the door as quietly as I could, I took a cautious step toward the park when I heard footsteps coming from behind me. I turned quickly to see a jogger coming down Pear Street. Letting out a long sigh, I watched her turn right to follow the capital trail that ran directly beneath the elevated railroad tracks and parallel to Dock Street along the Canal and, of course the shoreline of the James. With her earbuds firmly in place, and music so loud I could hear it clearly standing yards away, she continued down the path. I waited a few moments to be sure she would be clear should the worst happen and continued my approach. There was still no sign of Lilith, and I felt my body begin to relax.

"She is not here."

I spun quickly to see Inyoni leaning on my car with her arms folded across her chest.

"Damn it!" The words came out of my mouth much louder than intended. She was wearing a white sundress and sandals showing more skin than her normal business attire ever had. Her dark skin almost glowed in the sunlight contrasting sharply with the flowing white dress. She looked like a cross between a Greek goddess and an Egyptian warrior. Recovering finally, I found my words again "Why is it that everyone seems to be able to sneak up on me when I am supposed to have all of these hyper senses?"

"Because," she said, moving away from the car and toward me. "You are an ungrateful, ignorant adolescent who has been thrown into a world you know nothing about; you are trying to solve all the problems of said world without ever considering the fact that you may be wrong..." She cocked her head to one side as though contemplating something. "Which also makes you arrogant, especially considering you have not bothered to learn anything about your gifts or how to use them." Her last words somehow timed out perfectly with her squaring off and looking me right in the eyes.

"Wow, you're a motivational speaker on the side, aren't you?"

"You concentrate on only one sense at a time," she said, looking as though she was fighting the urge to roll her eyes at my humor.

"So, I'm supposed to concentrate on more than one sense at a time, is that it?"

"You are not supposed to concentrate on any of them at all."

Her answer took me by surprise and somewhere in the back of my head I knew it made sense, Yoda-type sense, but I really didn't have time for it right now. "Thanks for the tip but right now I am trying to..." A new question popped into my head.

"Markku sent me," she said, obviously figuring out what was in my head.

"Why?"

"To try and keep you alive in the event you are as idiotic as you seem."

"Thanks. You should write that one down for your next self-help book." This time she did roll her eyes.

"Go, try to save him," she said. "I think you will find he has other ideas."

I met her eyes for a moment then turned to find Todd. His scent led me across a small bridge to a wooded area on the other side of the canal. With Inyoni watching my back, I was able to move at a regular pace, not too fast, which might look like an attack if he happened to see me coming, but not too slow either.

Following a small trail down a set of wooden steps, I came to a path; my nose told me to go left, toward the banks of the mighty James River; that's where I found him.

"Hi, Detective," he said, smiling as I stepped into a small clearing about ten feet away from him.

"Hey," I replied, studying him, his eyes, his movement, anything that might tell me if he was under any kind of outside influence.

"Everything okay?" Todd furrowed his brow.

"I was hoping you would answer that question for me," I said, my steps getting slower the closer I got to him.

"What do you mean?"

His speech was normal, and he seemed alright enough, but how was I to know for sure. I had only seen him when he was all doped up on demon mojo. How was I to know what his normal was?

"You were a part of an investigation," I said, hoping the lights would come on in his head. When I didn't see any I pushed. "You've been missing for days."

"Oh, yeah... she came for me."

"Lilith?!"

"Yeah," he said, sounding almost embarrassed.

"Where is she? How did you survive?"

"She's coming back, but I should tell you—"

"Ok we have to get the hell out of here."

"Wait. I need you to listen to—"

"No, you need to listen to me! She's not the only thing coming, and if they catch you with her, it's over!"

"What are you talking about?"

"It would take too long to explain. Come on," I said, taking him by the arm and leading back the way I had come, trying to get him to my car before things got complicated. "You wouldn't believe me anyway."

"You don't know what you're talking about, man."

"Oh yeah?" I was almost dragging him now. A picture of a frazzled mother in Walmart dragging her screaming toddler popped into my head.

"She's not dangerous!"

"She's not what?" The sheer stupidity of the statement made me release my hold on his arm and face him, if only to give him the stupefied gaze I reserved for especially dumbass statements.

Then we heard it. The sound that I heard days ago in Todd's apartment, like the pairing of a hawk's screech and a lion's roar. Instinctively, I stepped in front of Todd to protect him while turning to face the danger. That is when I saw Inyoni, flying through the air in a sickening and uncontrolled cartwheel. Lilith was here, and she had just thrown my de facto bodyguard into the river.

CHAPTER 52

"You were saying," I said, not taking my eyes off Lilith. Todd's only response was to gasp. I didn't have time to console or even explain. All I could do was reach back with my left hand to make sure he was behind me, and as Lilith turned to look at me, put up my right arm in a feeble attempt to look protective.

"They sent you again?" Lilith was smiling. "My child, they *really* must not like you."

"As a matter of fact," I said, my words coming out slowly as I fought against her allure, "I chose to come."

"Did you? You must truly wish to die." Lilith began walking toward me, every step more luxurious than the last, sensuality radiating from her with every movement.

"Everyone has been telling me that lately." I felt my legs begin to tremble, but I held on. Knowing what she was gave me strength I did not have the first time, and having sated my lust probably didn't hurt either. "But... Right now, all I want is the kid."

"He is mine through choice, and I will destroy all who seek to end my peace." She was closer now and I felt my knees buckle. I didn't understand what she was saying, but I figured I was slipping under her power. "I have removed the stronger of the two, and now I will end the one."

"You have removed no one!" Inyoni's voice came from behind Lilith with a ferocity that chilled me. She emerged from the water with deliberate and heavy steps, planting each foot as though she were bracing for battle. As she made dry land, still twenty yards from Lilith, she reached across herself, peeling off the now soaked sundress from her already changing body. Her extremities were first, growing thick with light, golden hair now covering them. Then her head and trunk swelled well past what basic anatomy should allow; I stared in disbelief,my mind trying to reconcile what I was seeing. There she stood, changed but she was no wolf...she was a lion!

Tawny fur covered her entire body. Her form was still bipedal but coiled, as if holding back the power that would inevitably spring forth. With each step the powerful thighs rippled while her knees remained at acute angles, power at the ready. She spread her arms wide, a primal instinct to make oneself look bigger to your opponent, and roared her defiance, her gaping maw filled with elongated teeth and fangs.

Lilith turned and faced her, wings at full spread, crouching low at the ready, battle lines being drawn. From her stance, Lilith could defend or leap, flying high to evade any frontal assault, but she remained still, waiting for Inyoni to make the first move.

Step by step, Inyoni the lioness closed the distance between her and the Queen of the Succubi, the mother that had borne all the demons of the world, the first of the supernatural beings. It was horrific and beautiful, terrifying and mesmerizing, and it was the last that allowed him to get away from me.

"Kid!" I screamed, but it was too late. He was past me and headed straight for them.

Whether it was my scream or unfortunate timing, Inyoni sprang forward. The piercing cry of the succubus crackled through the air, and she crouched lower, bracing for the attack. Todd, running with all his might, stumbled and fell in the direct path of Inyoni's charge. Lilith, seeing him fall leapt forward, landing directly behind him dropping to her knees as she took hold of him bringing up her right wing up as if...

"STOP!" Todd's command rang out just before Lilith's wing covered his head. The instant recognition, the realization struck me dumb. Inyoni, too, was stopped in her tracks. Lilith was protecting him! Several moments passed with no one so much as twitching before Todd's voice was heard again, muffled but understandable. "Let me go, please."

Lilith's head slowly emerged from behind the wing she had proffered as a shield. She looked at Inyoni, now only a few feet away but no longer baring teeth. She then looked at me. Apparently deciding I was also no threat, she slowly lowered her wing and released him. She stood as she did so, now directly behind Todd, her wings folding slowly behind her. He turned to her and raised his hand slowly, caressing her now gentle face which seemed to grow younger and more beautiful with his touch.

Todd then turned again so that he could face both Inyoni and me. "This does not have to happen. You came here to save me, right?"

I nodded my reply.

"Thanks, but I'm okay," he said. "I love her."

"What!?" My mind raced. It had to be part of her magic. "But kid—"

"No, you have to let me finish. I know it's not perfect, and I know that you have a job to do and all that, but it's what I want... It's what she wants too," he said, turning to face Lilith who stood there watching him with loving eyes, "and the mutual wanting of something so beautiful as love, the wanting to connect with someone else, to give yourself to another instead of trying to take all you can get should beat any other argument." He turned back to look at me. "No one gets to decide who I choose to share that life with except for me."

I looked at Inyoni. She had already returned to her human form, nude but in no way ashamed. She looked back at me, her eyes revealing nothing of what she felt. I turned to look at Lilith; her form too had turned human in appearance, belying all that was inside her. I looked back at Todd. I thought of Leigh and the possibility of being loved. I even thought of Milagro, who had hated me and now cared for me even to the point of tears when she saw me in pain. I thought of all that might be if we could all just want the right things.

"Kid," I said finally. "She has killed at least two people, maybe more."

"And that," Inyoni said, "is what you have to decide you can accept or not, Regnum."

I looked at Inyoni who was making her way to the sundress she had tossed aside before she changed. "What are you talking about?"

"You, Detective Regnum," Inyoni said, stressing the word Detective while tugging the wet sundress back on, "an agent of the Vigiles, must decide if you can accept that the succubus Lilith and her actions are a part of the natural order of this world, or an aberration that must be dealt with."

"And if I decide not to let her go?" I was speaking to Inyoni but looking at Lilith. "You look like you are done helping me."

"My instructions," Inyoni said, "were to protect you."

"Protect me?" Now I did look at Inyoni.

"Yes," continued Inyoni. "So, if you choose to intervene, I will do so with you. Despite the very real possibility that we would both die."

I couldn't tell if it was the respect Inyoni showed Lilith, or if Lilith just wanted to defend herself, but she finally spoke. "I killed only two."

"Is that supposed to make it better? Are we talking about some kind of merit system?" My anger was getting the better of me and I did not care to try and hold back. "Oh, well then, why don't we just let the poor little man-juicer go because she only killed two people and not three!"

"Theodore would have been my third."

"Theodore?" My confusion begged the question just before I began putting it together.

"That's me," said Todd, stepping forward. "I guess now you know why I go by Todd, right?"

"Yeah," I said, still in a stupor at the absurdity of what I had just heard. "I suppose I would too."

None of this made any sense. I could not wrap my head around it. Morality, emotion, and the bizarre nature of what I was seeing and hearing was making my head ache. "So, you are telling me that you want to run away with a... with someone who was trying to kill you? Is that what you're telling me, kid?"

"Yes," he said.

"I don't fu..." I turned away fuming. I pulled at my hair in frustration before finally facing them all again. "I don't believe this!"

"Your perspective may be the problem, Detective," Inyoni said, stepping closer to me, but keeping a safe distance from Lilith. I figured she did it in case it did come to a fight. "It is her nature. She cannot help what she is."

"Her nature? That's like saying we should let out all the serial killers because it was in their nature, and they couldn't help it!"

"She is not human!"

"You don't think I know that?!"

"I was made this!" The sound of Lilith's voice and her words cut through like a gunshot. She was standing next to Todd now. "I was punished because I would not yield to the will of another." She looked at Todd, took his hand in hers then looked at me, pleading. My heart broke.

I tried desperately to reconcile all that had happened and what I was seeing before turning back to Inyoni. "What does it matter?" I shrugged my shoulders in resignation. "It's not like I could stop her anyway. Why bother explaining it to me?"

"Because," Lilith answered, "you seem in need of understanding, or the guilt of your choice will destroy you."

"What choice?"

"The choice to let us go."

"I have not decided whether I will or—"

"Yes, you have," said Lilith, interrupting but there was no anger in her words, no challenge.

"Why do you think that? Do you think I wouldn't try? Do you think—"

"No. If you believed it to be the right thing your possible death would make no difference. You have been ready to die for some time now."

"Why does everyone think that?"

"Because you have the eyes of one who is alone."

Her words hit me like a hammer, and I could feel the ache in my stomach as though someone had torn something out of me. I opened my mouth to protest but nothing came out.

Lilith stepped away from Todd and began to make her way toward me. "I have seen eyes such as yours. I have seen them at gravesites, not those that wail and scream, but those that are still, those that know they have lost the one person that kept them from the darkness." She moved closer, her eyes soft and full of a sadness of her own. "I have seen them in prison cells, on the faces of those who know they shall never see the light of another's loving gaze." She stopped only inches away from me and moved her hand slowly to my face so that her fingers gently rested on the crest of my cheek under my left eye. "I have seen them in the very mirrors I pass. Eyes that ache to be closed forever, eyes like yours."

Lilith looked into my eyes with an empathy so deep that the crack in my heart grew, spreading like a spider's web. My eyes began to well up, my mind knowing that all she was saying was true, but I would not let the tears fall. Her tears, however, did fall, and I knew beyond question that she had suffered as I had for eons.

Slowly, she let her hand fall to her side, and her eyes hardened. Her face was that of a woman determined. "But we must not let them." Lilith turned so quickly, I never saw the move. One moment she was looking into my eyes, and the next she had her back to me.

We followed along her sightline until we saw them.

Todd was the first to ask the question the rest

of us knew the answer to. "Who are those guys?"

The sound of Todd's voice was like a distant echo bouncing off the walls of a deep well, but it was just enough to pull me out of the shock at seeing them.

Lilith was standing defiantly just in front of me, and Inyoni had once again peeled off her sundress in preparation of her changing.

It was strange, the things that go through one's mind when you rationally accept the fact that you are going to die. I suddenly became aware of how fragrant Lilith's hair was. My eyes drifted back to Inyoni, who was now standing at the ready, her beautiful body glistening in the sun. Then a thought I did not expect. I did not want to die, but it seemed the point was about to be made moot.

I moved so that I stood next to Lilith facing what might be our doom, then answered.
"They're angels."

CHAPTER 53

"Do you love me?" Lilith asked.

Todd turned to look at Lilith, a look of confusion seemed to cloud his face. "Yes," he said.

"Then believe that what I do, I do for you," Lilith said, then walked briskly past him to stand as a physical barrier between him and the angels. "Change," she said, not taking her eyes off of the approaching angels.

"Me?" I asked, not sure who she was talking to.

"No, you have no control over your gift. You would surely kill him."

I watched, confused, as Lilith looked over at Inyoni who returned her gaze. I saw Inyoni nod ever so slightly and then start walking toward Todd, her body changing once again into the lioness. It was grotesque and awesome at the same time.

Todd took an involuntary step backwards as Inyoni, now the walking horror that was a fusion of human and lion, drew closer. He looked as though he was about to turn and run when Inyoni bolted at him. It was faster than I could have imagined. He didn't even scream, his gasp of surprise woefully late, as he was already suspended by his throat in Inyoni's left claw.

My surprise had stunned me to silence, but when I saw Todd dangling by the neck, I found my voice. "What the hell are you doing?" I yelled looking from the beast that was Inyoni to Lilith.

No one answered me but Lilith, apparently satisfied with what she saw, turned gracefully back to face the trio of angels. Wings slowly spread as if from under her hair, they were expansive, at least ten feet across and the color of rich earth, not quite black but a dark and deep brown. As though in response, wings that almost gleamed white shot out from each of the angel's backs as they began to spread out in a half circle around us.

"Amrit!" Lilith's voice almost boomed as if it came from another plane of existence.

The angels stopped in unison looking at one another. Lilith took a step forward as she pointed to Inyoni who still held Todd by the throat. "She will give him Amrita, the divine nectar, if you take one more step!"

The angels stayed perfectly still, neither advancing nor retreating. A look of comprehension and frustration hardened each of their faces. Emboldened, Lilith took another step, her wings still at full spread.

"You are not here for me; you are here for him. All of you know that you cannot take me! You tried at the shores of the Black Sea at the beginning of time and even then, when you were at your strongest, you could do nothing but speak your mandate and command without authority! For I am Lilith, and I yield to no one. I yielded not to Adam, I yielded not to you, and I will not yield to any who command it of me. But I will yield to him," she said, her voice now tender and full of love as she turned to Todd still gasping in a death grip. "And he yields to me. There is no commanding it, no request. We yield because we choose to."

She turned violently to face the angels again. "And if you try to take him away I will let the beast mark him and he will have Amrit; what the ancients called immortality. And though he will not live forever, he will live for thousands of years... and I will live with him."

There was a silence so loud it hurt the ears. The angels stared at Lilith, their faces now stoic. Then a twitch, almost imperceptible, and all together the angels' wings went to full spread. In unison they stepped forward when Lilith's hand shot up. Inyoni opened her mouth wide, wrapping it around Todd's shoulder without penetrating the skin. Todd squirmed, but only slightly, apparently understanding what Lilith was doing.

"If I drop my hand, it is done," Lilith said. "And if you fail to kill him today, your next opportunity to force me home will not be for millennia."

The angels held, their wings lowering slightly but not folding. Lilith took another step forward, her hand still raised. "You need me to yield," Lilith said. "You know that you cannot force me; I must come of my own will. That is the law. You cannot destroy me for we are of equal strength. You can only follow me, destroying what I love and making my solitude insufferable."

"And so, we must again kill what you love." It was Semangelof who spoke for the trio, unblinking and still as stone.

"Consider if you fail," Lilith replied. "If you attack, she will bite him, and should you fail to kill him today you will not find us for thousands of years. Think of the failure. If you leave us be, I will love him for the entirety of his mortal life and again be alone, perhaps even more broken hearted than when I left Adam. Perhaps then will be my time to return with you. But if you attack, if you manage to kill him today my spite will sustain me for centuries and I will plague you each and every moment of them." The angels' wings lowered a bit more and Lilith pressed them. "The choice is yours."

Abruptly, Semangelof's wings folded behind him and disappeared. Senoi and Sansenoi followed suit then, one by one, they turned and walked away. I watched as Inyoni slowly released Todd who collapsed to the ground, breathing raggedly. I turned to look at Lilith, but she was still staring at the backs of the walking angels.

"How did you find me?" Lilith called after them. "You have not been this close to me since the beginning of time."

The angels never broke stride but the voice of

Semangelof came to us like a punch to the stomach. "The vampire summoned us."

CHAPTER 54

"Markku!" Somehow, I was able to say his name while my jaw still hung open in surprise.

"No," said Inyoni, now back in human form and putting her sundress back on for the second time. "He would not do this."

"Really? Because it sounds exactly like something he would do," I said, turning to face her. "The first time we met... No, strike that because the first time we met he had just slaughtered an innocent woman." The words came out like fire. I felt betrayed and foolish. "The first time we spoke, he rambled on about how we should all expose ourselves and let anarchy reign! How is this not something he would do?"

"Because what he wants is for us to live as nature intended, not hide in the shadows!"

"This is not nature!"

"It is what nature has evolved into!"

"And you agree with him?"

Inyoni did not answer but looked over at Todd.

Lilith had made her way over to him and helped him to his feet. They embraced and looked into each other's eyes before she spoke. "I have to take him away from this place."

"Why?" I asked.

"The angels used their better judgment, but they may return. I am stronger than any one of them but all three..." She embraced Todd again, and he held her even more tightly. "I cannot risk what I have found."

"And what exactly have you found?" My confusion was still getting the better of me. My conscious mind was scratching at the surface of what I had just witnessed. "And while you're at it will someone explain to me what just happened?"

"I was invited by a vampire as well," Lilith said, finally releasing Todd.

"What?"

"He is very old," said Lilith.

"And how do you know that?" I was not going to let any detail slide.

"Only one of the oldest of the remaining vampires would know how and have the strength to reach out to angels."

"You're not an angel."

"I was."

We stood in stunned silence, and when Lilith spoke again, I felt my knees buckle. "Both Adam and I were granted awareness, desire, and gender in order to begin life on this earth, but we were also given consciousness, more so than the soldier angels who pursue me. We were granted emotions as well, to encourage us to perpetuate and protect all that we were here to help create, but I resisted that life and was punished for my choice. Since that day, I have been pursued, instructed that I must return to ignorance, forget all that I have seen and felt. They cannot force me, so they must break me; break me with solitude." She looked away, a slight shake of her head providing only a glimpse of the pain she kept hidden. "Cursed with a hunger that makes me kill." Her eyes found Todd, "But I have not yielded and now I have found a new Adam. An Adam who is worthy of my love."

Lilith took Todd into her arms, and they held the embrace for just a moment before she turned to face me once more. "I was invited here with the promise that there were evil men here, for that is what I choose to feed upon. I believe that same vampire summoned my pursuers."

"Fine," I said looking back at Inyoni. "If not Markku then his father, your boss."

"But why?" she asked.

"And if he invited Lilith, then he is probably the copycat!" My mind was putting together all the possibilities. "He lied to me about Lilith and then he wouldn't even talk about the..."

My phone rang and the caller ID said it was Ramirez. I punched the green talk button so hard I thought I broke it. "Jo, I think we know who—"

"Simon's alive!" Ramirez interrupted.

"What are you—"

"We thought he died when he was taking out the kid he turned, but he swapped bodies! He is alive and he's going after Isaac, the kid in foster care you've been helping."

The blood in my veins ran cold for an instant, and then the heat came like a storm. "I'll call you from the car," I said as I ran.

"What is it?" Inyoni's voice came from behind me.

"Simon is alive!" I yelled without breaking stride.

My car was only twenty yards away, but it felt like I was running forever. When I finally got there I went around to the driver's side and almost ripped the door off getting it open. No sooner had I thrown myself into the seat and closed my door, did the passenger door open and Inyoni dropped into the seat next to me.

"What are you doing?" I asked.

"I came here to keep you alive if I could and it seems you are still not done trying to kill yourself."

"Whatever," I said, starting the car and slamming into gear. The tires screeched when I hit the accelerator and the car skidded sideways. I fought with the steering wheel until I had us tearing out of the parking lot, heading toward the interstate. "Here," I said, handing the cell phone to Inyoni. "Redial the last incoming call and put it on speaker." She did as I asked, and Ramirez answered.

"I'm headed to the kid's foster home," he said. He sounded breathless, as if he were hurt or groggy.

"I am on the way there too," I answered. "What the hell is going on, Jo? Why is this guy going after Isaac and more importantly, why isn't he dead?"

"There was another journal."

"What?"

"Another journal like the one you found and turned into Zuñiga, but this one continued where the one you found left off."

"I'm not following you, Jo."

"You were right in your thinking. The guy that Simon turned, Andrew? Well, he went nuts after he changed. He started hunting down all the people that hurt him and made fun of him while he was a paraplegic. He tortured and killed them. He was beating girls to bloody pulps and leaving them deformed just because they rejected him when he tried to date them. He broke almost every bone in some jock's body because the jock had pushed him down some stairs. It was all there, man."

The car leaned hard to the left as I turned the wheel hard toward the on-ramp. "What does this have to do with Simon and why is he going after Isaac?"

"He blames you, man!"

"Blames me for what?"

"Simon was trying to finish killing the rest of the people on Andrew's list! He couldn't let his creation keep killing and exposing us or he would be held responsible by Zuñiga. But if he convinced a succubus that there were a bunch of evil men here that needed to be killed, he could keep killing Andrew's enemies and the blame would be on

Lilith!"

"He was the vampire that called for Lilith?" Inyoni asked.

"Who the hell is that?" Jo asked.

"Inyoni," I said. "You remember the wolf...I mean lycanthrope that almost took my head off in Hadrian's office. She is very pleased to meet you."

"What the hell is she... You know what, it doesn't matter. Yes, he called for the succubus and at the same time he called for the angels so they could drive her off, all so he could keep killing and not get blamed for it."

"But we thought he was dead. How could we blame him?"

"He would eventually be found out," Inyoni blurted out. "Sooner or later, he would have been found to be alive, and the penalties for exposing our world are severe no matter how long ago the crime occurred."

"Great," I said, wrenching the steering wheel to the right, cutting off a semi-truck in the process. "He doesn't seem too concerned about exposing us now. He is going to kill a kid in broad daylight!"

CHAPTER 55

Traffic on the off-ramp was backing up so I drove onto the shoulder, sirens wailing and lights flashing. I kept checking my rearview mirror, hoping that another police unit wouldn't see me and call it in, or worse, follow me to the house where a pair of lycanthropes were going to try and stop a vampire.

"We must try to keep him out of sight," Inyoni said.

"Good idea," I said, the sarcasm attaching itself to my words before I could stop it. "And how do you propose we do that?"

"Wolf!" Ramirez's voice over the phone was commanding. "That's not helping. Now listen. You guys are going to arrive first—"

"Wait," I said. "How do you know that?"

"Because it has only been five minutes since Simon walked in and found me reading his journal. But don't worry, he only threw me across the room and promised to take away everything you care about since you stopped him from avenging what he cared about! We all caught up now?"

"Yes."

"Good! Now, when I couldn't get hold of you, I called Milagro and she said you were over in Shockoe. Is that right?"

"Yes."

"And the foster home where Isaac is at is in Glen Allen right?"

"Yes," growing impatient to hear the idea it seemed was coming.

"Simon is coming from Midlothian. You should be able to get a few minutes ahead of him. See if you can get the kid and everybody else out of the house, and then try and talk Simon down."

"What?"

"Try and talk him down, Wolf. Tell him what we know and get him to stop before he exposes us for good."

The phone beeped and the call was over. I weaved through the traffic on Hermitage then took the right onto Brookland Parkway.

"He will not stop," Inyoni said as I turned left onto Chatham. "The vampire you called Simon, he will not stop."

"How do you know?"

"I did not know who he was at the time, but a few days before the bodies of Andrew and who you thought was Simon were found, he came in to see Hadrian and demanded the right to punish Andrew's enemies so that he could try and save his new creation, the newly turned Andrew."

"That's what Hadrian was hiding! He wasn't lying about Lilith, he was covering up what Simon had tried to do… what he eventually did!"

"You have to listen to me very carefully."

"We're here," I said, but when I tried to get out of the car, Inyoni grabbed my arm.

"Listen to me now!"

I looked at her, anger flaring at first. Then I saw the desperation in her eyes. "Okay."

"Simon is very old and very strong. If it comes to violence, we will both have to fight, but you must learn control."

"Now is not the time for a lesson."

"It has to be. If not, we all die, including the child you are hoping to protect."

"Fine, I watched you change back, and you didn't have to kill anything. How did you do that?"

"Do not fight the change, Regnum. The pain is what drives your conscious mind into hiding. Let it happen. Will it to happen and you will find your mind still aware of what you do."

"But what about the—"

"If we can get them out, we will, but either way, we must stop Simon." She was looking at me and I guessed that she could see the fear in my eyes, not fear of Simon but of what I might do. "There is much more I will teach you, but you have to survive the day, Regnum."

I nodded after a moment, and we got out of the car.

The lights and screeching tires must have gotten the attention of the household, because the front door to Isaac's foster home opened just as we hit the porch steps.

"What is going on... Oh, Detective Regnum, is something wrong?" Kelly was standing in the doorway, her eyes wide. I could feel the guilt like a stone in my gut. I could not help but feel as if I had brought this to her door, and now I had to look into her eyes and tell her.

"Kelly, I am sorry, but we need to go back inside," I said. She nodded and I walked past her to look inside; Inyoni looked up and down the street before following us in. "Who's in the house?"

"Just me and a couple of the kids. Why?"

"Isaac?"

"Yes, he's here." I could feel her fear growing as I searched all the rooms on the first floor. "What is it? What's wrong?"

"You have to get them all out."

"What?"

"Kelly, someone is coming to hurt Isaac, now get them out!"

She took a step back and looked at me in shock. Then, as though a switch had been flipped, she darted to the stairwell. Her voice filled the house as she called out the names of the children in such a tone that they all came running down the stairs. Isaac was the last one down. He looked at me with mild surprise, but once he saw my face, he followed Kelly toward the front door.

I smelled it just before... "No! The back door now!"

The front door was kicked open with such

force, the top hinge separated from the frame entirely and the bottom held on by a single screw. A figure stepped through quickly, barely stopping when he saw me move suddenly to the right. He countered left and saw Inyoni. The hesitation was enough.

"Get out!"

Kelly practically shoved the kids toward the back door as I drew my nine-millimeter pistol from my side holster. One, two, three shots to his chest. I knew it would not stop him, but I needed to slow him down. On the last shot, I started running at him. I buried my shoulder into his midsection in a football style tackle. Lucky for me, the strength of an immortal did not give them extra weight. The force of the blow knocked Simon off his feet.

But now he had a hold of me. With a powerful hand on my opposite shoulder, he pulled me in the direction of the fall. We landed together and rolled. He calculated perfectly, our momentum reversing our positions so that he straddled my chest, pinning my hands under his legs. I watched in awe as he raised both fists high above his head meaning to smash my skull.

A blur of tawny fur smashed into him before the fists descended. I quickly looked toward the back door and saw that Kelly and the kids had made it out. Jumping to my feet, I turned in time to see Simon struggling against the mass of fur I knew to be Inyoni before flipping her Judo style onto a coffee table.

With room to maneuver and regroup, Simon stood up slowly. He looked at each of us in turn, first to Inyoni who was rising from the pile of splintered wood, then to me. It was as though he was choosing his target, finding a weak spot he could exploit. That's when I heard the first popping of the tendons and bones in my extremities.

The initial shock of Simon's blitz attack, my concern for getting the children out of the house and the chaos that followed only delayed the inevitable. Fear and anger coursed through me; I had been attacked and was now preparing to attack and so came the pain. I cried out in agony as the tendons in my shoulders and the sinews in my thighs pulled, stretched, and separated from the shifting bones. Clenching my teeth, I was about to collapse to the floor when I heard a low and deep rumbling; it was like a cat's purr, but deep as the ocean and as lush as the rainforest. Looking over to Inyoni, I could see her eyes focused on me and I remembered.

My legs steadied beneath me as I willed my body to uncoil, allowing the change to flow rather than convulsing. Inch by inch, the waves of pain became more like ripples and I was able to open my eyes. As I watched my flesh grow dark with fur, I felt my center of gravity shifting forward and I leaned to compensate. As I did, I looked down and saw my hips become misshapen, my legs and thighs now jutting forward. That's when I panicked.

I looked at my shoulders, and the same was happening there. I cried out. My head jerked upwards as the pain returned. Fighting to keep my enemy in sight, Simon came into focus. He was smiling! Though only a matter of seconds, the pain made it feel as though time had stopped just to make me suffer.

What happened next was the last thing I expected, and that may be why it saved my life. Still looking into Simon's smiling face, I watched as his smile faded just as I felt a gentle touch against my cheek. Inyoni, the fearsome lioness that was poised for battle only moments ago, now pressed her face to mine, gently caressing my face with hers. The pain subsided; my eyes closed as the low, comforting rumble emanating from her chest cut through the haze of my senses. When I opened my eyes, I could see clearly but somehow differently. My peripheral vision was less, but my focus was enhanced. Every detail was magnified somehow, and now I could truly see my enemy, and his name was Simon.

He stood in the middle of the room. I had not really seen him until now, and there he was, feet planted wide, hands near his thighs but curled like vicious man-claws. His light brown hair parted slightly off center, dressed in cotton slacks and a button-down shirt gave him the look of middle management at a bank or insurance firm. Had it not been for the lips pulled back, revealing the elongated canines of the vampire, I would not have given him a second thought.

Inyoni stepped away from me, the sound from her chest turning from the low, soothing purr to full-throated menace. Her eyes never left Simon as she sidestepped further and further, forcing him to turn and step back in order not to expose his back to either of us.

Almost smelling her imminent attack, I crouched lower, my own growl vibrating throughout my chest. Simon's eyes darted back and forth between Inyoni and me, both of us fangs bared.

Then the fire in my blood cooled as I watched his lips curl upward around his fangs in a smile. I shifted ever so slightly, confused as to why he would be smiling, and that was the mistake he was waiting for.

Faster than I could have imagined, Simon launched himself directly at my chest to tackle me, much as I had done to him. It was all I could do to sidestep the attack, but the move was made as though I had human limbs, another mistake. My hips no longer spread wide enough to evade his attack, and though my chest had avoided the full impact, Simon simply extended his right arm up and out connecting with the side of my head and snout, tearing flesh and knocking me down.

Dazed but still conscious, I watched as my own blood streaked through the air following the arc of Simon's outstretched claw. I also saw Inyoni launch herself at Simon's back, but Simon had planned at least two moves ahead.

As my body hit the floor, I watched him land on his hands, curl into a ball and roll through his landing so that he finished the maneuver crouched with one knee planted as a fulcrum and his other leg tucked like a spring underneath him, his arms outstretched and ready for her. Inyoni was already committed, and her momentum carried her right into the clutches of our enemy.

Catching Inyoni by the throat and her left arm, Simon used the force of her attack and magnified it, slamming her onto her right arm effectively pinning it beneath her. He immediately pushed off his leg, pivoted on his knee and straddled the now helpless Inyoni.

I sprang to my feet preparing for another attack, but as I watched him raise his clawed hand, I realized I was not going to be in time. Inyoni was going to die.

CHAPTER 56

The wind buffeted me just before the screeching reached my ears. Without touching the ground, Lilith swooped through the room, plucking Simon from his perch atop Inyoni as easily as an eagle pulls trout from a stream. The house itself seemed to shake as Lilith slammed Simon into the far wall with enough force to stun him motionless, his eyes wide. Whether it was fear or surprise, I could not tell, but it made little difference as the look changed to one that I knew very well. It was the look of the woman in the kill club as she looked down at her disemboweled self. It was the look of that man from the same club as Leigh sank her teeth into his throat. There was terror and confusion in Simon's eyes now as Lilith covered his mouth with hers and turned those horrified eyes blank.

The body hit the floor, and Lilith stood with her back to us for a moment, her wings heaving slightly with every breath she took. Tentatively, I began to move toward Inyoni, my own breathing ragged and unsure.

Slowly, Lilith turned to us, tucking her wings behind her. Tears fell freely from her eyes, and she made no attempt to wipe them away. Inyoni had taken my offered hand and we both stood looking at the one who had saved us. Lilith now stood before us, distraught as though her heart had been stolen from her.

"Why do you cry?" Inyoni's clear voice startled me so much that my head snapped round to look at her.

To my surprise, she was completely human again. I looked at my own hand still holding hers, and I saw that I too had returned to human form. Then I quickly realized something else... We were both stark naked.

A sad smile touched Lilith's face as I scrambled about looking for anything to wrap around my nether regions. Finding nothing, I quickly pulled the tablecloth from the overturned dinner table, wrapping it around myself like a toga.

Inyoni snickered, then casually walked over to the far corner of the room, picked up her sundress and slipped it back on. "Perhaps you should start wearing a kilt," she said, smiling at me as she made her way back to Lilith.

Inyoni slowed, as if she were waiting for Lilith to acknowledge her, her expression now one of respect and empathy. "You did not answer. Why do you cry?"

"He was my child," Lilith said, her eyes drifting to where Simon had met his end. "You all are. I am the mother of all demons; all who are like you are in some way from me. Though, he was..."

She paused, turned away slightly as more tears fell, and I could not shake the feeling that there was more, much more than a bloodline that made her shed a tear for the madman she had just killed. "He was," she continued, "one of the earliest, close to the original strain. That is how he was still able to summon me."

"He could speak with you?" I asked in shock.

"No, but I could sense when he wanted me near. There are few left who are close enough for me to sense, very few, and I have just killed one. That is why I cry, lioness."

"My name is Inyoni, and it is an honor to know you, my queen."

Lilith nodded to Inyoni solemnly, then turned to me. "If it matters to you, wolf... forgive me what is your name?"

"Believe it or not," I said, standing just a bit prouder than before, "that is my name." I grinned sheepishly. "You have to appreciate the irony, right?"

"It is no irony.".

"I'm not sure what you mean."

"You were destined for it, my child." She looked at me intently, as if to drive home her sincerity. "So then, Wolf, if it matters, you made the right choice."

"Which choice was that?"

"Todd and I will live out the remainder of his days in peace and in love. He will live longer than most while in my care, and I suspect you will never see me again."

"Why do you say that?" It was Inyoni's turn to be confused.

"I have only loved three times throughout my existence. The first was Adam, but I would not sacrifice myself or my strength to feed his. Then there was Rome, where that love tore my heart in two. Each time I have loved, and each time I lost that love, I was unwilling to see or hear of any living creature for hundreds of years. This time will be no different, with one exception."

"Yes," Inyoni said inquisitively.

"We will not change who we are to be together." And without another word, Lilith walked out of the room, through the shattered door and out of sight.

We stood there, Inyoni and I, staring at the door. Perhaps we doubted our choice; perhaps we silently celebrated that we still lived. Or, and this is what I believe we both realized that we had just been in the presence of a true Goddess, terrible and beautiful, but a Goddess none the less.

"I should get going," I said, breaking the silence.

"You may want to find yourself some clothes."

"I got that covered," said a voice behind us that I recognized instantly. "No pun intended." Ramirez stood just inside the back door, holding a small duffel bag. He tossed it to me, and I caught it awkwardly, trying to keep my tablecloth toga in place at the same time. "Ever since that time in the park, I keep an extra set in the trunk of my car," Ramirez said as he took in what was left of the room.

"Thanks," I said, moving off to the side and dressing under my toga like I was changing under a beach towel.

"I assume that's Simon," Ramirez said, indicating the wrinkled corpse that lay in a heap against the wall. "And, it looks like he went by way of a sun-dried tomato. Anyone want to tell me what happened?"

"It's a long story," I said as I stepped back into the main area of the room, now fully dressed in jeans, t-shirt and a pair of those silly rubber shoes with the holes in them. He got the sizes right, but I hated rubber shoes.

"You got someplace to be, kid?"

"Well, I figured I should get back to the precinct so I can get fired, since I haven't closed the case on---"

"Actually," Ramirez interrupted, "A Mr. Gregory Langston waltzed into your precinct and confessed."

"What?" My mind started racing for explanations.

"Yeah," Ramirez continued, "Apparently, he was going on about how he felt it was inevitable that you were closing in on him. I don't have to tell you your lieutenant was pissed."

"I'll bet. But why the hell would the guy go and do that?"

"I may be able to answer that," Inyoni

said, stepping a bit closer to us. "Leigh, a recent acquaintance of yours I believe, paid the man in question a visit. Suffice to say he was convinced to turn himself in or suffer a bit more than he would otherwise."

"What?" I shook my head in disbelief. "Ok, so why did she do that?"

"Apparently you made an impression."

"Yeah... but... I mean how would she have known?"

"Markku."

The name hit me like someone slapping me awake. "So, he sends you to make sure I stay alive, and then talks Leigh into threatening this guy into confessing---"

"She did not require convincing, Wolfgang. She was more than happy to assist. As I may have mentioned, she is rather fond of you."

An image of Leigh draped across my bed, intoxicatingly beautiful flashed into my head. It was followed by one of her in a pair of my cargo shorts and button down, looking at me over her shoulder as she walked out, smiling that mischievous smile and making me ache to pull her back into my arms. Then the image of her bidding at the kill club crashed into my mind's eye; she was ravaging the man she had bought, feeding on him until there was literally, not a drop of life left in him.

I shook my head, trying to clear the image. "What does he want with me, Inyoni?"

"Perhaps you should ask him?"

CHAPTER 57

"Was my help not required?" Markku sat in the same chair opposite me, in the same room of his penthouse that he had when I first asked him for help.

"I asked you for help on the case. You went quite a bit beyond just looking at a body and answering some questions."

"I thought, and correctly so I might add, that you required a bit more from me than you realized at the time."

"Ok, but why?"

"Because you were facing things of which you had little or no concept." Markku sipped on a glass of something red and I shuddered to guess what it was.

"I get that part. What I'm asking is why help at all? Why bother?"

"It was nothing really."

"Nothing? Inyoni was almost killed, Markku."

"True, but the possible gains justified the risk, and she agreed."

"What gains?"

"Keeping you alive, Wolfgang." The words hung there for a moment, both of us taking measure of the other. "If it makes you feel more at ease, I did not order her to do anything. She volunteered."

"Why do you need me alive?"

"Need? No, Wolfgang, I do not think I need you alive but for some reason I want you alive. Need is a thing clear as crystal. You can see through it to its very purpose and reason for being. Want, on the other hand… It is the wanting that confounds us all. Wanting often has little to do with logic or conscious choice. Only when you find the true reason for wanting can you classify it as a need or merely a fancy, and I am not sure which you are to me just yet." He cocked his head to one side, his eyes narrowing, studying me. "But again, if it will put your mind at ease, something tells me that I will need you sometime in the future, and that is why I did what I could to keep you alive."

Despite the flood of thoughts running through my head, there was really nothing left to say. I stood, gave Markku a nod, to which he simply raised his glass, and made my way to the door.

"Oh," he said, placing his glass on the elegant coffee table and standing. "And, this might come as a bit of a shock. Your adoption request has been approved."

"My what?"

"Your request to adopt the boy. Isaac."

"I never submitted any request!"

"I am aware of that, Wolfgang, but it is what you wanted, yes? You feel somehow responsible for him, though I cannot understand why, and you want to protect him, do you not?"

"Yes, but that gave you no right to do what you did."

"I didn't."

"Then who…" More thoughts flooded in and a name came to mind. "Zuñiga?"

"One might think that but in fact, it was Hadrian."

"Why would… I am really not understanding any of this."

"Nor should you," Markku said, walking slowly across the room to stand in front of me. "Perhaps my father is just giving you something so that he can take it away later. Perhaps he wishes to establish some sort of control over you. Or, perhaps he wants you to stay alive as well. Either way your life is only going to become more complicated, not only because of the boy, but because you have barely scratched the surface of our world."

"I am starting to get that. So what do I do now?"

"Center yourself, Wolfgang. Embrace the life that has been given to you so that you can change what you wish to change and maintain what you wish to maintain."

"And what do you wish to change, Markku?"

"Everything."

"Why do you… it seems like you hate this world and still you are trying to keep me in it."

"I do hate it."

"Really… why? I mean, are you going to spout

some cliché about no one understands you and all that?"

"Wolfgang, I do not hate this world because it does not understand me, I hate this world because I do not understand it."

*****

It was surreal how much had changed over the last few days. I found good in evil and evil in what felt so good. I was going to be a parent. I was infatuated with a murderer ,and despite all that, I still felt like the loneliest being on the planet.

I sat in my car, still parked outside of Markku's building, and felt as though the air had been sucked from my lungs. I was happy to have Isaac, sad for his loss, confused by Markku and thrilled to be alive. I felt as though every emotion possible was bottled up inside ready to burst.

I picked up my phone, punched in Ramirez's number and began typing out a text.

Rain check on a beer at Legends, will tell you about what happened tomorrow over coffee.

His response dinged in a second later: *What's up?*

I just need to decompress, I replied.

Where?

The opera.

End

SPECIAL PREVIEW

HOMESICK
A Wolf Regnum Novel
By M. Angel

CHAPTER 1

Different, and yet somehow the same, that was the house at the corner of 25th and Q. The night sky was overcast but I saw everything; gone was the trash, the dilapidated siding and broken furniture. The entire neighborhood had, over the last year and change, been renovated, but that did not change what went on in this particular house.

"I'm in position," I said into the radio. From where I was parked I could see the front entrance where, according to the plan, my first team was going to breach. Me and the patchwork team I had put together over the last year had been watching the place for the last month or so. It was difficult for me to trust them, especially knowing where they came from, but I had no choice.

"Almost there," came the response from my handset. I checked my watch; we had all agreed on a three a.m. go time and there was still ten minutes to go.

It was almost surreal, watching the place; memories of what had happened, what I had seen, what it had done to me, always hummed in my brain like the beginnings of a migraine whenever it was my turn. The worst of it all was the thing I did not want to see, the person I hoped would not see going back into that house. Every time I had to sit in my car, parked in this very spot, I prayed I would not see her, be reminded of what she had done and how she relished it. Since we had begun seeing each other, Leigh and I never talked about the Kill Club, she never brought it up and I didn't want to know if she had ever gone back. It was not the sort of thing a cop wanted to know about his girlfriend.

"We're ready." The voice from the radio yanked me back to the present, and I immediately spotted the dark grey minivan now parked about twenty yards from the Kill Club.

"Copy that," I said, feeling ridiculous as I tried to sound official. Then I looked at the minivan and was reminded that I was most certainly not the most ridiculous thing about this little venture.

These guys weren't trained for this; hell I wasn't trained for it, not really but it had been over a year and the nightmares still came to me at night. So, I watched, I planned, and after weeks of watching I was able to get a rough count of how many workers were in the building, and at what times. The idea was to have a few of them against as many of us as I could wrangle.

"Us," I said to myself and shook my head. I was not wearing a badge tonight, and the Richmond PD had nothing to do with this raid. There are monsters in our world most of them are human, but some of them are not. It was the latter I was hunting tonight and I had brought some monsters of my own; I was one of them. "Just keep it together until I say go, alright"

"It's almost three!" The voice on the radio was different but I had not known these... creatures long enough to tell who was who.

"We have to be as sure as we can be about the numbers guys," I said going over the plan in my head.

"All we need to be sure about is that you keep our names out of this, like you promised."

That voice I did recognize, not because I knew him any better than I knew the rest of the group, but because it almost oozed out of the radio. It was one of two vampires; one spoke and the other did not, but they both gave me the creeps. "I found you-"

"-You mean arrested us," said the first voice.

"Whatever," I said getting irritated. "I contacted each of you on my own, and you agreed to help me get this-"

"-In exchange for your discretion as well as reduced punishment for what you call our crimes," said the vampire, reminding me that I had made deals with every one of these things.

"Hadrian Vanderbroek will not hear of your involvement," I said. "Hell, my boss doesn't even know who you guys are."

"Keep it that way," said voice number two who I now guessed was the troll, and not the social media kind. "Vanderbroek slaughter's anyone who crosses him, so keep your mouth shut. Or at least until he slaughters you."

He was right. There was going to be hell to pay after this, and I knew it. I just hadn't put it in so many words in my brain. "You worry about the plan and let me worry about who gets-"

"Someone's coming out the front door." It was a harsh whisper that was loud enough for me to hear from across the street, even without the radio.

There he was, the last one to leave the house for the night. The guy I affectionately called gimpy because of the ridiculous limp he would adopt just as he stepped out the door. Obviously the guy thought of himself as a thespian. "Alright, get ready and stick to the plan."

It took Gimpy about three minutes to make it to his car and drive off. That's when I picked up the radio and whispered, "Go".

The door to the minivan slid open and out came the two vampires, almost gliding out of the vehicle. The two front doors opened, and two more figures began making their way toward the house. Those had to be the wolves, they moved like me. Then the minivan rocked back and forth just before what looked like a seven-foot sumo-wrestler basically dislodged himself out of the side door. That would be the troll.

Getting out of my car I began walking toward the vampires as the wolves and troll headed off to the other side of the house. The plan was to have the troll and both wolves enter through the back door while the two vampires and I entered through the front. Having fought a vampire and lost I felt better going in with them since I knew how they moved. The main reason though, was that I didn't trust myself going in with other wolves, especially when there was a troll whose primary job was to bust things up. The last thing I wanted was to change tonight. I still didn't have enough control, so if I changed I would have to kill something... or someone.

ABOUT THE AUTHOR

M. Angel

M. Angel resides in Southeast Virginia, originally from Central New York he joined the U.S. Military just three days after graduation. That decision resulted in many years of travel as well as meeting people from many different cultures and walks of life. These experiences are what he hopes to bring to his writing.

Stay Connected:
www.wineywriter.com

Made in the USA
Middletown, DE
07 June 2024

55152164R00210